The Heart of The Beast

*A romantic adult fairytale revealing how the
power of love can overcome the hardest heart*

Susan Kohler

CCB Publishing
British Columbia, Canada

The Heart of The Beast: A romantic adult fairytale revealing how
the power of love can overcome the hardest heart

Copyright ©2007 by Susan Kohler
ISBN-13   978-0-9783893-6-9
First Edition

Library and Archives Canada Cataloguing in Publication

Kohler, Susan, 1950-
The Heart of The Beast: A romantic adult fairytale revealing how the power of
love can overcome the hardest heart / written by Susan Kohler.
Also available in electronic format.
ISBN 978-0-9783893-6-9
I. Title.
PS3611.O47H43 2007   813'.6   C2007-906904-5

Original cover art design by John Nofsinger.

Publisher: CCB Publishing
             British Columbia, Canada
             www.ccbpublishing.com

Dedication

To all my friends: your faith, your help, your suggestions and your encouragement were all priceless in writing this book, but it's your offbeat, risqué and slightly kinky sense of humor that really keeps me going. You're the best!

Other books by Susan Kohler

The Paddle Club

Hot Crossed Buns

Another Batch of Warm Buns

Prologue

Once upon a time...

There was a grand castle built high on a hill overlooking a small, poor village. The peasants living in the village had a rugged life, but overall it was a tolerable life. They worked arduously planting fields and groves, and tending the green pastures for grazing their small herds of cattle, sheep and goats. Small flocks of chickens, geese and ducks wandered near some of the rough cottages.

The surrounding countryside was lush and green, the nearby forest filled with wild game. Although they were rarely allowed to hunt there, and the penalty for poaching the lord's game was stiff indeed, sometimes a deer or boar would find its way onto a villager's table.

The villagers were, down to the last man, dirt poor, but most of them were decent and hard working. They had to be, for any man who thought he could gain by taking advantage of others soon faced the wrath of the ruling lord.

The lord of the castle was well liked and respected by everyone. He was a fair ruler. He could be fierce and stern, but oftentimes he would bring the villagers a bit of game for their tables. He would ask after their families, and when doing so he would show a kindly smile.

He had ample reason to smile. He had a beautiful wife, whom he loved deeply. The lord and his lady also had a wondrous family: Two strong, handsome sons: one nearing manhood and one still but a small lad. He also had a daughter, an exceedingly lovely daughter. She showed signs of becoming an extraordinarily beautiful woman, with intelligence and a good heart. Her strong will was already apparent, and the lord secretly feared that she might become too headstrong.

Even more secretly, he took pride in her strong will. Everyone should have lived happily ever after, and for a while, they did.

Until one day the invaders came. They came with a large army, heavily armed and well trained. There were dozens of foot soldiers, scores of archers and swordsmen, along with several dozen mounted soldiers, all led by a powerful knight and his retainers.

The old lord went out to meet them with his small army of guards and foot soldiers. The battle was fierce, bloody and very short. When it was over, the old lord was brutally slain and his fighting men were badly defeated; most of them died with their liege. His despondent wife and three children were feared slain, or so most everyone thought. Some claimed that his wife lived. There were faint rumours that although she was filled with grief, she survived, and that fearing for the safety of her children, she had taken them and fled never to be seen again.

Since the knight leading the assault on the castle was himself slain in the invasion, the distant King decided to reward one of his other young knights by granting him the castle and the surrounding lands to live in and to rule.

The knight he chose to reward was young, about twenty-five. He was very special to the King, although few knew the real reason why. The knight, who now was the new lord of the land, was widely known for his fighting skills and bloodthirsty temper. He was a cold and forbidding man, a knight whose very lack of mercy or human compassion gave him a strange and terrifying appellation, one that all knew but few were bold enough to say aloud. That his very brutality worried the King, a King who had shown himself to be harsh and brutal, was a strong testament to how cold and battle hardened the knight truly was.

Secretly, the King hoped that peace and a permanent home, along with the responsibilities that come with ruling, would tame the fierce, grim knight to some degree. Perchance his own land and serfs to rule would teach the fearsome warrior some basic human emotions, would teach him the import of a man's life and even the value of his own his happiness, without weakening him too much.

The King knew that to be a great man, the knight needed to add some human factors to his cruel disposition: Wisdom, mercy, a degree of patience and especially some compassion. Mayhap, the King reflected, now that the war is over, his knight would learn these things well enough so that he would no longer be called by that terrifying appellation, that he would no longer be known by the simple but dreadful name... The Beast.

THE HEART OF THE BEAST

Chapter One

Life in the small village had greatly changed since the day of the terrible invasion. Life was much more tenuous, survival more arduous, and death took many of the villagers through starvation and disease. The villagers were even poorer now than they had been before. Much of their livestock had been either killed outright in the fierce battle or stolen by the invading hordes.

The villagers had not been able to replenish their meagre flocks of chickens, geese and ducks. The herds of swine, goats and lambs had grown back a little but still remained greatly diminished. There were precious few cattle left in the herds. Virtually all the horses had been stolen or killed, so many of the villagers had to plow the land by hand.

It wasn't just the lack of livestock. Nature had conspired with the invaders, it seemed, and followed the invasion with a few years of bad weather, at least for farming. There was precious little rain, and the summers were warmer than normal. The crops had been very poor for the past few years, not yielding nearly enough to replenish the village after the invasion.

Several other things had hurt the small village as well: The new lord had raised the rents to be paid by the farmers but he saw no need to do anything for them. The villagers worked so hard to pay the rents that they had no time to even begin repairs on any of the small huts they lived in.

Even the sanitation in the village suffered after the invasion. The old lord had ordered the village to be kept clean, a rule many of the villagers thought to be foolish in the extreme. Still, the village had been spared many of the diseases that scourged the countryside.

Now, with no one to enforce the order and the villagers working so hard just to survive, filth had built up in the village. All vestiges of the old lord's sanitary rules were lost. The added waste and refuse had caused several diseases to sweep through the village, greatly decimating the population. Those who remained struggled to merely survive.

The villagers hunted for game in the forest but it was a very dangerous undertaking because poaching the lord's game carried a death penalty. The Beast imposed the penalty with absolutely no mercy. Bodies of hanged men lined the road to the castle, even though the Beast periodically ordered them cut down.

Worst of all, the new lord believed it was his right to use the peasants as he saw fit. There were rumours of women being dragged to the castle on his order. Few returned, and they were greatly wounded, left with scars on their young bodies and their minds that never really faded.

Beauty, the defeated lord's daughter, and her family had moved away from the village immediately after the invasion but wherever they travelled, life was extremely rugged. Poverty was rampant throughout the country. The new lord was rebuilding many things, but he had so far kept most of his efforts close to his own home. His reign was still new and tenuous, and he fought to establish control. Outlaying villages were barely noticed.

Although few in the small village knew the former lady and her family very well if at all, to them the small town still felt like home. They had roots there and a sense of connection to the past. In truth, they felt a sense of obligation to the villagers. So, even with living conditions as bad as they were in the village, the old lord's widow and her family chose to return there to live as simple peasants.

They had some fear of the new lord. There were rumours about him. It was said by some that the surviving families of the conquered lords had been hunted down and slaughtered. Nonetheless Beauty's family hoped the new lord thought them to be dead and would not look for them to be living in the very shadow of their old home.

It was a beautiful spring morning. The sky was clear and blue with just traces of soft, fluffy clouds. The surrounding hills were plush and green, and the crops in the fields were growing nicely, for the first time in years. There were a few lambs, young and frisky, grazing on a distant hillside. Even a few calves were nursing, but alas there were no playful foals. Wildflowers grew at the entrance to the forest, which abounded with deer, boar and other wild game.

Beauty surveyed her surroundings with a sigh. She loved this countryside and its splendour but there was always a slight tightening in her throat as she studied the huge stone castle that arose from the distant hillside, casting a shadow of dread over the entire countryside. Waves of emotions washed over her: Regret, longing, despair and resentment, even hatred. She shivered, although the day was much too warm for the uncomfortable way she was dressed.

She wore a bulky and ill-fitting dress, made of plain, thick, grey wool, with a high neckline and long sleeves. It was monstrous and unflattering, like all the dresses she was used to wearing. Along with the dress, she wore a long, heavy cloak and hood that covered her face, hair and body completely. Under the hood, her long hair was pulled back and crudely tied at the nape of her neck with a rough leather thong.

She hated the drab and concealing garb but she had no real choice in the matter. Her older brother, Tom, warned her constantly that if she let anyone see her, her unique beauty could be her downfall. She could fall prey to not only the crude attentions of the village men, but she might also be unfortunate enough to draw the barbarous lust of the Beast, the young knight who ruled as lord of the manor. Remembering the few times she'd seen the knight from a distance riding his great, black warhorse, she shivered again and knew her brother had been right.

Beauty sighed again, softly, and thought to herself, if she hid herself so completely, how would she ever find a man to marry? What man would ever notice her? Who could she ever meet? How could she ever fall in love? She had no idea where to even begin looking for a husband. In truth, she thought ruefully, she had no idea what station or rank of man she should consider since her family's fortunes had sunk so low. Should she try to make friends with one of the peasant boys? Or should she try to find her life's mate amongst the nobility? What about the displaced nobles?

She knew few men from either class, and the few that did know of her had never seen her without the bulky, concealing outfit which was hardly apparel destined to attract a man's attention or arouse his passion.

It seemed to Beauty that she was doomed to a life alone, without a mate or children. She could face life without a husband, if need be, but she longed for children to love. Her resentment of the bleak future was yet another fault she placed straight at the feet of the Beast.

The village men she could handle, it was mainly to avoid the Beast's odious attentions that she was forced to hide herself in such hideous garb, and it was because of him that she now had to work like the lowest field hand. Cursing the Beast under her breath, she smote the hard soil with her hoe.

The Beast ruled his newly acquired lands and peasants with absolute authority, dispensing his own form of law absent regard for justice, and wanting the smallest trace of mercy or compassion. Many men had been tortured or even hung after being accused of the smallest of crimes, and without the least question as to their guilt or innocence.

As lord, the Beast also truly believed he had the absolute right to take any of the women who lived in the village for himself or any of his men. If a woman belonged on his land, he reasoned cruelly, she belonged to him. Both of Beauty's brothers had told her countless tales of the young and innocent women he had taken to the castle. Wild stories of young girls who were both scared and scarred when they were finally returned, battered and bruised, and they also spoke of bastard children left to starve or to scratch out life as just another peasant.

The most frightening stories Beauty had heard were of the girls who never returned at all. There had been too many of them since the Beast had come to be the lord of the land. Some of the village girls had run away, to be sure, but others certainly had not.

There were reports of mangled bodies found in ditches by the roadside or deep in the woods. They had been slaughtered, bloodied and broken before being left to rot. The corpses showed signs of great violence: Bruises, broken bones, rope burns and a multitude of knife wounds. Beauty knew of at least six young girls who had been found murdered in the last five years, all since the Beast had come to rule the castle. More were missing and never to be found.

Beauty even personally knew of a lass named Molly, no older than herself, who came back from a night in the castle after being beaten so severely that she'd been left crippled. Although she never spoke of what happened to her, it was widely known that she was taken to the castle by the order of the Beast. Molly later found out she was pregnant. In desperation, the lass had killed herself and the babe within her. Beauty's older brother had been fond of Molly, had even thought of taking the girl as his wife.

Beauty sighed as she leaned on her crude hoe and rubbed the small of her back with one dirty hand. She paused, exhausted from the sheer drudgery of planting even a small vegetable garden in the rock hard clay, and reflected on the turn her family's fortunes had taken. Once, Beauty and her family had lived a truly happy life and the future stretched out in front of them like a jewel just waiting to be picked up.

Now her father was dead and her older brother worked in the stables at the castle, slaving for the same man he held accountable for so much grief, both for his own family and for the rest of the villagers. He truly believed the Beast to be a monster. The monster who was responsible for poverty and desperation in the village, his own family's downfall, and so many serf girls' bloody and violent deaths.

Tom despised the Beast with his entire being and hated working in the monster's castle but he well knew he had no choice in the matter. His family needed his meagre wages, along with the small amount they made from the crops that Beauty and his younger brother Nate worked so hard to eke from the land on their pitifully sparse farm.

Now, because their father was dead and their lives so filled with despair, their mother, once a beautiful and joyful woman was wasting away, desperately ill in her heart and mind.

For the sake of his family, Tom had swallowed his hatred and his need for revenge and taken the lowly job. Every instinct he possessed, to the deepest corner of his soul called for him to avenge the wrongs done both to his family and to the lass, Molly. Only the knowledge that to do so would not only further endanger his remaining family but also bring about their total ruination, stayed his hand.

At times, Tom hated himself, believing himself to be a weakling and a coward for not seeking his vengeance, but to Beauty he was a true hero for putting his family's survival above his thirst for vengeance. Beauty well knew Tom still held need for that revenge in his heart, only waiting until the right time to strike out and destroy the Beast. She feared the day when Tom's threadbare patience was finally worn through, when his iron control was shattered beyond all endurance. She feared that day for she knew its mark would mean the end of her brother's life.

Beauty returned to her chore, bending her back into the slow, painful job of breaking up the hard clay sod with the hoe, reaching down occasionally to pull up a particularly tough weed. Hearing a faint cry in the distance, she looked up from her toil and saw her younger brother, Nate, running toward her through the fields. She smiled, watching the lad of fourteen years run with all the boundless energy of youth but when he stumbled and almost fell, Beauty knew at once, somewhere deep within herself, that there was grave trouble running along with him.

"Beauty!" Nate was gasping from his desperate run, tears streaking his freckled face. "'Tis awful! The Beast is going to hang Tom!"

"What?" Beauty shrieked. "Nate, quickly tell me what's happened."

"The Beast has learned that someone's been stealing from the grain in the barn. Two of the stable lads were accused and the Beast couldn't decide which was guilty, not that he tried very hard." Nate took a deep breath, trying to choke down his tears. "Beauty, he's already had them both beaten and whipped to bloody pulps. Now they say he plans to hang them both from the castle gates at sundown."

"No!" Beauty's soul seemed to shatter within her and she screamed the single word as she dropped to the stony ground, sobbing.

"I've got to save him!" Nate choked out, his young chin trembling as he struggled to hold back tears. "Beauty, I have got to, but how?"

Instinctively, Beauty knew Nate had no chance at all of saving Tom. Terrified and grief-stricken, she tried to think. Before long, a faint thought came to her and a frightening plan formed in the back of her befuddled brain. She worked almost desperately to think of another plan. She tried to hide from the very idea, tried not to hear her innermost soul whispering the plan to her, but she knew deep in her heart there was only one chance to save Tom.

All her fears seemed to crowd at her, like a pack of wolves circling a spring lamb, and she wondered if she had the necessary nerve to follow through with her plan. She would need all the courage she could muster to do what had to be done but she could see no choice, no other course of action.

"No!" Beauty said firmly, gripping her younger brother's arms. "There is no chance. You cannot hope to save him, but mayhap I can. Go to our mother. Stay with her and comfort her. However this ends, she will truly need both your strength and your support."

"But Beauty, what will you do?" Nate sobbed, fearing the worst. "The Beast will never listen to you! He'll kill you... or worse."

"I have to try," Beauty said, her voice sounding strangely calm in spite of the terror beating like a second heart in her breast. "It would kill Mother if Tom were to be hung. Go to her, Nate, and pray. Pray very hard for Tom and for me."

"Beauty, you cannot go to the Beast. He'll rape and murder you and still hang Tom," Nate sobbed, giving voice to his inner fears.

"Mayhap Nate, but he would certainly murder you and still hang Tom. I have the better chance," Beauty said sternly. "Remember how desperate this is; without Tom, you and our mother would surely starve. I have to go save not only Tom but all of you. Now honour my wishes and give me a kiss before you go to tend to our mother."

When the boy opened his mouth to speak again, Beauty stopped him. "Promise me that you will not attempt to interfere or to rescue me, else what I am doing will be for naught, and the three of you will surely die along with me."

The boy flung himself into his sister's arms and both stood locked together for a long, timeless moment before he kissed her cheek and reluctantly left, headed for their primitive hut.

Beauty took a few seconds, drawing several deep breaths and watched Nate run home. She spent the brief time gathering her wits and courage before she resolutely began the long hike to the castle. She did not even think to take time to wash her face or to change into a clean, more flattering dress. In truth, if she had taken the time to do so, her meagre courage would have deserted her completely.

An all too short time later, she stood at the huge, wooden castle gate fearfully asking the fierce, grizzled soldier who stood guard there for a word with the Beast.

The guard leered as he looked Beauty over, noting her bulky, shapeless form and the dirt covering her hair, face and dress. "His strumpets dinna usually come here unless they've been dragged here. As a rule, they're brought here with their hands tied behind their back and their shoddy clothes ripped almost completely off. Unless they've been tightly bound and gagged, the dirty sluts are generally kicking and screaming their heads off," the guard sneered at Beauty.

"Then mayhap they're not sluts but were in fact pure maidens seeking desperately to preserve their decency," Beauty shot back, angered by the man's callousness.

"Tis highly unlikely, but of no real import." The guard snarled before he asked crudely, "Tis very strange for one of the local sluts to just walk up to the gate as ye did. Did the Beast summon ye?"

"No, but he will wish to see me," Beauty replied with all her dignity wrapped around her like a cloak sheltering her soul.

"Just how would ye be so certain of that?" The huge man leaned over to ask her, his foul breath hitting Beauty in the face. "The master likes his sluts to be beautiful."

For her answer, Beauty silently pulled back her hood, letting him see her face for the first time. Without another word or question the shocked guard admitted her and summoned the nearest serf to take her to the Beast.

Walking behind the skinny, young peasant, a youth Beauty recognized vaguely as the son of one of her neighbours, she was led through the cobbled courtyard. She tried to ignore the catcalls and crude remarks the knight's men directed her way. She kept her head high but her eyes lowered to avoid stepping into any of the filth, mud and horse manure thickly scattered on the smooth, worn cobblestones around the courtyard. Silently, much too frightened to speak, she held her head erect as she followed the lad into the castle, into the very lair of the Beast.

In spite of the day's heat, Beauty shivered as she was led into the great hall, a huge, drafty room with high stone walls, huge beams in the ceiling, and straw strewn on the stone slab floor. There were various carved wooden chairs around the sides of the room, some with dirty brocade seats. In the centre of the room there was a long wooden dining table with great long benches along both sides. There was plenty of room around the great table for servants to move around freely when serving the soldiers and guests who dined there. A smaller, more ornate table and two large, wooden chairs, both carved intricately and having padded brocade seats were set on a raised platform near the end of the room. Iron stands with candles and wall-mounted torches provided faint, barely adequate illumination. An empty fireplace took up most of the end of the room, next to a long, winding, stone staircase.

Tapestries sewn with great detail and care by the former lady of the castle were hanging on two walls. They depicted either hunting and forest scenes or Biblical stories. Seeing the tapestries brought tears to Beauty's eyes until she remembered her quest. The youthful serf quickly left the hall and Beauty stood, quaking and silent, before the great warlord himself.

The Beast stood, still and distant, leaning casually back against the end of the great table. He seemed relaxed as his arms were casually crossed and one knee slightly bent, but instinctively Beauty knew his careless demeanour was deceptive. He was as ready for action as a wolf was ready to spring on its unsuspecting prey. Beauty well knew she was that prey.

He wore a plain, white shirt of soft linen; it was loose with a soft open neckline that showed his lightly furred chest and billowing sleeves gathered at his wrists. The shirt was long, hanging almost to the tops of his thighs, and a wide leather belt circled his waist. He had leather boots that reached his knees. The thick leather gloves he used for fighting and his brown doublet were on the table beside him.

Although Beauty had seen him from a distance, she'd never been close enough to the Beast to make out his features or even his build. Beauty was shocked down to her bones at the sight of him. The man who ruled the land with such brutality, wielding his power with an iron fist and legendary cruelty was not ugly. He bore no resemblance to the ogre or monster he was said to be. To the contrary, he was very handsome! Breathtaking!

Tall and well formed, he was very muscular, without a trace of fat. He had long deep chestnut hair pulled back at his neck. His eyes were a deep, vibrant green, although they were cold and emotionless. He had a surprisingly young face with firm even features, and such a full sensuous mouth that in spite of her terror, Beauty felt a quiver run down her spine, a quiver that was not entirely born of dread.

The Beast never even looked at her; he stood motionless, seemingly at ease, waiting for her to speak before he finally barked, "Who in hell are you and what do you want?"

"M'lord, I am the sister of one of the lads you propose to hang this evening, and I have come to ask for your mercy," she replied with deceptive calm.

"Haven't you heard, lass? I have no mercy," the Beast said coldly. "The two lads are thieves and deserve to die."

"I don't believe you. They're just two lads who were accused. There's no evidence, there's been no hearing. You don't even know which one is guilty, or even if either one is. You are sentencing two innocent young lads to death. It's not right." Beauty's voice quivered. "And my brother Tom is so young, barely more than a boy."

"I am the sole judge of what is right. The lads are both over twenty, certainly old enough to know the penalty for theft is death and they will indeed both hang as I have ordered." The Beast was implacable.

"But, M'lord, I know my brother well. I swear before God, he is no thief," she said meekly as tears formed in her eyes and ran silently down her face.

"Your brother is naught but rabble and all the rabble steal or would if they did not fear me enough and that is why the two lads will make such a good lesson. I care not which of them stole from me, or even if neither of them did the deed. They will serve me well as a warning of my justice and that is reason enough for me to hang them." The Beast looked at her for the first time noticing her covered face and bulky, dirty clothes. "You'll have to give me a better reason than your cries and protests that he is innocent to persuade me to show mercy." His eyes raked insolently over her body, concealed as it was. "A much better reason."

Beauty dropped to the floor and sobbed aloud for a while before gathering her wits. In an act of desperation, she reached out a hand and grabbed the Beast by his ankle.

"Please M'lord, I beg you. I will do anything, I will give you all that I have to save him. I need him, else my mother and younger brother will starve and also… " her soft voice faltered, "I love him. What can I do?"

The Beast sneered at her pleading, but he reached down and pulled her roughly to her feet. "Love? What is that but a soft women's word? I have never known of love and I do not believe in it."

"You've never known love? Not even from your parents?" Beauty was so shocked she forgot herself, looking him straight in the eyes for a quick moment before lowering her gaze and adding, "M'lord."

The Beast thought of himself as a very private man who had long closed himself inside a wall as thick and solid as those enclosing the castle grounds, and nearly as impenetrable. In truth, deep in the core of his soul, he hungered with an ache he would never acknowledge, even to himself. He hungered for just one person to see past the stern warrior to the man buried deep inside.

To be certain, he was not thinking of the peasant girl before him as that person. He thought of the girl as being worthless, of no more importance or intelligence than one of his dogs, but she was the first person ever to pose such a question to him, and almost against his will he answered her truthfully, surprising even himself.

Mayhap a dam broke deep inside his soul releasing a flood of buried emotions or mayhap he was angered by the nerve of the girl and just wanted to let her see herself as the weak fool she was, speaking of wasted emotions like love and mercy.

"I very seldom saw my parents when I was an infant," the Beast scoffed. "From what I've heard, they hired a nurse to care for me. If care is what you'd call it."

"What do you mean, M'lord?" she asked quietly, sensing that he was telling her things he had never spoken aloud before.

Beauty felt a pain coming from within this proud man and knew she had to tread lightly, not letting him see any trace of sympathy. Sympathy that he was sure to take as pity or weakness that he could use to his advantage.

"The nurse kept me swaddled. I was bound so tightly I could barely breathe, or so I've been told, and left hanging from a nail on the wall in filthy rags until I was thought old enough to begin learning to walk and talk. I remember naught of it, of course, but whilst I was in the King's guard I learned that most infants are cherished and well cared for." The Beast paused and shrugged, "It probably did me no harm, and mayhap it even strengthened me."

"And when your parents felt it was time to begin teaching you?" Beauty prompted, heartsick at this tale of abuse.

"All my memories of my parents are the lessons I learned from their fists or their whips. Is that love? Sometimes, if they were too tired or busy to whip me properly when they thought I needed punishment, they had their executioner do the task. A man known far and wide for his brutality. Is that love?" the Beast sneered, not even fully realizing why he was telling her this story. "They fostered me out to another knight for training at the age of seven. He beat me even more often than they did; was that love? I was told constantly that to show any hint of mercy or tenderness would make me seem weak and foolish, that I would be judged not worthy to be a warrior, a knight, or to rule a castle such as this. The lesson was beaten into me daily. And since I've grown up I've seen the truth of their teaching. I have seen naught to change my mind. I've seen the hopelessness of life and the cruelty of war, and I've known men so depraved as to make me seem a weakling, but I have never, ever seen love. I do not believe it exists."

"You have seen love, M'lord. You see it now. It's standing here, now, before you, begging with you," Beauty said proudly. Then she paused and lowered her voice, "I fear you as I have never feared any man before. I have been raised hearing tales of your heartless cruelty, and I have known of women who have been brought here against their will. They've been murdered or killed themselves both before and after submitting to your cruel and lustful attentions. They died in pain and disgrace. With all of that, and knowing full well the risk I take, I stand here offering you anything I can give to save my brother. Is that not love?"

The Beast did not let her see that a touch of her reasoning had struck a spark deep within him. A trace of wonder and a hint of admiration for her courage.

"Why would any woman kill herself after I honoured her with my attentions?" the Beast puzzled out loud, ignoring the shock that threatened to ruin his composure.

Could it be true? Gathering himself, he shoved off the uneasy feeling. Certainly spending a night in his bed, even by force, was not enough to cause a woman to take her own life in despair. What disgrace could there be in pleasuring the lord of the castle?

"It's only a wild story, made to frighten young girls into obedience. It can not be real." He then asked bitterly, "Who told you these tales of my cruelty? I should have him hung as a traitor!"

Beauty saw the trap but knew not how to avoid it.

She dropped her head and whispered softly, "Many have said it, M'lord, tis common talk in the village."

"Including your brother?" the Beast asked quietly; he was no fool.

"Yea, M'lord," Beauty admitted softly, her voice barely a whisper. "Including my brother. He is the one who suggested I dress like this to avoid catching your attention."

"I gave him a decent job and a chance to earn a little money to help his family. Does that not warrant some loyalty? Why should he spread these tales to you? 'Tis nigh treason? You have not helped his cause by telling me thus," the Beast roared.

"There was a lass in the village who he was fond of, he might have even married her until you… took her," Beauty said meekly. "She was a virgin."

"It is my right to claim the maidens. What harm did that do? She could still marry your brother." The Beast was unconvinced.

"She was beaten so badly that she was crippled when you let her return to the village, M'lord, and soon found herself to be pregnant with your child." Beauty met his cold stare head on. "My brother still would have wed her, I think, but she killed herself in despair. Please, M'lord, understand that he did not tell me these things to be disloyal to you but because he fears for me, that I might meet a similar fate."

"Yet you stand before me, having come here on your own accord, offering yourself to me. What would he think of that I wonder?" the Beast taunted her. "Would he be pleased that you offer to give yourself to me?"

"He'll know why I did it, and understand, I pray, but he will still be furious." Beauty swallowed before she continued, "And I will be, in truth, eternally dishonoured. If I can save his life, it will be well worth the price."

"And will he not try to take vengeance for you?" the Beast sneered and wondered aloud. "Against me? I would, for a sister well loved, if I believed in love at all."

"He will not. I swear it," Beauty said steadily. "I have a mother and a younger brother for him to protect. He would not abandon them or put their lives at risk to save me."

The Beast paced the room, agitated at this glimpse of the girl's mind. Finally he paused, tamping down his fury before continuing, "What exactly are you offering? For all your fine talk, so far as I can tell, there's nothing at all about you to interest me in the least."

Beauty silently pushed her hood back, letting him see her face for the first time. She reached up and pulled the leather thong, releasing her dirty but long, flowing hair.

The Beast stared at her, amazed and stunned. He struggled to maintain his icy demeanour, to hide his disconcerting reaction from her. Beauty was the most beautiful woman he'd ever seen, at least her face was, even covered as it was with dirt. She was young, maybe eighteen, barely more than a girl, and seemed very petite. She had clear blue eyes, perfect cheekbones, a generous mouth with even white teeth, smooth clear skin and thick dark blond hair.

The Beast found his voice and snarled, "You've been working in the fields too long, lass, and you are very dirty. Indeed, right now you look more like a plough horse in need of a good grooming than a lass I wouldst bed, but I will admit you could clean up passably well, and your teeth do seem to be decent. Now drop your cloak and let me see if there's a body worthy of my interest under all that wrapping."

Beauty was torn between being insulted, defiant and afraid. Her eyes flashed as she struggled to hold her tongue and her mind worked feverishly to figure out if she was helping her brother at all or hurting his cause. Slowly, her eyes down, she removed the heavy, concealing cloak, dropping it to the floor.

The Beast was no stranger to a woman's charms so he could tell that she had a stunning figure beneath her loose, bulky dress. Her breasts were very full and round for someone so slender. They stood out proudly against the rough material. He was amazed and more than a little angry that she'd been hidden from him. After all, she was his property!

He decided to get a little revenge. It would be fun to see how long it would take him to shatter her spirit. Even through the dress, he noted her shaking legs and wondered if she would even last out the night.

"You still have too many clothes on. For all I can tell you have no shape at all," the Beast snarled. "I said disrobe."

"M'lord!" Beauty blushed.

"Is not your brother worth it? What did you think would happen when you offered to do anything to save him? Didst you think I would leave him go without demanding payment?" The Beast was without mercy, leaning into her pale, ashen face as he finished with deadly quiet. "Without seizing payment from your body and your very soul?"

"I am more than ready to do anything you ask of me to save my brother's life," Beauty replied softly as she slowly struggled to remove her clothes with numb fingers. "But, M'lord, I am an innocent, a virgin. No man has ever seen me undressed or touched me. I admit

I'm afraid of you, yet I will do whatever you ask if you will but free my brother."

"You will do whatever I ask of you whether or not I free your brother." That it was a statement of cold, hard fact, and not a threat made the utterance even more chilling. "If I wanted to bed you in the shadow of your brother's hanging corpse, you would obey."

She gave a soft involuntary gasp at his bitter statement. She had undressed down to her soft shift and knew it offered no protection from his piercing eyes. She stood still before him, her erect nipples clearly outlined against the thin fabric, eyes down and knees shaking. The Beast looked her over, noting the firm thrust of her breasts, the curve of her tiny waist and the soft flare of the hips. His eyes skimmed down and he realized that her legs were long and well formed. She seemed flawless. He felt himself grow hard with desire.

"The shift too, if you think your brother's life is worth it," he growled roughly.

Without a word she slowly slid the straps of the shift off her shoulders, letting it fall gently to the floor. She raised her eyes, staring straight ahead. Naked, she stood before him, looking proud and unafraid. It was a sham; although she appeared outwardly calm, inside her stomach was roiling, and she struggled hard not to faint.

The Beast knew well how to read the tension in her face, the slight clenching of her jaw, the furrow between her brows. He knew the effort she made to appear calm and felt a faint hint of admiration for her courage. Knights had shown more fear facing him than did this lass.

He tamped down the admiration and sneered cruelly, "Why should I release your brother? You are mine anyway, and I can have you anytime I want. I should hang your brother for trying to hide you from me, and if I could do it twice, in all likelihood, I would. God's truth, I should have you whipped for hiding yourself from me but I'd hate to mar that silky skin before I had a chance to touch it. You were very foolish indeed to come here. Now, go upstairs and prepare yourself. I'll attend to you shortly, after I have hanged your brother."

Chapter Two

"No!" Beauty shrieked.

In that instant, all her attempts to appear calm and unafraid were for naught. She struggled to control her sobs as her legs gave out and she slumped once more to the cold stone floor. She raised her teary eyes with tremendous effort, and for the first time deliberately met the Beast's gaze head on and held his eyes.

What she saw in his eyes both amazed and strangely saddened her. The eyes of the Beast, eyes that were known far and wide to be merciless and cold, filled with cruel rage and hate were instead bleak, touched with pain, filled with loneliness and hopelessness.

"M'lord, I am not a fool. I knew well the peril I faced coming here. Truly, you can and probably will ravage me anytime you feel the urge, and do anything with me, however vicious and cruel, that fills your dark desire. I know I cannot withstand you or refuse you anything, including my own death. That is the power you hold over me, over all of us in the village. It is your privilege by right of conquest and by sheer strength." She swallowed a few times, still holding his eyes. "I am only a commoner and a woman, a small woman at that. You may take my body and demand anything you want to from me, but there is still one thing you cannot take from me by force, something I can still give or withhold from you only at my own will."

"What is that?" She'd barely managed to pique his curiosity but it was just enough to bring the question out.

"The thing you claim never to have felt or known, real affection, mayhap even love." Beauty paused, choosing her words with care. "You can rape me now, 'tis true, but if you will release my brother unharmed, I promise I will stay with you willingly tonight and do anything you ask, freely and with affection. If you release my brother unharmed you can do anything you want to me: Rape me, beat me, use me in any odious way you choose, and I will still strive to love you and serve you faithfully in any way I possibly can all through the night."

"All through the night? What if one night isn't enough for me?" the Beast asked sourly. "What if all the things I want to do to you, to your body and to your very soul, take more than one night? Is the rest of your brother's life only worth one night of yours?"

"Truly, I meant to put no limits on what I would do for you, M'lord, or how long I would stay with you," Beauty told him seemingly calmly. "'Tis just that it's well known that you only use a woman for one night. No woman has ever been known to hold your interest any longer than that. Why should I think to be any different from the others?"

"If I were to free your brother, I would ask much more of you than one night in bed, even with your willingness. I would ask that for as long as I want you to serve me, you would do so. I would ask for the use of your body in my bed and for you to service me in any way I wish during the day, either as my lowest servant or as my whore. If I tire of you, I would put you away from me in whatever manner I wish. I may give you to one of my soldiers as a reward for his good service or I may even decide to kill you," the Beast glared at her sternly. "In other words, Beauty, to save your brother's life, you must give yourself to me completely and forever. You must become my chattel just like my horse or my dog. Is your brother worth such a sacrifice?"

"Yea, M'lord. I would agree to anything to save him." Beauty's voice trembled.

"And knowing I think of you as a possession, could you still do anything I ask freely and with affection as you said you would? Could you even begin to try to love me?" the Beast challenged her.

"M'lord, I give you my word." Beauty broke away from his gaze and lowered her eyes, her voice was hardly more than a whisper. "And I meant it. I knew it would not be easy."

For a long moment, the Beast made no reply. Silently, he studied Beauty with a guarded expression as he considered the situation.

Against his will, the spark of interest she had ignited within him began to grow. What was it like, the Beast wondered, to bed a woman without terror in her eyes? Without knowing only her pleading and her tears? To have sex with a lass who wasn't scared and begging for mercy?

Once he'd been at court and soon learned that even the town whores feared him when he sampled their crude wares. They put on a brave face when they saw his purse, but they plied their trade reluctantly and quickly, disappearing as fact as they could.

How could it feel, he wondered, to have someone stand by his side willingly? To have someone he could go to for comfort and companionship, even someone who would come to him for the same. Someone to spend the long winter evenings relaxing with him. Possibly even to have someone reach out for him with affection. Would it be wonderful? Was it even possible or was this just a woman's trick? He debated whether he could release the boy without being seen as too weak and soft to rule. He decided that he could.

Without a word, he determined it was worth the boy's life to find out what a willing, affectionate woman was worth. After all, he could always hang the rascal later if he changed his mind.

Keeping his thoughts and longings to himself, the Beast growled, "How could you promise to love me? Lass, you don't know anything about me except for all the tales you've heard. All those wild stories of my cruelty."

"Are they true?" Beauty asked softly, hesitantly. "Those reports of your cruelty, could they possibly all be true?"

"Most of them, the worst of them, probably are true. I am a very hard and harsh man," the Beast answered coldly. "Anyway, it makes no difference, I will take you to my bed tonight and then you will know for yourself. But make no mistake, Lass, I will take you with or without releasing your brother, whether you want me or not. It matters little to me how you feel about it. If I'm the monster you believe me to be, can you still promise me your love?"

"I can and will love you, in a small way, for the saving of my brother's life but 'tis true it's not the same deep, abiding love, filled with passion, that's said to be found sometimes between a woman and a man. It's not the romantic love that poets sing songs about. I, myself, do know that sort of love truly exists, as my parents felt it for each other, but I've never found it. I can, however, promise to give you my admiration, my deepest loyalty, my lasting respect, and even my real affection."

Unexpectedly, the Beast hid a grin. "I note you didn't promise to give me your obedience. I want one more promise from you."

"What more can I promise you, M'lord?" Beauty asked shyly, still shaking. "The obedience I just now failed to mention?"

"Nay, I can assure your obedience without much effort on my part. Be defiant if you like, for a while. A small woman like you is pitifully easy to bring under control. I'll even enjoy bending you to my will, if you can manage to make it into enough of a challenge. The last promise I want from you is this: I want you to swear never to see any of your family again, even when I tire of you and send you away or give you over to one of my men as a plaything." The Beast had no faith at all in her promises and protestations of loyalty so he decided to test her, to push her as far as he could.

Bleak despair washed over her. It took a moment for her to manage to say the words, her voice was trembling and her throat seemed frozen shut.

"Yea, M'lord, I swear it," she whispered in heartfelt anguish.

"Then, I'll consider it," he curtly replied. "Be quiet, wench, and let me think."

Without realizing why, he felt compelled to goad her into backing out of her oath. To prove she was treacherous like all the others in his life had been, men and women both.

There was only one woman who had stayed beside him throughout his life. She was a young widow who once served as a maid in the castle of the knight he was fostered to. At the time she became his maid, she had just recently lost her young son, along with her husband, to the great plague.

The sad young maid, Gwyneth, had taken to the small boy she helped care for. In him, she saw only the loneliness that mirrored her own grief, not the budding cruelty of the Beast. She had mothered him tenderly when she could, but the knight of the castle and the

Beast himself made it difficult. Now she was growing older, without a husband or children of her own.

She had returned with the Beast to his father's castle when he was a grown knight. The Beast even heard rumours that Gwyneth had for a short time been his father's mistress, as he had begun to recover from the death of his second wife. The Beast never knew or even cared if the rumours were true.

Still, she stayed with the Beast, following him to this castle. She worked hard, managing his castle and worrying over the man he'd become. Gwyneth was the only one who truly cared for him. She was also the only person who felt comfortable enough around the Beast to nag him, and even that was very rare indeed.

Everyone else had deserted him. They had all proven to be shallow and uncaring. If Beauty were to prove truly as loving and steadfast as she appeared to be, then he feared her instinctively, for she was a threat to everything he was raised to believe in. Still he had to know.

He gestured to her clothes strewn about on the stone floor. "Get dressed."

"M'lord, whatever you decide, may I go to see my brother? Just to say goodbye since I will never see him again once he's been hung," Beauty choked out the last words and paused, swallowing several times and breathing deeply before she could continue. "Or, with hope, once he is freed and my promise to you takes effect."

Beauty rose quickly and pulled on her shift and the loose dress with shaking fingers.

The Beast pondered for a moment then called for a servant, his eyes never leaving Beauty's.

To her surprise, the servant who answered his summons was known to Beauty from the past. She was so upset that she couldn't place his name at that moment but he was an older man, probably in his fifties. He was trim and spry with a handsome face, and he was surprisingly well groomed compared to most of the village people Beauty knew.

The servant was dressed in brown hose, a white shirt and a dark brown doublet with no trim. His simple clothes appeared clean and neat, and he seemed to have bathed quite recently, a rarity indeed.

He showed no sign of recognizing Beauty, although she learned later that indeed he had. She also soon remembered that his name was Seth, and that he'd once been the personal servant to the old lord.

"Send for the maid, Gwyneth, to clean this girl up and get her in my bedchamber ready for me," the Beast growled, ignoring the servant's start of surprise.

He paused, and Beauty's knees buckled before the Beast continued, "And get word to the stables to release... " his voice trailed off and he cocked his brow at Beauty.

"Tom." Beauty supplied quickly, a stunned smile lighting her face for the first time.

"Tom. He's tied up in the last stall. He's to go free," the Beast ordered, mesmerized against his will at the force of Beauty's smile.

"M'lord," the stately servant hesitated, almost scared to believe what he'd heard.

He avoided looking at Beauty, now fully realizing why she was there. Without any words, he knew exactly what bargain she'd made and why. A curious mixture of relief and abhorrence filled him. Not that he judged her harshly for the bargain. Knowing her as he did, he knew she had no choice in the matter. He sighed for the old lord, and wondered how such things had come to pass.

"What is it?" The Beast held Beauty's gaze, amazed, almost speechless, at the joy in her eyes.

"Both of the lads are named Tom," the quiet servant pointed out.

"Then set them both free!" the Beast bellowed in a sudden temper. "I'm tired of this business and I have better things to do."

"M'lord," Beauty asked timidly, repeating her request, "may I see my brother for a moment before I go with the maid?"

"You will return to fill your promise?" the Beast asked.

"You have my word," Beauty replied.

"I have never trusted in promises, very few men of my acquaintance are worthy of trust and none of the women," the Beast snarled.

"Then let me prove myself to be the first," Beauty said calmly. "Truly, I am yours willingly and I do not seek to escape, but I would like to see my brother safe."

"Then it's you who does not trust me or my word," the Beast's tempered flared quickly and Beauty realized there was still the very real danger of losing her fight to save Tom.

"I do, M'lord, truly. 'Tis just a woman's way to want to reassure herself that her loved ones are all safe, that all is aright with them. Also, I would like a moment to calm my nerves before…" her voice trailed off.

"You said you'd be willing," the Beast growled, reaching out and grabbing her by the arms.

"M'lord, I am willing, truly," Beauty stood in his harsh grasp without flinching. She looked him in the eyes and smiled shyly, "But I never claimed not to be nervous, as is a virgin's right. Even a virgin who marries for love can be nervous the first night. Please, M'lord?"

"All right, but return shortly," the Beast told her gruffly. "And remember that I can always hang him later, so warn him and be warned yourself: I will only keep this bargain as long as you keep it and as long as he gives me no more problems as he works."

"You still want him to work in the stables, M'lord?" Beauty was surprised. "After all this?"

"Why not? He does his job well and I wondered who I would find to replace him." The Beast was surprised at her question, as though a narrow escape from the gallows should not matter a whit to her or to her brother. "Now go!"

"Yes, M'lord." She turned and moved quickly to follow the servant. "And thank you, M'lord."

The Beast watched as she walked away, noting the grace of her stride and the sway of her hips. How long, he wondered? How long will it take for me to prove her to be the liar she has to be? How long before she loses her resolve? The game would be fast and furious but he already knew the outcome; Beauty would soon prove to be as inconstant as everyone else in his life.

As soon as they were out of earshot, the servant asked, "Beauty, how is your lady mother?"

"She is very ill," Beauty told him gently. "I think it's mainly from sorrow. She misses my father deeply, and she has lost much."

"Oft I've wanted to leave the castle and see her but I wasn't sure if

31

it would be wise," he said with quiet dignity. "Or if I would even be welcome."

"You are always welcome, Seth, but 'tis true we have as little to do with the castle inhabitants as possible," she shrugged sadly. "I never thought I would step foot into the place again."

The servant looked at her gently and said, "I sent the word to Nate about your brother but I was torn apart by it. I both hoped and feared that you would come, Beauty. I fretted over it all day for I knew of no other way for Tom's life to be spared, but it breaks my heart to see you come to such a state. I feel as if I've failed your father."

"Seth, my old friend, that's not true," Beauty told him gently. Her quiet acceptance of the situation had increased as soon as the Beast was out of sight. "Do you disapprove of me?"

"I disapprove of the situation, lass, never of you," Seth told her gently. "I will strive to help you in any way I can."

"Thank you, Seth." She gasped as a thought hit her. "How is it that you had to ask which Tom should be released? You know my brother well."

The servant shrugged, "I hoped the Beast would be so blinded by your beauty that he would do just what he did. I took a chance that he would let both lads go. The other poor lad had no one to save him. It worked, did it not?" The servant winked as he held the barn door open for her.

A short time later, after a tearful exchange with her brother, Beauty returned to the great hall and presented herself to the maid, Gwyneth. She soon found herself in the knight's great bedchamber, a large room that seemed to be barren except for a fireplace, a wardrobe against a wall, a small table, a mirror, a chair and a great big bed. There was a large fur rug on the floor in front of the fireplace.

The bed seemed to Beauty to take up all the room. It was a four-poster, made of rich dark wood and covered with deep intricate carving. There was a deep feather mattress, crisp linen sheets, and great piles of fur coverings for warmth and comfort.

The fireplace was already lit against the evening chill. A large metal tub was brought into the room and placed before the fireplace. Men had been ordered to bring hot water to fill the tub.

The maid had brought a silver platter of food with her, tender meats, bread and ripe fruits. She ordered Beauty to eat as they waited for the tub to be filled. Beauty's nerves were stretched so tight that her stomach rebelled at the thought of food but she had not eaten since early morn. She was hungry and she knew she would need her strength to get through the night ahead. Flashing a grateful smile at the maid, she picked at the food.

When she'd eaten all she could force down her tight throat, Beauty stood beside the tub, submitting herself to the dubious ministrations of the maid. The maid was a middle-aged woman, maybe forty, dressed in a plain, straight grey dress, with white lace at the neck and cuffs. Her brown hair was lightly streaked with grey, and pulled severely back into a tight bun. There was no welcoming light in her soft brown eyes. She seemed to take Beauty's presence in the castle as just another distraction, a source of still more chores to be done.

She barely spoke to Beauty, and when she did, not in very civilized tones. She barely let the two men finish pouring boiling water into a large metal tub before she stripped Beauty's clothes right off her body, ripping them, and silently pointed at the steaming bathtub.

Without a word Beauty stepped into the water, visibly flinching at the scalding heat. She gave control of her body over to the austere servant who bathed her, scrubbing her vigorously and roughly all over. The maid then washed and rinsed her long hair. Beauty stood as the maid dried her with a rough towel. The maid towelled her hair, then brushed it dry. Lastly, she rubbed scented oil over Beauty's skin, frowning as she noted the calluses on Beauty's hands.

Finishing her silent inspection, the maid finally spoke to Beauty.

She asked coldly, "Who are you Lass? And why are you here?"

"I'm just a peasant from the village," Beauty answered softly, shyly. "And I'm here to save my brother's life."

"Your brother was one of the lads who was supposed to be hanged?" The maid was surprised, muttering, "Queer business that."

"How so?" Beauty's interest was piqued and she forgot her nudity.

"Tis a bit of a mystery how the theft came to the master's attention. No one actually saw the theft and no one noticed any grain missing, so who told the head guard? 'Twas Gerrin himself told the tale to the master," the maid puzzled. "Anyway that's not what I was asking you. Who are you?"

"Just one of the villagers. They call me Beauty," she replied calmly.

"'Tis fitting enough," the maid chuckled almost against her will. "But it's not your given name, I'll wager, and you are not just one of the village maidens."

"I lived there before tonight," Beauty asserted, uncertain just what this woman knew about her. "In the village."

"Sure lass, if that's what you want me to believe." The maid paused. "Be ye a virgin?"

"Yea." The reply was soft and nervous, the truthfulness of the claim written all over Beauty's face.

"Have courage, lass," the maid said softly. "Many of the stories you've heard about my master are not true. He's a rough man to be sure, but he's a good man inside. I believe he has love and mercy locked away somewhere inside him but he doesn't know it yet."

"How can a man not know when he holds human emotions deep inside his soul?" Beauty puzzled aloud.

"He was raised not to show any emotion at all, except anger and ferocity. Any trace of humanity was soon thrashed out of him. He needs a strong woman who can show him the secrets of the heart, one who can teach mercy to the Beast. 'Tis a job that will take a great deal of inner strength." The older woman looked Beauty over carefully and poured her a glass of dark Spanish wine.

Her manner gentled and her tone softened. "You just may be the one."

"What one?" Beauty refused to see the woman's point and ignored the proffered glass.

"God's truth, the woman who can tame the Beast!" The woman smiled softly as Beauty gasped. "It'll be the hardest thing you've ever tried. Take the wine." She paused until Beauty did so. "You'll need the courage of a legion of fighting men and the patience of a saint, and all the endurance you can muster. You might be able to do it though. I've a feeling."

"Why would I try to tame the Beast? Right now, I just want to survive the night," Beauty said softly, sipping the rich wine. "I want to serve the Beast well enough so that he doesn't regret the bargain we made."

"Someone has to reach his soul, to find the man within. With courage, you will be the one. Me name's Gwyneth. Seek me out in the kitchen in the morning if you need aught. And drink at least one more glass of the wine before he comes to you, maybe two, but no more," the maid told her softly before putting a soft, sheer gown of linen and delicate white lace over Beauty's head and leading her to the bed. "Two or three glasses may help ye, but any more would truly make things worse."

The maid waited for Beauty to get into the bed before she stepped out into the hall and ordered the men in to empty the tub. Alone in the huge bed waiting for the Beast to come to and take her, Beauty was more than nervous, she was truly scared. She sipped a second glass of wine as she looked within herself, deep into her heart and soul. She decided that the only way she could keep her promise to the Beast and her own self-respect was to accept the promise she'd made, within her own heart and mind at least, as a marriage vow.

After she spent time with the Beast she knew she would be ruined, far too much in disgrace to ever marry another man anyway. To her, for the sake of her sanity, this had to be a marriage and she would honour it as such even though there was no priest and even though to the Beast it would be a mere dalliance. Her resolve was firm as she came to a kind of peace within her own mind. As the maid had suggested, a third glass of wine helped.

Waiting alone in the huge bed, she clung to the thought of her brother and remembered their hurried conversation earlier in the main barn.

The barn was a large wooden shed, with stalls for more than twenty horses, a hayloft, and piles of deep clean straw and sweet smelling hay. A room off to one side held tack and armour, while off to the other side stood a forge where several blacksmiths constantly laboured over the making of horseshoes, swords and arrowheads, along with other weapons and crude tools.

Both of the condemned men were held deep in the far end of the stables. She found her brother Tom chained to the wall in a stall filled with dirty hay. He and the other Tom, a lanky youth, were both considered too lowly and unworthy to even be taken to the dungeon. Both of the men had soiled their clothes from being tied up all day unable to undo their pants, and the stench in the stall was foul. As soon as they were unchained, the other Tom ran home, leaving Beauty alone with her brother.

Tom was covered with filth. He had been beaten almost beyond Beauty's recognition. His handsome face was covered with bruises and his dark brown eyes were filled with despair and fear. His dark blonde hair was dirty and matted. Tom loved his sister dearly and once he learned of the bargain, he had pleaded with her to leave him to his fate and save herself but she held fast. She could not bear to see him hung. He wanted her to run but she refused to flee.

"He'd just hang us both! You know there is no escape from the lord," Beauty sobbed. "Furthermore, I gave him my vow. You know I cannot break it."

"I know you always honour your word, Beauty, but I don't want you to end up like Molly!" Tom protested, tears in his eyes. "I cannot leave you to the Beast. It would kill our mother."

"I can only hope and pray that I don't meet the same fate as Molly. You know that I have to be the one who stays here, brother. First, because I love you, but also because I have looked at the facts with a cold reason. See it like this: If you are hung, we will not be able to keep from starving, lest I turn into a whore. If I stay with the Beast, you will be able to provide for Nate and mother, and only one of us will be lost. True, he will certainly disgrace and dishonour me, he may even kill me, but as long as the three of you are safe I know I will, in some small way, manage to be content." Beauty said before adding cautiously, "I do believe however, against all reason, that all will turn out well in the end."

"Sister!" Tom was shocked. "Could it be that you are attracted to the Beast? Do you have soft feelings for this monster of a man?"

"I confess that he is the most beautiful man I have ever seen, brother, but I am deathly afraid of him. He scares me with his smallest glance. Indeed, he is almost inhuman, with no trace of compassion or mercy in him." Beauty lowered her gaze. "Nevertheless, I did give him my promise. I will strive to love him and to give him my affection for showing you mercy. I will try to keep my word, in all ways. 'Tis true, I fear him greatly but I made my choice and I gave my word. I'm glad to be able to save you. Pray for me, please God, pray that it will all be well for me."

"I'll pray for you, Beauty." Tom hugged her tight before he let her go reluctantly, ignoring the tears in her eyes. "And I'll work to find a way to save you."

"Do not. Do not even think of it," Beauty replied firmly. "And please God, Tom, do not attempt any vengeance. 'Twould be the death of us all, Nate and our mother too." She held his eyes and put all her love into her words. "From this night on, I will be dead to you and our family, and disgraced as well. My only salvation, Tom, is you. As long as you are safe, dear brother, I will find some happiness. Go home now and see to our mother and Nate but remember to return on the morrow to work here."

"How can I work here knowing what must be happening to you inside the castle?" Tom muttered.

"You have to, else our mother and Nate will surely perish. It might be that your job will even give us a chance to see each other once in a while, even though as of now he commands me to swear never to see any of my family again. It's a small barn, and mayhap I'll get to ride with him sometimes," Beauty whispered, hugging him close. "Go now. Be strong and pray for me that I'm all right."

The poignant memory of those few precious moments with her brother strengthened her resolve to please the Beast. Beauty waited in his bed, dreading the arrival of the Beast, and yet hoping he'd come soon so that she could find out what fate held in store for her. The wine helped a bit but the waiting was fearful and seemed to last forever. Before long however, she heard his footsteps, sure and heavy, coming up the hall. In that instant, it seemed to Beauty that the wait had not been long enough, that the Beast had come to her all too soon.

Chapter Three

The Beast entered his bedchamber and slammed the door. Suddenly the large room appeared to grow smaller to Beauty. The very walls seemed to be closing in on her and she felt trapped. Her breath caught in her throat and she struggled to breathe as the very air surrounding her seemed to suddenly turn thick and sluggish. In spite of the wine, she began to tremble, shaking uncontrollably. The Beast appeared to ignore her completely, not looking her way or speaking as his hands went to the fastenings of his clothes. His very silence further unnerved her.

Lying there on the bed, looking at him as he quickly shed his clothes, she was both terrified and mesmerized by his strong, muscular body and his physical perfection. In spite of what she'd heard both from him and about him, the real shock though came when he removed his tunic and saw the multitude of scars covering his perfect form. As he briefly turned his back, she gasped as she noticed that although there were several obvious battle wounds on him, his back was almost completely covered with old scars that seemed to have come from countless merciless whippings.

"Is something bothering you, lass?" the Beast mumbled, irritated and still looking for her to try to back out of her agreement, "Or are you finding your agreement easier to make than to keep?"

"Nay, M'lord, I was but shocked to see the proof of your words about how you'd been raised, M'lord, and the reminders of how many battles you've fought. 'Tis rare for one so young to have been in so many wars, but the truth of your words is reflected by the great number of scars on your body." Beauty met his gaze and whispered, "Any man who has lived the life you must have lived and seen such ugliness as you've witnessed would surely have to be completely hardened to the softer emotions, truly."

"You think my body's ugly, lass?" the Beast growled, deliberately misunderstanding her. "It makes no difference to me."

"No! I think you have a truly well made body, M'lord, 'tis strong and well muscled. You have a very pleasing face too. 'Tis what's been done to you that's ugly." Beauty paused, not realizing that her words had pleased him strangely. "I don't like to think of anyone, let alone the one man I have promised to love, undergoing so much torment and suffering. Remember, M'lord, I have promised to love you in my own way."

"Rest easy, lass." The Beast almost smiled in spite of himself. "It's far too late to change the past and it served to toughen me, to make me fit to lead vast armies, to fight battles and to win wars, and to rule."

"I don't believe you have to be so hard to rule. The old lord ruled this land wisely and yet with compassion, M'lord. He was clearly respected by the serfs but also well loved by them. He knew how to rule reasonably with justice tempered by mercy. The local peasants prospered but so did he and his family. He was widely known to truly love his wife and children, and they loved him deeply," Beauty pointed out, a slight tremor in her voice. "He was truly a fair and just man."

"And now the old lord is dead," the Beast countered coldly, stalking over to the bed.

He sat on the edge of the bed and removed his hose and boots. "And his family has disappeared. Now his castle is mine to hold, his lands and peasants mine to rule. Does that not prove he was too weak?"

"And would you, with all your cold, bitter fury and strength of will have withheld against an invading horde any better than he did? Your King sent ten times as many men as the old lord had, all of them well trained and heavily armed. It was not lack of strength or courage that brought the old lord down but overwhelming odds, lack of trained fighting men and good weapons," Beauty pointed out.

"What brought this matter to your mind now? Do you seek to argue or reason your way out of my bed?" The Beast stood up and walked over to fetch the wine, then returned and stood looking down at her.

"No, M'lord, I went at it clumsily but I wanted to point out that here, in this one place, the warrior can also be a man. You can drop your guard and still be safe," Beauty said proudly. "I will not betray you but will stand proudly beside you in times of strife."

"Be warned, lass, for I am not a fool. I know what is said behind my back, that someday I'll meet the woman who can tame the Beast. I think there's something more on your pretty mind. I think you seek to be that woman, to be the one to tame the Beast. The woman who can teach me what love is," the Beast grinned without any humour in it. "Beware my lass, for it cannot be done, and certainly not by the likes of you."

"Tame the Beast? Ha! What mere woman could manage such a miracle?" Beauty responded with seeming calm but somewhere deep inside her soul the idea had taken root.

She looked up at him as he stood by the bed, naked. Her emotions were jumbled but her mind was clear and fixed. She knew the risks she took by being there with the Beast, not only in his bed but also in his hands, and under his control. In her heart, mayhap to ease her conscience, she saw this pact much as an arranged marriage.

She also realized that the real key to her survival, not only the survival of her body but also the survival of her spirit and her soul did indeed depend on her being able to tame the Beast. She had to succeed or he would surely crush her. Not that she needed to tame him by making him into a weakling, she grasped intuitively, but simply by showing him how to trust someone enough to lower his iron guard and reveal the man hidden deep inside the facade.

She needed to show the Beast that the peasants whom he took for no more than mere animals in the fields were indeed real human beings, with all the hopes, despair, love, fears and dreams of any other people. It was her only chance, albeit a faint one, to improve things not only for herself and her family but also for the villagers.

She also needed to discover his dreams and strive to make his dreams hers, to help him achieve them. She would have to learn to share his goals, worries and responsibilities. The hard part was that she needed to do all this without his knowing it and most certainly without his cooperation; she only needed to overcome his lifetime of hard fought training and deeply held beliefs to achieve it.

The Beast, pouring himself a goblet of wine, climbed into the bed. It was a measure of his lack of regard for Beauty that he simply didn't consider offering some to her.

Drinking deeply, he turned to her and asked gruffly, "What do they call you, lass?"

Beauty struggled not to shrink away from him, but she was nervous in spite of herself. "They call me Beauty, M'lord."

"It suits you, lass," he grinned and reached out for her. "But I doubt it's your given name."

In spite of herself, she shrank slightly from his reach. Her trembling increased and she seemed to shrink back into the mattress.

"Breaking your word already?" the Beast growled. "You said you'd be willing and loving."

"I am," Beauty protested softly, "but I am also still nervous, M'lord. Even a true bride on her wedding night is entitled to be a little timid. I know nothing of the things that happen between a man and a woman in bed. I don't know what you expect me to do, or what you want to do to me. Please, M'lord, be just a wee bit patient and show me what you want of me so that I can please you. You made me very happy today when you released my brother. Let me do the same for you."

Without a word, the Beast stretched out his arm and pulled her over to him. His action was not as rough as it was before but it was implacable and there was no escape. Instinctively, Beauty reached out her small, work-roughened hand and placed it on his chest. She stared into his eyes and gently rubbed a small circle on his chest, feeling the slight coarseness of the light covering of dark hair.

"What do you want me to do, M'lord?" she whispered softly. "What pleases you?"

"Your hand, touching me, pleases me." The Beast was surprised at the answer that came out of his own mouth. "Have you never touched a man in such a way before, lass?"

When Beauty silently shook her head, the Beast lay back and

relaxed slightly, reining himself in and forcing himself to hold back his desires for just a minute. He decided to slow down a bit, even though he was more than ready. He would let this sprite of a girl-woman get to know him just a little before he took her. He wasn't being weak or kind, his mind whispered defending his decision to himself, he was simply prolonging his own moment of pleasure.

"Then, lass, feel free to explore," he whispered as he cupped her hand with his own and dragged it softly along down his body.

"Truly, M'lord?" Beauty was shyly pleased in spite of her fears.

"Truly," the Beast grinned at her, already finding her timid willingness strangely touching. "I'll bear up under it somehow."

Beauty tried to ignore the quiver she felt, seeing him grin. She stroked his hard chest with her delicate hands, exploring and tracing his old wounds and his firm muscles. She delighted in the hard contours and light furring of his chest. She rubbed one finger lightly over one of his nipples and felt his body jerk in reaction.

"Is that bad, M'lord? Did I do something wrong? I'm truly sorry." Alarmed, she looked up into his face, afraid that he might be displeased with her actions.

The Beast clenched his jaw, "No lass, do not be sorry. It feels very good, almost too good. Pray continue." He finally smiled and said a word he had seldom used before. "Please."

Slightly reassured, she returned her attention to his chest. With one small hand she was once more touching one of his nipples and flicking her thumb over its nub.

The Beast found himself fighting for control over his body and his urges but he also realized he was actually enjoying the sensations she roused in him.

Beauty kept up her sensual exploration, her hands moving ever so slowly downward. She teased his navel, explored his hips and muscled abdomen before going ever lower, and even encountered the thick thatch of dark curls below his waist.

She paused before she finally teased the wiry curls but she carefully avoided touching his erect manhood until the Beast quickly took her hand in his and firmly guided it to him, showing her the motion he hungered so much to feel. She blushed as she felt the length and thickness of his fully erect penis. As she slid her hand along its length, she marvelled at the texture of it, the soft skin covering the hard muscle inside.

"It's so big! Doesn't it get in your way?" she asked, completely without guile. "All hard and sticking up like that?"

In spite of himself, and for the first time in a long time, the Beast laughed openly. "It's not like that all the time, lass, only when I'm ready for a woman."

The timid, sensual stroking continued for a moment before the Beast continued in a tight voice, "Lass, if you truly want to please me, you should know one thing: Any place you explore with your hands, you can also explore with your mouth."

Beauty blushed furiously but she mumbled, "As M'lord wishes."

Gingerly she lowered her mouth to his chest, shyly licking and kissing him. Remembering his reaction to the touch of her hand on his nipple, she gently licked at the nub with her tongue before nipping it. Her hands were still stroking his erect manhood.

Suddenly, the stroking of her hands and the gentle touch of her mouth was too much for the Beast to bear. With a low growl, he signalled that her brief respite was at an end. He ripped the thin gown from her and rolled over on top of her without a word and used his knee to spread her legs apart. He entered her quickly and roughly, ignoring her scream of anguish.

She felt a pain like she'd never felt before as he shredded her virginity. He used no care or finesse with her. He thrust hard and fast with no thought of tenderness or mercy. He thought only of his own pleasure. She held onto him with all her meagre strength, determined not to cry out again as he rode her roughly until he climaxed and collapsed in a heavy heap on top of her. In spite of herself, she wept softly, too spent and too hurt to even attempt to hide her tears.

"You didn't know it was going to be so hard to keep your bargain, did you my little lass?" the Beast muttered against her neck, softly taunting. "Have ye no mother? No sisters? Did no one ever tell you that the first time for a woman could be very painful?"

In spite of his taunting words, he held her gently and stroked her hair with a tenderness that would have shocked him if he'd only realized it. Almost against her will, she relaxed slightly in his arms.

"No, M'lord, my mother is very ill and I have no sisters," Beauty replied softly. Then she looked up at the Beast and asked shyly, hopefully, "Only the first time?"

"I know it gets easier, that the bleeding stops and the sharp tearing pain is gone after the first time, but there may be some tenderness for a while," the Beast told her softly. Then he surprised both of them by adding, "I've never kept a woman around long enough to find out if she ever comes to fully enjoy it as much as I do, but I've heard rumours that some women do."

"Would the women who come to enjoy mating be sluts, M'lord?" Beauty asked. "Or whores? Or do decent women ever come to enjoy it?"

"I know not for sure, but 'tis probably not the common sluts or whores they speak of. Those women care not for the size of a man's tool, they only enjoy the size of a man's purse and the colour of his coin." The Beast pondered this before he mused aloud, "I wonder if there are any places on your body that please you when they're touched like there are on mine? Strange that I've never thought of it before."

"I don't know of any such places, M'lord, but if it pleases you to find out, then please feel free to explore," Beauty offered smiling softly, still nervous but trying not to let it show. "I'm here to do whatever you want."

Amused at both her suggestion and her nerve, the Beast decided to comply. With hands that felt rough from years of battle, he gently stroked and explored her soft body. He spent several long minutes fondling her full breasts, gently teasing her nipples. To the surprise of them both, she squirmed and gasped under his gentle touch. By his very nature, he was bolder than she had been when she explored his body. His mouth quickly followed the path forged by his hands and he savoured the taste and texture of her soft skin.

He soon learned that touching and suckling her full breasts both gave pleasure and caused her to moan and writhe with sensuality so fierce that it almost crossed the border into pain. He let his hands move slowly downwards, with his mouth still suckling her breasts. He discovered that she responded almost as wildly as he did when her sex was touched.

Knowing from long, lonely nights that touch alone could bring him some satisfaction, he slid a long finger into her, gently stroking her. His thumb brushed the nub of her sex and he quickly realized this coaxed an even greater reaction from her. She writhed and squirmed, her legs clasping around his hand. The Beast watched her face as he gently fingered her and heard her soft moans. He kept up the gentle stroking for a long time, repeatedly speeding up and slowing down. He felt her wetness and knew a strange pride that he could coax such a reaction from her.

In a combination of wonder, pleasure and curiosity, he lowered his mouth to her soft curls and kissed her there. His tongue teased the nub even as his fingers slid quickly in and out of her. In mere seconds, she was writhing in a frenzy that he recognized from his own release. He was so amazed that he almost raised his head and stopped, but she grabbed him by the hair and held him to her until her body shook and she gave a startled little scream.

While she lay sighing and panting cuddled by his side, he realized that he was ready again. Quickly he got her into position and thrust into her. Although she was still quite tender, his recent ministration with hands and mouth had readied her, making the entrance moist and the passage in easier. Her still aroused body slowly began to respond to his fast, hard thrusts. She was just beginning to get a hint of the pleasure that they could find together when he moaned aloud and climaxed inside her.

After his breathing returned to normal, the Beast did something that surprised both of them very much. He got out of the bed and walked nude over to the small table. He poured some water from the pitcher sitting there into a small bowl. Then he dampened a soft cloth and walked back to the bed. He pulled back the covers and sheets, ignoring her blushes, and very tenderly washed her virgin's blood from her body. He also discarded the shredded remnants of her gown, and then slid back into the bed.

"You didn't feel so much pain this time, did you lass?" the Beast asked her gently, his large body wrapped next to hers, relaxing fully for the first time he could ever remember.

"It was much nicer. I admit I enjoyed having you explore my body," Beauty responded shyly, blushing furiously. "Do I please you, M'lord?"

"You please me well, Beauty." The Beast kissed her soundly, tasting the sweetness of her mouth for the first time before he continued, "But beware, this is only a pleasure for me, a trifling. Don't expect there to be anything more between us. You're a possession, merely a possession. I will still take you whenever and wherever I want. I will still do whatever I wish to you and I will not hesitate to take a whip to you if you fail to please me."

"And when you are done with me?" she asked timidly. "What then?"

The demon hidden not so deep within the Beast rose up unexpectedly. He was still trying to test her resolve, to prove to her and to himself that she was no more faithful and trustworthy than countless others in his life had been.

He replied coldly, rolling her over, partially atop him, "Why do you ask? It is none of your concern what I do when I am done with you. You are mine, like my horse or my hawk. When I tire of you I will replace you with another even more beautiful woman in my bed. Possibly, I will give you to one of my men as a reward, or mayhap send you away. I could even decide just to kill you or to have you killed. It matters not."

"It matters somewhat to me, M'lord," Beauty stated wryly and proudly, hiding the wretched fear his cold words aroused in her heart and soul. "But I know not what you say when you accuse me of trying to tame you. Your proclamation is no more than I expected from your treatment of me."

"Liar!" The Beast taunted her sharply before he unconsciously voiced his own hidden fear, "You enjoyed the treatment I lavished on you or shall I put my mouth to your sex again and see if I can make you scream? I know you expect much more from me, in bed and out. You hope and pray for my kindness, my consideration and even perhaps for my affection. You but fool yourself, for I don't have it inside me to give, Beauty. I know you even think to tame the Beast and I warn you now, it simply cannot be done. Life has hardened me overmuch."

Beauty kept silent but somewhere deep inside herself, perhaps on an instinctive level, she recognized the basis of uncertainty and the defensive quality behind his declaration. He's unsure of himself, she realized, and afraid I might gain some small degree of power over him. Her heart leaped in her chest and a few short words began to form in the back of her brain: We'll see, my fine Lord, we'll see who tames the mighty beast.

She kept her thoughts carefully hidden and remained compliant beside him. It was a long and exhausting night for Beauty. She was far too sore to sleep easily and still very nervous around the great knight. Of course, every time she did drift towards sleep, he reached for her yet again. Towards morning, he pulled her to him and simply pushed her head down towards his erection.

"Pleasure me with your mouth," he commanded firmly.

She was shocked and very unsure of exactly what to do but she tried to comply. She quickly learned how to pleasure him and soon tasted him as he reached his peak.

When morning finally arrived Beauty was completely exhausted and very stiff and sore. She snuggled deeper into the cushions and tried to ignore the stern, male voice telling her to get up. That was her first mistake. Suddenly she was wide awake as she felt the Beast's large, rough hand descending harshly on her bare buttocks. She found herself pinned to the mattress, her hands grasped behind her back by one of the Beast's hands while his other hand punished her.

It was a long, sharp spanking. She screamed and squealed as his hand descended rapidly and harshly on her bare bottom. A loud crack accompanied each quick slap. The punishment was causing a pink blush to spread quickly all over her pale skin. Her flesh jiggled slightly under each separate spank. Soon, even the pink blush began to take on a darker hue, turning cherry red. When her whole bottom was fiery and hot and she was crying like a baby, she heard the command repeated.

"Get dressed, go down and tell one of the servants to prepare my bath. Then go to the kitchen and tell them I'm awake and to start preparation of the morning meal. Come back straight away and help me bathe or I'll spank you again, and this time I'll make sure your bottom is so red you can't sit down," the Beast was implacable.

"Yes, M'lord." She scurried to obey, pausing only to quickly rub her throbbing, sore bottom.

The Beast watched with relish as she rubbed her tender red butt while trying to avoid his eyes.

"Hurry girl, or do you want some more?" he growled, amused. "You seem to find that wee taste of a slappin' so interesting."

Wee taste indeed, she thought as she quickly pulled on her torn gown, my whole bottom hurts and I'll not want to sit down for a long while. Does he think I'm still a young girl to be thus punished? Although as a young child she'd had much longer and harsher spankings, as an adult she felt above such things. I'll get revenge on you yet my fine lord, she thought.

As he watched her practically run from the room, the Beast thought to himself: Who would have thought a wee bit of a lass could be so amusing and could pleasure me so much. It might be worth it to keep this chit of a girl around for a bit.

Beauty practically ran into the kitchen, struggling as she held the shreds of her gown together. She called out to a servant to help her find the maid, Gwyneth.

"Quick, Gwyneth, I need your help," she told the maid. "The Beast is up and growling."

"Don't ye call him the Beast in front of me, lass." Gwyneth rebuked Beauty sharply although she was secretly pleased to realize that the lass' spirit was not yet broken.

"I've already got things ready for him," she told Beauty. "Milord's bathwater is already boiling. I'll tell the lads to take it up. His meal is almost ready for him to break his fast."

"Thank you, Gwyneth," Beauty told the older woman with a shy grin. "Truly, I meant no disrespect earlier when I called him the Beast. He really did seem to be growling this morning."

"He must be very tired then, as sometimes he's in such a mood when he fails to get enough sleep," the older woman grinned. "Was it from poking you so often or was it from struggling with you to accomplish the deed at all?"

"'Twas not from any struggle I gave him, he had no problem at all with me," Beauty blushed fiery red, "except getting me up this morning to do his bidding."

"Be ye well, lass?" Gwyneth asked gently.

"Passably well, I guess," Beauty grudgingly admitted as she gingerly and unconsciously rubbed her sore bottom, "except for some stiffness, a sore butt, and his lordship's infernal impatience to get his bath and some food this morning."

Gwyneth smiled to herself but said only, "Then 'tis best if ye get back up there to help him bathe and dress or he'll pull you back over his knee and spank you again. He likes to do that. There's a spare gown for you in the wardrobe. I think that one's ruined."

"Really?" Beauty shot back, hiding a rueful grin. "What makes you say that?"

Beauty hurried up the stairs. The Beast had just seated himself in the steaming tub. "It took you long enough. Get over here and scrub my back, lass. Be quick about it or do you need another spanking?"

Beauty quickly picked up the sponge and began scrubbing his back. Was it her fault that later, as she washed his long, dark hair, she managed to get some soap into his eyes? Was it her fault that the rinse water she poured over his head had turned so cold?

The Beast reacted instantly as the cold rinse water hit him. Reaching out a long arm, he quickly pulled Beauty into the tub on top of himself. She wound up sitting on his lap, feeling his hardness beneath her in the rapidly cooling water.

"You'll pay for it dearly if you ever pour water that cold on me again," he growled.

"I'm sorry, M'lord." Beauty did not sound repentant as she hid a grin. "It was but an accident."

"Sure it was," the Beast muttered, meeting her lips with his in a quick kiss. "I know you would never do anything like that intentionally; just remember, an accident like that could cause you to get another spanking or your brother to hang."

Beauty stiffened at the threat. The Beast rose from the small tub with Beauty still in his arms, a feat requiring considerable strength considering the awkwardness of his body and hers entwined in the small tub. He carried her over to the bed and lowered her to the mattress, covering her body with his.

"M'lord!" Beauty protested. "We cannot, it's daytime."

"What on earth does daytime have to do with anything?" the Beast asked her amused.

"Well, 'tis indecent," Beauty said uncertainly, "isn't it?"

"According to you, everything we do together is indecent, Beauty." The Beast slid into her in a firm thrust. "So what difference does the sunlight make?"

Beauty never answered. The Beast stroked her body with his hands even as he thrust in and out of her moist body. She was beginning to learn how to respond to his movements and his rhythms, but he finished too soon for her to get any real enjoyment from it.

At the knock on the door, he covered their bodies with a luxurious fur pelt and yelled for the servant to come inside. It was Gwyneth carrying the tray filled with their morning meal. She had brought fresh fruit, cold milk, hot bread straight from the oven, fried potatoes and porridge with honey.

The Beast balanced the tray on his lap and began to eat with relish. "Eat up, Beauty."

She began to pick at the food with little enthusiasm but gradually her appetite got the better of her and she ate heartily. The Beast noticed her appetite and smiled to himself.

"I guess you're hungry," he commented casually as he watched her eat. In spite of himself, he felt a little guilty. "I hope you had dinner last night. I never thought to ask you if you required anything."

"Gwyneth took care of me, M'lord," Beauty replied quietly, pausing in her dining. "As you knew she would."

Instinctively she realized that his statement was an apology of sorts, probably as good an apology as she would ever receive from him.

"If you ever have any hunger or thirst, just mention it to one of the servants. They will take care of you," the Beast told her. "Don't wait for me to order food or drink for you."

"How can I order your servants about?" Beauty asked, protesting.

"I'm only one of your servants myself."

"You have a special status, and I will make sure they all know it," the Beast promised.

"I'm your whore, what status is there in that?" Beauty hung her head and whispered.

"The strange thing is," the Beast reached over and lifted her chin with his hand, looking into her eyes as he replied, "I don't think of you as a whore." He saw her open her mouth to protest and continued rapidly, "I'll admit I use you in bed, and I intend to continue doing so. I just do not think of you as a whore, not even mine. Please don't consider yourself such."

"I will not, M'lord." Beauty paused. "But what am I then? What is my status in the castle?"

"Consider yourself my companion and my mistress," the Beast replied, setting aside the tray to take her into his arms again. "And my lover."

Chapter Four

For the first few weeks they spent together, the Beast very seldom left Beauty's side except when he was occupied with the running of his lands or when he went to train with his guardsmen. He worked constantly to keep himself ready for battle. He also left her side when he went to patrol the surrounding countryside, searching for any sign of raiders. The crushing poverty surrounding the countryside, indeed the whole land, had greatly increased the number of miscreants willing to kill for a mere pittance. Some of these vile thieves formed brutal packs. The roaming bands of thieves were vicious thugs who would steal anything they could get their hands on and leave a trail of burned out huts and dead serfs in their wake.

There was only one other time the Beast would leave Beauty alone. That was when he had any reason to go into the village. He stoutly refused to let her accompany him; it was his means of blocking her from any chance of seeing her family. Her hopes that she would get to go riding with the Beast, and therefore have at least a chance to see her brother Tom in the stables, also never came to fruition.

During the days when he was working and too busy to spend time with her, Beauty was kept inside the castle walls and was always well guarded.

She wasn't so well guarded because the Beast had any emotional attachment for her or even because he was concerned about her safety in any way. Although he fully enjoyed her in bed, he still distrusted her. He thought of her as a possession and he was a man who safeguarded his possessions from anyone who would attempt to steal them away. As he had told her when they first made their arrangement, even when he had no need of her, no desire to spend time with her, she was not allowed to go to the village to see her family or even to the barn to see Tom.

She was watched constantly, and not only by guards; there were many on the household staff who reported her every movement to the Beast. The watchfulness did more than ensure her safety. She knew the guards were also watching her to report any improprieties or suspicious activities to the Beast. For the most part, the guards had nothing to report except that she read the Bible or some poetry, or embroidered, usually as she sat on a marble bench in the ornate flower garden. Sometimes, when she was particularly restless, she even worked in the garden planting new roses or other flowers, trimming away dead leaves and pulling weeds.

Once however, she did manage to smuggle a brief note to her brother, Tom, as he worked in the stables. The Beast found out about the note, of course, and read it through without Beauty's knowledge before letting it be delivered to Tom. It read:

My Dearest Brother Tom,

I write this at some risk to us both but I wanted to reassure you that all is well with me, at least as well as can be expected. The Beast is fierce indeed and growls at me often, but all in all, he treats me with a fairness that is at odds with his reputation. Life here is not perfect but much better than I expected or feared.

So rest easy, my dear brother. Please take care of our mother and Nate and comfort them with the knowledge that I find life here at the castle to be tolerable. I miss you all. Godspeed,

My deepest love,
Your sister,

Beauty

The Beast was at first angered by the mere fact that she had enough nerve to write the note, and then by its contents, secretly pleased. He realized she was, in a small way, content with him and that she had not used the note to berate him or to encourage her family to attempt to rescue her.

He considered spanking Beauty for defying him by the mere act of writing such a missive but decided to let the matter go. Although she never even knew about it, it was one of the few times he was lenient with her.

He let the note be delivered to Tom partially because he was intrigued by it. Not only by the contents, but also by the very fact that a simple peasant woman could read and write. Such a thing was unheard of! He was already suspicious of Beauty, having realized almost immediately that she was no ordinary peasant girl. He had soon realized that Beauty had many qualities not commonly found in the villagers.

Once he really looked at her as a woman, he realized that she walked, spoke, and at all times comported herself with a dignity and poise not found in the rest of the vassals. As proven by the note, she was well educated in reading and writing, and she was also quick with numbers. She knew the gentle art of embroidery and took it upon herself to repair a small flaw on one of the tapestries.

She had become interested in the day-to-day chores involved in running the castle. Although some of the servants clearly resented her status, indeed, some of them whispered behind her back that she was no more than the Beast's whore, she slowly gained their grudging respect. She worked hard right along with those servants. Things that had been broken or fallen into disrepair over the years were soon fixed or replaced. Things that were once seldom cleaned now shone brightly. Meals suddenly had more taste and variety. The account books showed that she was frugal, managing these improvements without wasting very many of the Beast's precious coins. Someone had trained her well in the running of a large estate, trained her to be a bride to someone important. The Beast was no fool, for he knew she was definitely no ordinary serf.

The Beast held these thoughts to himself, noting them but not confronting Beauty with them. Instead, he gradually left more and more of the domestic responsibilities in her hands. She handled them capably. He stood back and watched, and puzzled as to her real identity. He had an idea who she really was but was unsure why she kept it secret. He knew he would one day confront her about keeping her true identity a secret from him.

Beauty was pondering a mystery of her own. She was trying to find out how the two Toms came to be accused of the grain theft. There could have been no missing grain because there had never been a theft. The same with witnesses; who could come forward to be a witness when there was nothing to see? Who had carried the tale to the Beast? Why had the Beast believed the accuser without any doubts or questions? She wanted to know who was behind the accusation and what his motive was.

Beauty also wondered who was really behind the killing of the peasant girls. Although she would be the first to admit that this was no tame beast she lived with, indeed he was rough and insistent and never questioned his right to use brute force to get whatever he wanted, he was not needlessly cruel. As far as she could tell he was heedless to the pain of others and desensitised by his upbringing, but she sensed he derived no dark pleasure from inflicting such pain. She would never believe him capable of cold-blooded and savage murder.

She had to admit he had committed the rapes, even the Beast admitted to them. He simply refused to see them as rapes, but he admitted them as a part of his life. Like so many men of his station in life, he considered the use of the village women as just one of the privileges of his rank.

He really was a beast, Beauty realized, yet she just could find no hint of the monster in him. He never really beat her, except for the spankings, and most of the time they weren't exceedingly severe.

Although he often left her bottom well warmed and reddened, he had never left a bruise or a welt on her. It was a measure of restraint and control that the Beast never admitted. Indeed, he would deny any hint of gentleness as if it were the vilest accusation Beauty could make against him, but for the most part he wasn't especially harsh with her.

By contrast, those murdered girls had been savaged and mutilated. They had all been beaten half to death, and then stabbed numerous times, some almost hacked to pieces. It just was not him, and Beauty knew it. She refused to let herself see what that bit of unwavering faith might reveal about her own growing feelings for him.

All her inquiries led to one man as being behind both problems, the accusation against the two Toms and the girls' murders, but she had no evidence, nothing yet that could be put before the Beast as solid proof. She even believed this man might be behind other accusations against unfortunate men over the years. Men who had already been hung for petty crimes they might not have committed.

She began to believe there was indeed a real monster in the castle, one who did these things just to gain pleasure from watching the sufferings of others. She knew she would need a great deal of solid proof because the man she suspected was one of the few men the Beast trusted. She bided her time and watched, pondering what the future could hold for her and the Beast.

Life with the Beast was not easy at all. She did anything he asked, true to her word, and she acted loving and obedient at all times. It was hard for her though because she had to defer to him in all matters, in spite of the fact that sometimes she ached to speak out to him about her feelings and opinions. She longed for the freedom to defy him, or to even argue with him.

Still, she'd become more relaxed around the Beast even though she often admitted to herself that she'd not yet come to feel truly comfortable around him. She had a long way to go before she could come to love him. He was still too rough and far too unreachable. Sometimes she wondered if she would ever come to care for him in even a small way and at other times another faint hope floated through her mind. Could she bring him to care for her? Could she teach him to have any small trace of tenderness or compassion? Could she tame the beast that she'd given her life over to? Would he ever come to love her? Although she admitted to herself that it was barely possible, the only way she could see to improve her life was to try to teach him how to love. The task was more difficult for her because she herself knew nothing about the love found only between a man and a woman.

He still kept her clothed in dresses that were almost as bad as the dress she'd been wearing when they met, little more than bulky rags. They were better fitting and of much softer wool and finer linens, but they were starkly plain with no decoration. The colours he chose for her dresses were drab greys and browns, even solid black.

He still slapped her rump at the slightest provocation, and still bent her over his knee and spanked her fairly often. The strange thing was, the very spankings themselves reassured Beauty about the Beast. Not because she enjoyed them in any way, but because even when he spanked her, he kept his temper under tight control. He was never unduly harsh or savage with her. The reason she found this so reassuring went back to her childhood.

Beauty had rebelled during the turmoil that erupted around her several years ago when her father died. She had fought against the pain and upheavals in her life by acting spoiled and childish. Her brother, Tom, had stepped in and taken over the raising of the barely teenage girl. He took her in hand, literally, and frequently spanked her for her disobedience. Usually he spanked her over her clothes but sometimes, rarely, Tom had even spanked her bare bottom.

The spankings Beauty got from the Beast were no worse than she'd gotten as a rebellious young girl from her own brother, who was at heart a gentle man. They were not the beatings a brutal man inflicted on a helpless woman, meant to cause real injury, possibly cripple, and even kill.

The Beast also seemed to relax and open his mind and heart ever so slightly to Beauty every time he spanked her. Afterwards, he'd hold her and talk quietly about his life and whatever problems he was facing. She knew he didn't realize that he did it and she didn't quite understand why it happened. Mayhap it was his unconscious way of making things up to her, but she enjoyed those quiet times with him, cuddling up to him and talking. The cuddling almost made the spankings worthwhile. Almost.

Sometimes the spankings didn't even hurt her at all, and she didn't think they were really meant to. Sometimes they almost seemed to be in fun, almost a form of teasing. It was as if they were merely a part of the Beast's sex play. Those times, the light spankings ended with the Beast laughing and throwing himself onto her, pressing her down deep into the mattress as he drove himself home.

So she settled into life with the Beast. He kissed her very seldom but often used her sexually. The sex became less painful and hurried, and even more frequent. He usually took her very fast and hard with very little preliminaries. At first, the few moments of tender touching he'd given her that first night were almost never repeated. Slowly however, he began to take his time with her. He started to spend more time touching her, stroking her, preparing her body to welcome him inside her.

Part of this was the Beast's subconscious reaction to the extra passion of the responses he drew from Beauty when he took his time and showed her some tenderness and built her passion. He never quite took enough time though, and Beauty secretly hoped to find a way to show him what she needed. When the quick flashes of tenderness she saw buried deep within this fierce man did occur, Beauty was touched to her soul by the warmth and gentle nature hidden away inside this wounded man.

For the most part, Beauty was philosophical. In her experience, for a woman to be frequently beaten by a husband or a master was commonplace, but for a husband or lover to care about his woman's satisfaction was rare. In truth, she realized she fared no worse than most of the married women she knew except that she was not married; therefore she lived in sin and disgrace.

Her only real complaints were that once or twice she had gotten a faint glimpse of what real passion and tenderness could be and she wanted to feel its full reach. She wanted that deeply. She also missed her family and her freedom. Aside from these things and her loneliness, Beauty was fairly content.

She was learning to live with her rugged companion without angering him. She was fairly confident that the Beast would never really hurt her. About a week later, when she went with the Beast on a short hunting trip, she found out that she was wrong, painfully wrong.

Beauty was thrilled as she waited outside the stables for her mount to be saddled. Not only was she eager to ride again, for it had been years since she had been on a horse, but she was hoping to get a chance to see Tom and mayhap have a quick word with him. The Beast brought her a horse, a gentle but spirited bay mare, and helped her to mount. The other Tom, the man who was almost hung alongside her brother, and another man Beauty did not know brought out the dogs. They were off!

Although she didn't get to see her brother, Beauty was still excited to be riding out with the Beast. It was the first time the Beast had ever taken her with him anywhere, even hunting. Beauty did not enjoy the hunting itself. She had never come to enjoy the sight of animals being chased down and slaughtered. She revelled in the beauty of the countryside and the feel of a horse beneath her, even knowing she would be sore from the unaccustomed hours of riding.

The Beast and a few of his soldiers were replenishing the castle's supplies of meat. They loosed the dogs to run down the wild boars. They used short stout lances, easier to work with in the thick forest than their regular lances, to kill whatever boars the dogs ran down. They dressed down the day's catch in the forest, salting some of the meat, drying some, and cooking the rest.

The Beast was angered by the signs of poachers he found in the forest. Standing over the carcass of a slaughtered deer, his temper raged.

"I'm going to find these poachers and hang them!" he bellowed. "That would teach the scum that poaching in these woods is the same as stealing from me."

"It makes me wonder, M'lord," Beauty said thoughtfully, eyeing the spoiled remains with distaste, "why would any of the villagers be willing to run the risk of poaching? How desperate must they be to be willing to face your wrath?"

"Do you seek to excuse them for poaching?" the Beast yelled at her. "Or do you attempt to persuade me to show them mercy for the crime?"

"Neither M'lord, I but wondered what led them to take such a risk." Beauty met his eyes openly. "They must know what penalty you would put on the killing of your game."

The Beast turned away from Beauty without answering her but he pondered her remarks for a long time. He knew full well that the villagers feared and even hated him. Her questions ate at him. Why would they take such a risk? The thought came to him of what risks he would be willing to take if it were his family that was starving. He said no more about it but the thought remained in his mind for several days.

The next day, disaster struck! As the small band of hunters was fording a swift but shallow river, one of the younger guards lost control of his horse and was thrown. The guard probably could have stood up in the shallow water but between his panic and the weight of his clothes, boots and sword, he could not get a purchase with his feet. He thrashed about in the water, panicked and unable to swim. The Beast leaped off his horse to rescue the lad and handed his heavy sword to the nearest person. It just happened to be Beauty.

Beauty's horse was also spooked, panicked by the guard's horse bumping into him and the shouting of the men. She struggled to keep her mount under control but her horse slipped on a wet rock and almost went down. As Beauty wrestled to remain seated and to help her horse regain his footing, the sword slipped from her grasp. She gave a startled cry as she saw it fall over a small waterfall and squarely into the one deep pool in the river.

The Beast was soaked and irritated as he carried the unconscious young guard to the shore. He struggled to revive the man but his efforts were to no avail. The Beast turned away, coldly ordering the other guards to bury the body. He was exceedingly angry and frustrated. His clothes were stuck to his body and his best leather boots were probably ruined. That was when he realized that Beauty had dropped his sword. It was the final straw. That was also when she found out that the Beast could and would indeed hurt her.

She found it out the hard way, bending over a hollow log in the forest, naked from the waist down with the Beast using his thick leather belt on her buttocks and legs without the least hint of mercy. It was the first time he'd ever hit her with anything but the palm of his hand and it hurt greatly.

He ignored her screams as he lashed at her red ass repeatedly; each swing of his strong arm causing a welt or a bruise. The whole of her bottom was covered with painful red stripes and purplish blotches.

Worst of all for Beauty, the Beast's guards were well within earshot, and even as she writhed in pain she knew they heard and enjoyed every swish and crack of the belt, every sob and every scream.

Finally the Beast stopped and coldly ordered, "Stand up."

He put his belt back on. It was over. The voice he commanded her with brooked no denial or disobedience. Beauty tried to comply but she was too stiff and sore, and much too shaken to her core. Her legs failed her and she sank to the ground, weeping openly.

"Cease that at once, woman!" he commanded, but without any real anger behind the words.

The Beast started to reach down to her then hesitated and sat stiffly on the hollow log. He pulled her onto his lap, ignoring her sore bottom as he cuddled her gently. She clung to him as she continued to cry. Her sobs seemed to last forever, but when her tears finally began to ease the Beast quickly shifted her position until she was face down over his knees.

Beauty panicked and struggled to right herself but to no avail. Holding her in place with one iron hand, he stroked her hot, flaming ass, gently touching the welts. He explored her moist femininity with his fingers before he withdrew his hand to spank her with lightly stinging, almost gentle spanks.

For long moments he held her like that, alternately stroking her hot bottom, fingering her moist core, and almost gently spanking her. Finally, he used his hands to bring her to the heights of ecstasy.

After she came, he held her shivering body until the shutters stopped. Then he coldly pushed her off his knees and ordered her to stand up and straighten her dress. Although she was shaking with both pleasure and pain, this time she did as he ordered without any further delay.

When she finally walked stiffly behind the Beast as he led her back to the camp, the men were staring at her and laughing. Crude remarks floated towards her on the cool night air. The Beast suddenly picked her up and carried her over to a small tent set a small pace apart from the men. He threw her face down onto a soft pallet of furs. He grasped her hips in his hands and pulled her roughly to her knees. Without any preliminaries or finesse he entered her, sodomizing her even as she cried anew. She gasped and even screamed several times at the unfamiliar pain.

61

She was still sobbing as he rolled away. "That hurt!"

"It's just the first time, like the other virginity," the Beast murmured. "It gets easier with time."

"M'lord?" Beauty asked gently. "Why haven't you done it that way before?"

"I prefer the usual way," the Beast replied. "I usually only do it that way if the woman wants to prevent a pregnancy."

"Then why tonight?" Beauty asked curiously.

"Because I was irritated with you and I felt like it," the Beast told her sternly.

"I'm sorry, M'lord," she sobbed, her hands gently grasping her own butt. "Truly, I didn't mean to displease you."

"Displease me?" The Beast was once again furious. "You dropped my favourite sword into the deepest part of the river and you think I'm displeased? I'm far past displeased, and if you don't know that maybe I better take you back to the log and add to your welts."

"If that's your wish, M'lord, I await your pleasure," Beauty said softly, still crying. "But I truly am sorry. I'll swim out to get it tomorrow."

"You can swim?" The Beast felt his anger fade.

He was amazed since none of his men could swim. He was a poor swimmer himself, as the day's disaster proved.

"Yes, M'lord," Beauty sighed wearily, ignoring his surprise. "Shall I prepare myself for another whipping?"

"Nay, lass," the Beast told her softly, "I think I have another use for you tonight."

To her amazement, he got a moist cloth as he had on their first night together and washed her, soothing her tender parts. After he finished the task, he proceeded to spend an eternity loving her slowly and thoroughly with his hands and mouth, even turning her over to gently kiss her welts. He lightly nipped her round firm buttocks, then licked the injured spot. Finally he turned her onto her back and lowered his mouth to her soft tangle of moist curls. It was a long time before he entered her, and for once he moved slowly, almost leisurely inside her before picking up the pace. In spite of her welts and tenderness, for the first time she felt the full measure of a climax with him as they reached the peak together. One of the young foot soldiers sleeping nearby heard her scream her release as she reached her climax.

"God's blood!" the young man exclaimed. "Isn't he ever going to cease beating the poor girl?"

An older guardsman sleeping nearby laughed openly, "Lad, we need to find you a woman and quickly!"

"Did I whip you too hard?" the Beast asked as he held her gently before they slept. "I was angry and so frustrated by the death of the guard that I may have overreacted a bit."

"It's not my place to say, M'lord. Indeed, I am at your disposal," Beauty replied calmly, but inside her heart leaped as she realized that for the first time ever the Beast had almost admitted he was wrong and had even come close to an apology. "Do with me as you please."

"And if I decided to kill you or turn you over to one of my men for a plaything?" the Beast asked.

"It's your decision, M'lord." Beauty kept her eyes downcast, hiding her quick spark of temper from him. "I have no say in the matter."

"How about a kiss instead?" the Beast whispered gruffly, bending down to her.

"If that is your wish, M'lord." She smiled at him, a wide dazzling smile. "I but seek to obey you and please you."

The Beast stopped before kissing her, his mouth almost touching her soft lips as he whispered softly, "I just love meekness in a woman, Beauty. It's too bad your meekness is a sham. Did you think I was fooled?"

She reached up a slender arm and stroked his long, silky hair. "You're no fool, M'lord, and I'd fight anyone who dared say so."

The Beast laughed softly as he kissed her. Beauty met his kiss willingly, responding with a passion of her own. It was still rare that he kissed her. Then she pulled him down on top of her, ignoring the ache in her bottom, as she sank back onto the soft bed of furs. He didn't press her back into the furs and enter her however; to her amazement he lowered his mouth to her breasts, nibbling them before he traced a line of kisses down her soft belly to the thatch or curls guarding her femininity.

For the only time since their first night together, he brought her to the heights of ecstasy with an intimate kiss that seemed to fill her very soul with sensuous joy.

This time, the young soldier merely pulled a blanket over his head and ignored her cries.

The Beast reached for her as her shivers ceased but she said softly, "Not this time, my fine lord."

She pushed him gently onto his back and he went willingly. He let her do what she wanted. He could scarcely believe the depth of his emotion, his joy and his pride, as she returned his intimate kiss. Although she did whatever he asked, it was the first time she had ever initiated such an action. He soon found out what difference there was between compliance and enthusiastic participation. Before they slept, they made love again. This time she rode astride him, completely wanton in her passion.

The next morning they sent most of the guards back to the castle, keeping only two men with them. The two guards, experienced hunters, were stalking deer with their bows. The Beast had been craving fresh venison for his table. This day Beauty and the Beast did not hunt; instead they tarried by the river, resting and talking softly. For once, the Beast asked her opinion on several minor matters before he came to the one thing that had preyed upon his mind.

"Beauty, if you were me, what would you do about the poachers?" the Beast asked, lying beside her on the riverbank.

"I know not, M'lord, for 'tis not an easy problem. The serfs have to have enough to eat but your game should be protected," Beauty smiled as she stroked back a lock of hair from his face. "Not just for your use, but to ensure that game will always be plentiful in these woods. Some of the serfs, not all, but some are so lazy that they would rather poach than toil on their farms while some others are truly starving. I think they deserve different punishments, even though the crime is the same."

"But there should be some punishments?" the Beast asked pointedly.

"Yes," Beauty admitted against her will, "but the villagers should have some protection against starving and their awful poverty too."

"I'll think about it." The Beast reluctantly stood up and pulled Beauty to her feet. "We had best return to the castle as these woods are not safe without a guard nearby."

Back at the stables the Beast helped Beauty dismount, overlooking the presence of her brother Tom. She was thrilled to see her brother but afraid to let her emotions show. Not by word or gesture did she acknowledge his proximity or their relationship. The Beast ignored Tom too. In fact, he talked to Beauty about the poachers right in front of her brother.

Handing the reins of his charger to Tom he said, "I think I'll start sending a small group of guards out to patrol the woods for poachers. Not with Gerrin, but mayhap I'll put Gregory in charge. He needs more experience. I'll tell him to go out every third day and order that he should bring all the poachers he catches back to me, still alive, to await my judgment."

As they walked back to the castle Beauty whispered to the Beast, "M'lord, if you truly want to catch the poachers, you should not have let Tom hear the schedule for your patrols. He can warn the villagers. And why did you put Gregory in charge when Gerrin is so much more experienced and ruthless?"

"Because, my dear Beauty, Gerrin really is so much more ferocious," the Beast grinned. "And I hope Tom does warn the villagers. Why do you think I said it in front of him? I'm not a fool."

He whistled as he strode into the castle, leaving Beauty staring after him with her mouth agape.

Chapter Five

After the hunting trip many things changed between Beauty and the Beast. In spite of the harsh whipping he'd given her, Beauty began to relax even more and feel much more natural and comfortable around the Beast. She began to feel that she'd seen him at his worst, that he would never get angrier or hurt her worse than he had in the woods. Even then, as furious as he was with her, he had given her a few bruises but caused her no serious or permanent injury. She began to feel confident that he never would.

The sex between Beauty and the Beast also grew more intense and passionate, especially on Beauty's part. Something during the long night following the whipping had finally unlocked the full range of her passion. Was it his hands, alternately lightly stoking and comforting her and slapping her gently before he used them to finger her femininity bringing her to the heights of ecstasy? Was it his manhood, large, firm and erect, causing her to scream with the sheer pleasure of his loving? Was it the unfamiliar and painful but somehow exciting feeling of him using her from behind? Was it his mouth nibbling her and the slight scratch of his stubble on her inner thighs? Or was it the time he took with her now, every loving act stretched out to its fullest extent? Could it even have been his acceptance, nay enjoyment, when she took the lead in lovemaking, closing her mouth gently over him or riding atop him? No matter the reason, a real passion grew between the pair.

But passion, as good as it was, was still all there was between them. There was some trace of affection but still no real love had taken hold. The Beast was sometimes polite and usually kind to Beauty, but he still treated her like a valued servant or mayhap a favourite horse instead of a beloved woman.

For her part, Beauty still held something of herself back from the Beast. She rarely spoke up to him. She seldom argued or even ventured to give voice to an opinion. Her feelings on many things were kept to herself. She had more feelings for the Beast than he had for her however. She had even started to feel that her one true purpose in life was to stand by the side of this dangerous, difficult man and give him her support, if not her love. She continued to find more and more ways to help the Beast around the castle. She laboured long and hard to make the castle a refuge for the Beast, a place where his stress and responsibilities could be put aside for his relaxation and contentment.

She began to make rare little gestures of affection towards the Beast. They were comfortable little touches, with nothing planned or even passionate. She just began reaching for his hand when walking beside him, stroking his hair back when a lock fell onto his forehead, or touching his shoulder as she stood by his side.

She even began to feel comfortable being in the castle, especially in the master bedchamber. She gained a sense of belonging, of being home, that gradually replaced her feelings of being out of place, of being held against her will as a prisoner or a hostage. The servants, many of whom had shunned or ignored her at first, began to treat her as the lady of the castle, coming to her and asking for her advice and bringing the mundane domestic matters to her instead of the Beast.

The Beast changed also. He relaxed quite a bit and even came close to having a bawdy sense of humour. Slowly, he began to care about Beauty's appearance. One day he went so far as to bring in several bolts of expensive cloth and a team of seamstresses who made Beauty a wardrobe full of gowns that were more colourful and of richer fabrics than the ones she already had. These were no meagre rags; they were the finest silks and satins, decorated with rows of embroidery or pearls and trimmed with the finest furs.

He even brought her small presents, among them expensive lotions and soaps for her skin. He noted with pride that her hands no longer held any trace of the roughness they had when she first came to him. They were now truly a lady's hands, soft and silky, meant for no harder task than stroking her lord as they loved each other.

Truly, the Beast had learned how to coax the most passionate responses from her, and he soon enjoyed feeling her climaxes. He had learned well that pleasure was a game best played by two. It still took his complete control, but finally he admitted how much he enjoyed it when he allowed her to explore his body as he had hers that first night.

And she did explore and play with his body, thoroughly. It was not the halfway and tentative exploration she'd been able to give him before he ended matters by entering her so brutally when he took her virginity, but instead it was a full exploration of a man's body by a woman who matches his passion. Those times when she took the lead, he forced himself to relax and enjoy it as she explored his chest and his manhood, stroking him and gently cupping his balls. She suckled his male chest, licking his nipples, and trailed her mouth down his rippled abdomen before finally she took his penis into her mouth. He exploded with the sensations she brought him. They often made love long into the night.

The Beast even learned how to really kiss, with nibbling lips, duelling tongues and tender caresses. The funny thing was that the better he got at it, the more he liked it and the more Beauty liked it too.

His quick temper faded and he seldom spanked Beauty unless it was a playful tussle, a game meant to arouse and not to hurt. A few quick slaps that pinkened her skin and barely stung, followed by hours of lovemaking and laughter. His belt now only held up his pants.

The Beast still had rough edges though, a quick temper and a thoughtless lack of concern for her feelings. He still barked out orders and expected them to be obeyed instantly. He still refused to consider Beauty as anything but a possession, refusing to give her the consideration and respect due a mate. Nevertheless, Beauty began to feel cautiously happy. It was only a fool's paradise however; the Beast was not yet tamed, far from it.

Several weeks passed peacefully, and the summer's heat was fierce. The summer crops were practically burning in the ground and there was a rare shortage of water in the village. The villagers feared for their lives, for without the crops they faced starvation.

More than a few reports came to the Beast of roaming bands of thieves robbing villagers and travellers, but until the end of summer none of the reports amounted to anything. One day late in the summer, the Beast saw one of his lookouts riding up to the castle at breakneck speed and knew instinctively that their relative peace was at a sudden and violent end. He ordered the guards and soldiers to arms before the rider even reined in at his feet. Without the Beast's bidding, Tom saddled another horse for the lookout and took care of the sweating, exhausted horse he had ridden into the courtyard.

The Beast called Beauty, kissing her goodbye in front of his men, before riding out to catch the villains. The thieves were an ignorant lot with no knowledge of battle strategy and very few weapons. They were used to preying on the weak and helpless, unprepared for the fury of a well-trained knight and his armed guards.

It was a fast and furious chase, and in a very short time the Beast and his men had the small band of thieves cornered. The hapless miscreants had not gotten anywhere near the castle or even made their way to the village. They had, however, murdered a helpless old woman who had a hut on the edge of the woods outside the village. The Beast and his men found the hut almost burned to the ground. The old woman's body was nearby, badly battered with her throat slashed. It made almost no sense to the Beast; the old woman's hut was so poor it seemed rank insanity to rob her.

The wanton brutality the thieves had committed on a helpless old crone sickened even the Beast, though he gave no outward sign of his feelings to any of his men. The anger he felt on the old woman's behalf shocked the Beast to his core. Was he beginning to have feelings and to care for these serfs?

One of the Beast's foot soldiers hesitantly told the Beast that he thought the old woman might have had a young granddaughter, a girl around twelve. They searched the area but found no trace of the girl. Finally, they stopped searching for the girl and resumed the hunt for the thieves.

The Beast's men caught up with them at the edge of the forest. They surrounded the band of thieves and the fight began. It was one-sided but still a fierce and furious battle. The thieves were out numbered and not well armed but they knew they fought for their very lives, and they fought with the fierce desperation of men with nothing to lose. The Beast fought savagely, swinging his broadsword with all his might. He turned his horse and ran after one thief, a quick thrust putting the sword through the man's back. He chased ruthlessly after another. This man turned to face the Beast, a sword in hand. It was a feckless touch of bravado and it was useless as a fast slash of the Beast's sword took his head from his shoulders. The Beast dismounted and entered the fray on foot, killing two more thieves as his men captured or killed the rest.

When the battle ended, six dead thieves lay on the ground along with two of the Beast's guardsmen. Three other thieves were taken prisoner. They were bound tightly with rope for the long trek back to the castle and to their doom. The Beast and his men rested and tended the worst of their wounds. In a rare show of concern for the well being of others, the Beast himself tied a bandage to the wounds of two of his guards.

A short distance from the fight, the guards found the young girl's battered body. She was stripped nude and was badly beaten and bruised. The Beast could tell she'd been used sexually for there was blood streaking her legs and between her thighs.

For the first time, looking down at the small bruised and bloody body, seeing her torn clothes on the ground beside her, the Beast felt a flash of empathy for a woman. It was a brief glimpse of how it felt for a woman to be brutalized and taken against her will. He squelched the feelings deep down, refusing to let himself examine why the small body affected him so much. In spite of his effort however, the girl's bloody image remained in his conscience.

"Bury her," the Beast ordered his men as he turned away from the pitiful sight.

"But M'lord... " a young guardsman protested timidly.

"Doest ye think to be too good to be digging a grave?" the Beast asked harshly. "Bury her now or you'll need two graves, one for yourself."

The young guard straightened and faced the Beast. "Then you'll need two graves, M'lord, for I'll not have any part of burying a living girl."

"Living?" the Beast examined the small girl closer.

He looked up at the young soldier with a trace of quick sardonic humour in his eyes. "Remind me to reward you for your courage before I beat you for your insolence, lad. You have saved a life this day. Mount up."

The Beast himself bundled up the girl and placed her gently in front of the young soldier for the ride back to the castle. He had the men take her back to the castle, hoping Beauty would know how to treat her and what to do with her. He never acknowledged this sign of his reliance on Beauty, not even to himself.

"I have to stay here and make sure none of the thieves escaped." He ordered the young soldier, "Take her to my lady. She'll know how to treat the girl. She can save her if anyone can. Take a few men with you, the wounded ones. She'll also see to their wounds. Tell Beauty I'll return shortly."

The Beast searched the area for a few more hours but could find no sign that any thieves had escaped. Later that same evening the Beast would hang the captured thieves from the castle gates. The meagre possessions found on the thieves were given to the guards and foot soldiers.

As he rode back to the castle eager to see Beauty, the Beast pondered several troubling things. Was his reputation as a warrior being undermined or were these men just ignorant of whose land they had crossed? He also realized that he needed to find a few more guards, and that the guards he already had needed to train much harder. He also wondered about his head guard. Was Gerrin getting slack or soft? It did not seem possible as Gerrin's bloodlust was legendary. Was he trusting the man too much? He'd heard several strange rumours about the fierce warrior he had beside him for so many years. The one thing he refused to ponder was his eagerness to return to the castle and to Beauty.

While Seth and Gwyneth and even Beauty's brother Tom tended the wounded soldiers, Beauty had taken charge of the young girl, doing all she knew to bring her back to health. She was badly injured and feverish, and some of her wounds were festering already.

Soon Gwyneth joined Beauty. It took both Beauty and Gwyneth working together using all their combined strength and skill to care for the girl. They worked for several days but gradually the girl, whose name was said to be Claire, began to recover. Her outward wounds healed, the swelling in her face went down and thankfully, her fever broke. Her mind and spirit remained injured however, and Beauty feared that she would never fully recover from the trauma she'd suffered.

Every night Beauty clung to the Beast and wept for the girl whose suffering touched her so deeply. The Beast would never admit it as he fought to keep from weeping himself, but he drew a curious comfort from giving succour to Beauty.

Summer lingered and for the most part, a fragile peace was enjoyed by both Beauty and the Beast. The nights were filled with passion and hot sex. During the days, they got along fairly well, with affection and understanding growing between them.

Life was peaceful and they were content enough except for one thing: The presence of the girl, Claire, who was still terrified of all men but most especially she feared the Beast. She ran screaming from him every time he tried to approach her. Beauty used all her patience and quiet strength to build an uneasy truce between the two but it was an almost impossible task. Gradually the girl put a strain on Beauty's own still fragile relationship with the Beast.

Real trouble between the Beast and Beauty came without warning on a hot summer evening almost two weeks later. Its cause was so simple as to be almost laughable. The Beast happened to overhear some of his guards talking. They were drunk, having spent the evening drinking stout ale and not as cautious as they should have been.

One man belched, "Things are much nicer around here now that the little bit of fluff has tamed the mighty Beast. His lordship seems almost human."

"Beast! The skirt's turned him into a lady's lapdog," another man laughed drunkenly.

"And the little miss is holding tightly to his leash," another hooted,

72

slapping the rough wooden table.

The head guard, Gerrin, remarked in a snarl, "I can't wait until he tires of the little slut; then I'll get my chance to crawl between her thighs and show her what a real man is. I guarantee it'll be me what tames her and not the other way around. The Beast has grown too soft."

Overhearing this, a lifetime of beliefs, habit, training and painful memories built up within the Beast. He was a warrior! He was bred and trained to be strong, fearless and merciless, to protect his lands and serve his King! Long ago all signs of mercy or compassion had been literally whipped from his soul. It had been drummed into him that any of these emotions weakened him as a warrior, a knight, and a man.

God above, he raged, he was no tame little lapdog and he certainly was not on Beauty's leash! No woman ever born could bring him to heel!

It was sheer chance that he was in the height of this rage when he next saw Beauty. It was a trick of fate that gave her terrible pain and great hope, great hope indeed.

The Beast stormed into the castle and found Beauty busy talking to one of the servants from the kitchen. He was a young and very handsome assistant to the cook. Beauty was laughing as she stood close to the man and whispered. The rage simmering in the Beast exploded. Without a word, he grabbed Beauty by the hand and dragged her up the stairs. He never saw the terrified eyes of the lass, Claire, as he dragged Beauty past her on the stairs.

"Beast! What's wrong?" Beauty cried, sensing his anger. "What have I done to anger you?"

"For one thing, I saw you flirting with that lad downstairs," the Beast bellowed, unfastening his belt. "Disrobe."

"Flirting! Beast, no!" Beauty cried, ignoring his order for once. "I was not flirting!"

She'd never seen him this mad, and for once she was truly afraid of him. "Why would I flirt with a lad like that when I have a real man like you?"

"I do not understand the ways of women," the Beast snarled,

catching her and using a bit of cloth to tie Beauty's hands together, he then tied her to the post at the end of the bed. "Perhaps you think that I've become a weakling. That I'm too tame for you."

"M'lord! I know you are not a weakling or tamed." Beauty tried to speak calmly as she struggled against the bonds but it was difficult.

Desperately she continued, "I have never tried to tame you, M'lord, only to make your life easier, to give you a quiet place where you could relax from your toils and worries and to make you happy. And why, M'lord, if I were to turn away from you because you've become a weakling, would ever I turn to an even weaker lad like the one downstairs?"

"Because you can control him easier than you can me. You can use your wiles on him to make him do anything you want!" he roared, so angry that he failed to see how illogical his reasoning was. "Will you bed him too?"

Unwisely, Beauty lost her own temper. "Oh yes, I'm such a slut that I'll bed any man I can find, M'lord, even a mere boy like that. That's why I was a virgin when I came to you. Remember, I'd be a virgin still if you hadn't decided to hang my brother for no reason!"

"But you're no virgin now! You know full well the meaning of passion." The Beast shouted as he then accused her, "Mayhap you're yearning to try another man's bed, to see if you can find pleasure in another man's arms."

He's jealous, Beauty thought! In spite of the danger she was in, her heart leapt in joy.

Sensing peril but unable to resist goading him, Beauty asked, "Well M'lord, you claim not to love me; in fact, you swear to be incapable of loving me. So why should it matter? How would you feel if I bedded another man? Any other man? Why would you even care?"

"I'd kill you both!" the Beast snarled as he exploded. He pulled her skirts up throwing them over her head and exposing her to the waist. His action was so sudden and forceful that he tore the fabric of the dress.

In a temper he'd seldom felt before, he swung the belt. The blow landed, catching her full across her buttocks causing the skin to go white for the merest second before a long red welt appeared. The beating that followed was even longer and harder than the one in the woods. Beauty screamed and cried continuously throughout the ordeal. She begged for mercy, sobbing. She had welts all over her backside and even down her legs.

Amazingly, the Beast was not totally out of control; he managed to stop himself short of drawing blood or causing her any severe or lasting injury.

Trying to avoid feeling the pain, Beauty tried to keep her mind on something else. With every swing of the belt, Beauty asked herself over and over, is it possible? Is the Beast jealous? Does he really care enough to be jealous? For once, she almost enjoyed the beating. Well, not enjoy, but she felt hope at the motive behind it.

Finally, the Beast threw down his belt and untied Beauty. He stood by the bed watching her sob into the pillow. As his temper faded, he began to feel something very unfamiliar to him. For the first time in his life he felt doubts and even a touch of shame for his actions. Clamping down those feelings made him even harsher.

The Beast turned and left the room abruptly, leaving the sounds of her weeping behind him. As he entered the main hall, the first thing he saw was Claire, her small face pale and terrified, her eyes red with tears. He tried to ignore the girl as he strode through the hall and left the castle but he felt the accusation in those eyes boring into him, almost burning his back. He went to the training field and worked his men brutally hard until he was exhausted. It was a long time before he returned to the castle.

Without speaking a word to anyone in the hall, he climbed the stairs and entered the bedchamber where Beauty still lay on the bed.

"M'lord, may I ask you, calmly, what I did to anger you?" Beauty asked, looking up at the sound of his return.

She was surprised by the coldness in his eyes and his voice as he answered, "I'm not sure, mayhap nothing. What does it matter?"

"I'll admit it matters little to you that you've hurt me very much but I wouldst do whatever I can to avoid angering you so much again," Beauty replied softly. "Please M'lord, what was my fault? What offence did I commit to anger you so terribly?"

"Flirting," the Beast replied. "I saw you with a servant."

"Look at me, M'lord." She met his gaze with quiet strength. "You know I was not flirting with anyone, let alone that servant boy. Think! What man can compare with you? You are handsome, rich, powerful, and a good lover. There was no reason for you to be angry or jealous."

"Jealous?" the Beast gaped at her, shocked even as a nagging doubt formed in the back of his mind. Sternly he squashed it down. "I cannot be jealous of a possession. I but seek to hold onto what's mine."

"You had no cause to worry, M'lord," Beauty repeated, her voice sounding firm and calm even though she was far from it. "No other man can take your place."

"Mayhap not," the Beast muttered wearily. "It matters not. I think you still mean to tame me, to make me soft and weak."

"What?" Beauty was genuinely astonished. "Why on earth would I want to do that? I admire your strong will and courage, truly. I but seek to give you my companionship, my support and my affection."

"I do not know," the Beast sighed, feeling drained and tired. "Mayhap... "

"Mayhap M'lord admits he could have been wrong?" Her eyes flashed in spite of the pain she still felt.

She saw the muscles in his jaw twitch in reaction and hastened to add, "Calm yourself, M'lord, I do but jest. Tell me what happened to cause this, please."

"I heard the soldiers, my own guards, they were drinking and laughing," the Beast admitted slowly. "They claimed that you had tamed the Beast. They said that you had made me a lapdog and that you held the leash."

"And were they right?" Beauty asked meeting his eyes with a quiet, soft gaze.

"I'm a warrior," the Beast answered shortly.

"Were they right?" Beauty repeated her question more firmly.

"No," the Beast replied indignantly. "I am not weak nor tamed, nor any woman's lapdog, not even yours, wench."

"So why do you let a few words from drunken fools bother you?" Beauty asked with a trace of anger. "Ignore them, or better yet work them so hard on the training field that they know you're as strong as ever. Why take it out on me? Does that make you feel stronger?"

"I took it out on you because I was still angry when I saw you with that lad downstairs," the Beast admitted, feeling like dirt.

"We were just planning a special feast for you this evening," Beauty explained, making the Beast feel even worse. "M'lord, you have no cause to be jealous, I promised you my loyalty and I will never break that promise."

"I told you before, I was not jealous!" the Beast roared, covering his guilt with a show of temper.

Beauty turned her back to him and stood there silently. Long minutes passed without either of them speaking a word. Finally he lowered his voice and asked her a question that he'd never in his life asked anyone before.

"Forgive me? Please, I promise Beauty, I will never punish you so harshly again." His voice was so soft she could scarcely hear it. He walked over to her and placed his hands gently on her shoulders.

"Never again with the belt?" Beauty whispered, pleading in spite of herself.

The Beast felt her shiver through his hands. She turned to face him as he answered.

"Never," the Beast said softly. "I give you my oath."

At the sight of such a strong, proud man humbling himself to her, Beauty's heart soared. In a wordless answer, she sank to the bed and pulled him down atop her. Ignoring the pain from her welts, she kissed him with all the joy and promise she didn't dare give voice to. Not yet. She still had a long way to go to convince this stubborn beast of a man that caring and tender emotions strengthened a man instead of making him weak.

They made love passionately long into the night. After their first passion was sated, as they lay there recovering and relaxing, the Beast kissed her welts. He felt sick inside and more than a little guilty as he looked at the dark stripes covering her buttocks and legs.

"M'lord?" Beauty murmured softly. "Might I talk with you freely?"

"Of course, Beauty," he replied, waiting for her to tear into him for his brutality.

"You've used a belt on me twice now," she began, "and it seems to me both times were triggered by someone or something other than my own actions. The first time, you were so upset over the loss of that young guard, whether you will admit it or not, that you overreacted when I dropped your sword."

"I gave it to you to keep safe while I tried to save the man," the Beast pointed out.

"But I could hardly help it that my horse slipped, almost going down, and I had to struggle to stay on him, could I?" she countered.

"Your horse slipped? I never knew." The Beast looked sheepish. "I was too busy trying to rescue the man. My God, Beauty, I'm sorry."

"I know you are, I understand. I even understood it at the time. I also know those words were very hard for you to say," she told him calmly. "Truly, I'm not trying to place the blame on you. I just want you to realize that what caused your anger, in both cases, was not me. I admit, I resent it a little, being the target of your bad temper."

"Like tonight? I was really aggravated with those drunken fools and not with you," the Beast admitted.

"All I ask is that you stop for a minute and use your judgment to see if I am truly at fault before you beat me," Beauty requested. "Rein in your temper that much and I'll accept your decision without complaint."

"Without complaint?" The Beast quirked an eyebrow at her.

"Well, without too much complaint," she smiled softly at him.

"I'll try, Beauty." The Beast kissed her. "But it's hard to break a lifetime of habits."

"Actually, you treat me much better than I expected when I first came to the castle door," Beauty told him.

"Really?" The Beast was pleased. "Are you content here Beauty? Would you stay with me if we had no bargain between us?"

"I am content, even happy here," Beauty said, "but without the bargain I could not stay whether I wanted to or not. My conscience would not let me stay here unless there was a compelling reason. If I were here just because I care for you, I would indeed be a slut."

"You could never be a slut, Beauty." The Beast kissed her softly.

"No matter what any man says. I am glad for the bargain though, I don't think I will ever release you from your promise."

"I'll just have to bear up as best I can," she smiled at him. "Disgrace can be very pleasing, M'lord."

Realizing that she'd given him plenty to think about, now she sought to reassure him about many things. She wanted him to know of her loyalty, and she wanted to let him feel good about their relationship and about himself. She decided that words weren't always the best means of expression, so she began to love him tenderly and completely with her hands and mouth.

Chapter Six

The summer continued on at an almost leisurely pace. In spite of the unsettling presence of the young girl, Claire, a deceptive peace and calm reigned over the castle. The girl was even more frightened of the Beast after seeing him drag Beauty up the stairs and then hearing the obvious sounds of the whipping and Beauty's piercing screams. She continued to run from the room every time she saw him. Beauty oft found her afterwards, sitting huddled in a corner, shaking with fear and her small face wet with tears.

Beauty tried to explain to the lass that she was in no danger from the Beast. She gently held the girl, comforting her when she cried and listening to her as she voiced her inner fears. She also comforted the girl after her worst nightmares, when she woke screaming. Beauty told her, gently, that it was the Beast who had hunted down the band of raiders who had killed her grandmother and raped her in the forest. That it was the Beast who had taken her in so that Beauty could nurse her back to health. She tried to make it known to the girl that the Beast only wanted to act as her protector, to make sure she was safe and that she had shelter, clothes and food.

Claire refused to see the truth behind Beauty's words. She saw only a man who was coarse and rough, demanding in a loud voice to have everything his own way. She saw a brutal man who beat Beauty, but she never saw the hidden tenderness within him. She saw the rage of the Beast and not the pain and loneliness buried deep inside his shell. Every time she saw the man she went pale, her slender frame quaking visibly.

So things remained until one day, about a month after Beauty's fierce whipping, another problem between Beauty and the Beast came to a head. Actually, it was more or less the same problem, jealousy, but this time it happened in reverse.

The Beast had begun to feel restless. He grew impatient with the servants and short-tempered with Beauty. He fought furiously and endlessly on the practice fields, tearing the straw dummies into pieces at an alarming rate. Another servant had to be hired and put to work full time making and repairing more of the dummies and targets.

The Beast rode his horses to exhaustion. More than once, the castle inhabitants and even an occasional village family had fresh game for dinner thanks to his restless roaming and ready bow. Sometimes he even brought home enough for the guardsmen. Ofttimes, he paced the castle and grounds like a caged animal desperately seeking release.

He knew what was happening to him but he wasn't sure why. There could be many reasons behind his overwhelming disquietude. Was it merely that he was a warrior without a war, growing bored with the relative peace and routine of everyday life? Was the girl, Claire, getting on his nerves? Was her constant, unrelenting fear of him preying on his spirit bringing memories back to him, memories of the women he had forced to his bed? Did her very presence prick his conscience, reminding him of the pain he'd caused others like her, thinking it was his right?

The Beast, who had never questioned his own actions before now wondered, am I still the man I used to be? Did I force Beauty to my bed as surely as I did the others? Did it matter at all that is was a different kind of force? That she had been the one to come to him? He remembered her statement that without the bargain she would leave. Did that mean she was with him against her will? That her affection for him was a sham? He pondered these things but could come to no definite answers.

Could his restlessness be laid at Beauty's feet? Was he bored with Beauty? Or was he fighting, somewhere deep within himself, his true feelings for Beauty? His reliance on her quiet wisdom and unfailing support had grown. He trusted her more than he ever had any woman. He still fought against those feelings, the sense of being settled down; even his subconscious avoided the dreaded word *tamed*.

It didn't help that the girl, Claire, followed Beauty everywhere. Her big brown eyes, filled with fear and accusation, seemed to constantly pursue the Beast. Her thin, budding body trembled visibly when she was forced to stay in the same room with him for even a short time.

She was a mirror to the Beast, reflecting back to him the kind of man he was. She was his first contact with a rape victim after the rape was over, and he felt guilty and tainted in her presence.

Barely thirteen, she was not only a reminder of a past that the Beast had yet to come to terms with, but she was a constant companion to Beauty. Frequently, she inhibited the Beast when he wanted to take Beauty into his arms or into his bed. It was difficult to rouse Beauty's passions when there was a young girl who needed to be comforted. For whatever reason, Gwyneth did not seem to be able to give the girl comfort as well as Beauty. Gradually, Claire had become used to the many castle inhabitants but she still shrank from any contact with the Beast.

Although part of him knew why she was so terrified of him and understood it well, it still pained the Beast in a way that he could hardly have imagined; to see such abject terror aimed at him, reflected in the eyes of an innocent child.

Finally his restlessness came to a boiling point. For whatever reason, even though Beauty did everything he asked and more, a part of him wanted to seek out another woman. He himself did not know why. His mind was fighting against the trap he'd walked into when he'd taken Beauty into his life. He remembered a woman he'd seen the last time he'd been to the village. She was young and beautiful. He thought of her often, once even mentioning her casually to Beauty. She had kept silent, but the Beast saw traces of tears in her eyes and felt a strange guilt that he refused to acknowledge. Determined to break his ennui, he sent for the woman. One of his soldiers brought the maiden bound and gagged to the castle. Following Seth's orders, the young soldier carried the girl up the stairs and tied her to the bed in the Beast's bedchamber.

Gwyneth did the best she could, ripping off the woman's clothes, cleaning the woman up and preparing her for the Beast, but she disapproved of the situation. Gwyneth had no words to say to Beauty when she walked into the chamber and saw the naked girl tied to the bed being readied for the Beast's arrival. Beauty was hurt and stunned to see the lass in the bed, almost as afraid as the bound and gagged woman was. She barely had time to react when the Beast walked in.

The Beast was truly confounded by Beauty's reaction. First and foremost, she was hurt as if he'd betrayed her, even though there were no marriage vows between them and never would be. Then there was the anger, simmering just below the surface as if she were ready to explode. She stood there staring at him for several minutes, never saying a word. Her eyes did her talking for her and they spoke volumes. Finally, she asked the Beast in a very cold and stiffly formal voice if she could leave the castle and return to her home.

"But why Beauty?" the Beast asked completely puzzled. "Why would you want to break your vow?"

"I'm not staying here to watch you carry on with another woman!" Beauty's temper flared quickly but she struggled to hold on to it.

"Why?" The question was low and ominous. "What do you care if I bed another woman? Remember, you did not wed me, you sold yourself to me for your brother's life. You're not my wife truly wed before God. You're just a possession, like my falcon or my horse. By what right do you have any say in what I do?"

"Idiot! You mangy cur of a man!" Beauty's control snapped completely. "I'm not a falcon or a horse, I'm a woman who did what she had to do to save her brother. No man owns me, not even the mighty Beast!"

She slapped him sharply across the face and trod sharply on his foot, then drew back her leg to kick his shin; her hand reached for the small dirk she wore at her waist before she realized what she had done. She had attacked the Beast!

Both of them stood there stunned and shocked for a long moment before, with a sharp cry, Beauty gathered up her skirts and ran. She made it down the stairs and into the great hall before the Beast followed in a rage. He ran, catching Beauty just outside the great wooden door.

As soon as Gwyneth saw the Beast follow Beauty, she took some initiative for one of the few times in her life. Smiling, she went upstairs and untied the helpless woman. She gave her a few coins and sent her back to the village with Seth to accompany her.

Furious, the Beast dragged Beauty kicking, punching and cursing him, into the stables and threw her down into the straw. She looked up at him and berated him with words he was shocked to hear falling from her lips. Indeed, he was shocked to learn that she even knew such words. Standing over her, he reached for his belt.

"Nay!" Beauty pleaded, tears streaming down her face. "You promised, not the belt, not ever again!"

The Beast gave a mighty roar of frustration before bringing his fierce anger under control. Looking down at Beauty he remembered his promise. With considerable effort, almost a visible effort, he calmed himself down and thought for a moment. He soon realized that Beauty was jealous of the woman and he became secretly pleased by Beauty's reaction to the maiden.

A long-abandoned, nearly forgotten devilish streak took the place of his anger. Lowering himself to the clean, fresh straw beside her, he rolled her over, lifted her skirts and began to tickle and spank her playfully. He covered her bottom with loud, stinging slaps without any brutality behind them.

The spanking was more love play than anger, so it wasn't very harsh. Nevertheless, Beauty's bare bottom began to blush a becoming pink. He leaned over to nip one pink cheek. She yelled angrily at him, kicking him and calling him names as she struggled to get free.

As she struggled, she got her mouth filled with straw and had to spit it out in a very unladylike manner in order to continue to berate him. Suddenly the struggling, shrieking and cursing, not to mention the unmistakable sound of slaps connecting with bare skin, drew an observer.

"What are you doin' to my sister?" Tom bellowed, his love for Beauty overcoming his common sense and blinding him to his fear and hatred of the Beast.

"What does it look like?" the Beast yelled back as he continued to spank Beauty. Indeed, the slaps became quite a bit harder now that there was a witness. "This hoyden actually had the nerve to strike me! She even drew her dagger on me!"

"Beauty! You struck the Beast? Threatened him with your dagger? Are you crazy? He could have you hung for that!" Tom was shocked to the core.

"He deserved it!" Beauty screamed. "It was one thing when he told me he was thinking of taking another woman to his bed. I thought I was angry then but now, now he actually has some strumpet in the bedchamber stripped naked and tied to the bed. Now I know what real anger is!"

"Beauty!" Tom was even more shocked. "Are you jealous? Is that possible? Have you come to care for him that much? Have you forgotten who he is?"

"Fool! You're as daft as he is!" Beauty gasped as the smart spanking continued. "Jealous of the Beast! How could I be jealous? This lout thinks I'm just another possession like his horse or his dog."

"More like a bitch," the Beast said roughly. Staying his hand for a moment he asked, "Are ye jealous, lass?"

"Nay!" Beauty spat out the answer.

"Are you?" His voice dropped ominously and the spanking resumed. In fact his hands came down a little faster and harder.

"Dolt! Idiot!" she yelled, still squirming and struggling to get away. "Bastard!"

"Are you jealous of me, lass?" His tone was implacable as he spanked a little harder still.

Beauty stopped squirming and turned her head to look back at the Beast. "Please M'lord. I am not jealous of you. How could I be? By your own words, I'm just a possession like your horse. Is your horse jealous when you ride another?"

"Since when has my horse been as difficult to get along with as you are, and given me trouble the way you do?" the Beast mused aloud, laughing. "Mayhap there is some difference between you and my horse. I'll admit that you are much more fun to ride."

The spanking abruptly stopped.

There was a long moment in which no one spoke before the Beast quietly said, "Leave us, Tom."

As Tom hesitated, the Beast repeated more firmly, "Your sister's all right, man. Now go. Leave us!"

Tom paused to take a quick look at Beauty's red bottom. "You're right M'lord. I myself used to spank her harder than that when she was a fractious child."

"Traitor!" Beauty snarled. "Men!"

"As you can see, Tom, she's still fractious, although she's no child." The Beast grinned at Tom, something he'd never done before. Quietly he repeated a third time, "Leave us."

Tom met the Beast's eyes and for the first time in as long as he could remember, felt some hope for Beauty's future. There was a slight easing of the hatred in Tom's heart, a small lessening of his thirst for vengeance. A tenuous smile passed between the two men. It was the tiniest hint of a truce between them; the universal and timeless acknowledgment amid men throughout the world about the vagaries of a woman's nature. One male agreeing silently with another over the problems caused by a woman. Without another word Tom turned and left, locking the barn door behind him.

As soon as Tom left, the Beast rolled Beauty over. He ignored her soft gasp as her tender bottom found the rough straw. He grasped both her hands in one of his and held her arms over her head.

He grinned and lowered his mouth to hers whispering gently, "Is it true, lass? Are ye jealous? Have you come to care so much for me?"

"Of course not, you fool," Beauty said very softly, but her eyes were soft and half-closed, her breath was coming slowly, and there was the hint of a smile playing on her lips.

"Little liar," whispered the Beast, grinning as he reached for her and gathered her in his arms. He kissed her gently and began to remove her clothes. "I thought you were always truthful."

She met his passion with a need of her own, matching him kiss for kiss and caress for caress. He played with her with his mouth and hands before thrusting his manhood deep into her and bringing her to a furious climax.

"It seems there's another difference between you and my horse," the Beast mused aloud, teasing Beauty. "My horse doesn't get as much pleasure from being ridden as you seem to."

"I but feign my pleasure to boost M'lord's fragile ego," Beauty said primly.

"Feigned?" the Beast teased softly. "You bit my shoulder."

"I was exceedingly hungry," Beauty said sternly, her eyelids almost closed. "'Tis long past time for the noon meal."

Those were the last coherent words she said for a very long time as the Beast took her yet again. Later, still lying in the hay, Beauty snuggled contentedly in his arms.

"Why is it that whenever either one of us gets jealous," she ignored his derisive snort and continued, "I'm the one who always winds up with a sore butt?"

"That's the way of things, Beauty," the Beast grinned, teasing her, "luckily for me."

The pair put their clothes on and made their way back to the castle. Heads held high, they walked past several soldiers who noticed the dirt and straw sticking to Beauty's torn blue silk gown and to the Beast's shirt and hose. They walked past servants who noted the bits of straw in their hair and their dirty faces. They headed up the stairs and straight to the bedchamber. Neither one of them noticed the absence of the woman who had been tied to the bed. The Beast ordered Gwyneth to send their supper and hot bathwater up to the bedchamber as soon as possible. He wanted this private time with Beauty to continue.

Soon they were squeezed into the bronze tub together, soaping each other. A large tray of food was placed within reach. There was roast chicken, candied peaches, bread, cheese and fine red wine.

"M'lord?" Beauty ventured timidly, holding a slice of the peach up to his mouth. "Why would you be interested in any other woman? What am I lacking? Do I not do anything you ask? Am I not compliant with your every wish?"

He took the bite and poured a single goblet of wine, drinking from it before holding it up to her lips.

"Beauty, you do indeed do everything I ask, and you are very amenable. That may be part of the problem. If you go on being so compliant, you may begin to bore me." The Beast looked at Beauty and demanded, only partly teasing, "Where is the woman who stood up to me, in spite of her obvious fear, and bargained for her brother's life?"

"Wouldn't I be breaking the agreement if I quibbled with you and argued all the time?" Beauty asked as she reached over and tore a leg off the chicken.

"You agreed to love me and to do anything I asked. Telling me your true feelings on things won't break the agreement. Don't you think wives who love their husbands ever speak back?" the Beast asked, taking the chicken leg from her and eating it himself.

Silently she tore off the other leg and held it out of his reach as she ate it quickly.

"You want me to speak back to you? To fight with you?" Beauty asked astonished to the core as soon as she had swallowed her food.

"Nay, but I want your honesty and I don't think I have it yet. It makes me distrust you," the Beast told her, handing her the goblet of wine.

"You think I'm disloyal? I've done everything you asked without question. What more can I do?" Beauty was puzzled as she sipped her wine.

"You misunderstand, lass. I know you to be completely loyal to me. But I also want you to be true to yourself whilst serving me. I saw the real you once, terrified and pleading, but still you stood toe to toe with me and bargained with me. I'd like to see that lass again." The Beast gazed at her.

"Really?" Beauty's voice was deceptively soft. "How can I bring out that innocent girl, with a mind of her own and just barely enough courage to speak her piece? How, I ask you, when every time I disagree with you or displease you in any small way, I wind up over your knees with a stinging bottom?"

"And you probably always will," the Beast grinned openly before reaching for a crust of bread.

"Why?" Beauty puzzled.

"Because I enjoy taking you over my knees. I enjoy spanking you and making you squirm. I love to see the colour come into your cheeks and feel the heat where my hand has been," the Beast smirked, watching the colour come onto her cheeks. "Not hurting you, mind you, but playing with you."

"Oh? Sometimes your play does smart and sting quite a bit," Beauty said quietly, wishing she wasn't blushing.

"Sometimes I really am punishing you, and sometimes my temper gets away from me," the Beast admitted. "Still, if you want to hold my interest, you'll have to find a way to stand up to me once in a while."

"Or?"

"Or I'll send you home." His voice was deceptively steady and firm.

Although it was delivered in a flat, calm voice it was an empty threat. The Beast would never send Beauty away and though neither had admitted it yet, even to themselves, they both knew it. By now the Beast had all but forgotten the oath he'd forced out of Beauty. The oath that she was never to see her family again.

Suddenly, Beauty exploded in magnificent anger, shocking the Beast. "Now if that isn't just like a man! If I do what you want, I'm too boring. If I argue, I get punished. If I bore you, you'll send me home to see the family that I love so much I was willing to die to save one of them. What a stupid threat! Only a man could be so dumb! If I argue and get punished, not only do I lose any hope of seeing my family but I also have to stay here with you! And what have you ever done to make me want to stay with you anyway? Spank me? Rape me? Use me as the lowest servant? I'd sure miss all that if I went back to my loving family, wouldn't I?"

She drank deeply from the wine goblet before pouring more and downing that too.

Shocked, the Beast responded with a rage of his own. "What have I done to make you want to stay? I've treated you better than I ever have any woman before. Your chores are few and easy. Your beatings are not severe at all, I'm almost gentle with you."

His eyes narrowed ominously as he snorted, "I try to give you all the loving that I can. What more do you want?"

"I want the right to disagree with you, even argue. I want to share laughter with you and offer you comfort when things aren't going well for you. I want your affection when we love, as much as your passion. I want to be free to see my family and to be trusted to return to you." Beauty paused before continuing softly, "And I want two more things: I want to know what happened to leave Molly crippled and pregnant... "

"And?" the Beast growled lowly.

"And I want to know what would become of me and the child if I were to become with child," Beauty whispered softly.

"That's quite a list of desires, my love." Both of them tried to ignore his use of the term, even though it was the first time he'd ever addressed her so affectionately. Outwardly, only a brief flicker of shock in her eyes acknowledged that Beauty had even heard it. Inwardly her heart threatened to beat its way out of her chest.

Finally the Beast recovered from his own shock and continued, "I do not know what I would do if you were with child. If you had any noble blood, I could marry you so the child would be my heir."

"What?" Beauty almost shrieked.

She was so astonished, she dropped the goblet into the rapidly cooling bathwater.

"Why not? I have no desire to tie myself to any woman but I do need an heir. One woman is as good as another," the Beast shrugged, grabbing the wine goblet and drinking directly from it. "The only difference I can see would be her title and her dowry. If you had those things, you would do me as well as any other, nay even better, for I know you and have trained you to my ways. Well, almost trained you."

Beauty fumed as a longing she didn't want to admit, even to herself, filled her soul. She wanted no man to marry her on those terms, she decided. She wanted the man she was to marry to be doing it for only one reason; because he wanted her as his mate for life. Something that would never happen, now that she'd given her future to the Beast. Wisely, she kept her feelings to herself. It was only one of her many secrets.

Without knowing her turn of mind, the Beast continued, "But as it is, I do not know. I still refuse to give you permission to visit your family. As for the rest, you are arguing with me right now or hadn't you realized it? And I notice you did not ask me to stop spanking you, or did you forget to mention it?"

"I don't mind it so much." Beauty blushed as she admitted, "As long as you love me afterwards. It's only after you spank me that you open up and really talk to me and cuddle me, like you are now."

She wiggled against him as she continued, "I didn't like the belt though, it stings and hurts exceedingly."

"You minx!" the Beast exclaimed, as her foot gently explored and teased his burgeoning manhood.

Then he faltered. "About the girl Molly. Yes, as is my right, I took her. At least, I probably did. I really don't remember her. Then I must have left her, maybe to attend to a squabble in the village, or handle a crisis in the stables. I don't recall. I just know I didn't cause her injuries. I know I've done many things you disapprove of but I swear to you before God, I've never done that kind of injury to any woman."

"I can only guess what happened. I probably left her in the great hall unguarded. Someone must have dragged her into the barn, raped her and beat her senseless, leaving her crippled. I know not who. I would have wanted her to stay with me so that Gwyneth could care for her if I had known aught of her injuries." He paused before admitting, "I do know that girls have been attacked after being here, even though I started sending an escort to see them home. That's why you're always so well guarded."

"So you only raped her?" Beauty accused.

"It wasn't rape. If I had her, it was my right," the Beast shot back. "It's how I was raised."

"I know," Beauty admitted, "but I still can't believe it's morally right."

"We'll argue about that later." The Beast pulled her to him. "Right now I have better ideas. Let's leave this tub and get into bed."

"Tired, M'lord? 'Tis early," Beauty teased.

"I'm not a bit tired, as you'll soon find out." The Beast gathered her into his arms and dropped her, dripping wet, onto the bed. He grabbed a few of the candied peaches from the tray and spread them, artistically, on Beauty's breasts.

"I think I'll have dessert now," he grinned, lowering his mouth to nibble on the sweet fruit.

"Whatever M'lord wishes," Beauty murmured, her eyes closing in passion as she savoured the feel of his tongue on her breasts.

"M'lord, I also crave dessert," Beauty moaned as the sensations washed over her.

Reaching out one arm, she grasped the bowl of candied peaches. She pushed against the Beast's muscled chest until he lay back on the mattress. Beauty poured some of the peaches on his chest and began to nibble and suckle until the fruit was removed. The Beast nearly went wild. She poured some more of the fruit onto his erect maleness and ate that right off his body. This time the Beast did go wild, his whole body buckling under her tender, sensual ministrations.

As his breathing returned to normal, the Beast reached out for the bowl of fruit. "'Tis my turn, you've already had two portions," he said gruffly.

He poured the fruit onto the juncture of her thighs and put the bowl aside. Slowly, with his eyes holding hers, he grinned. That grin sent shivers down her spine. Those shivers were nothing compared to the sensations that followed though. He lowered his mouth to the tangle of curls and drove her out of her mind. Before he finished driving her to the heights of ecstasy, he had her legs resting on her shoulders and her heels around the back of his neck. She clenched her thighs so hard when she climaxed that she almost strangled him. For once, after her orgasm, he was the one struggling to catch his breath.

As soon as she slowed her own breathing and brought it under control, she noted, "I'm truly sorry, M'lord." She giggled, "I hope I've done you no harm."

The Beast leered at her and wiggled his eyebrows. "I doubt if you did any permanent harm. In fact, I think I can prove it to you."

He entered her in one smooth hard thrust and the ageless ritual of passion began again; so familiar and yet so new, and so incredibly erotic. Again and again they almost reached the peak, only to pull back. As if they were one, they slowed the pace almost to a stop. The Beast slid his manhood in and out of her so inconceivably slow that it seemed he would never get himself all the way into her. Ever so slowly he picked up the pace. Beauty was with him every second. She moved with his passion and his thrusts so perfectly that he felt joined to her permanently.

The speed built up again. Again they almost reached the peak. Again they slowed to a crawl. Finally, moving as one they moved towards the peak and went over. The feelings washed over them as they each held onto the sensations as long as they could before returning to the solid reality of the bed.

"M'lord," Beauty breathed on a sigh.

"What is it Beauty?" he asked without even opening his eyes.

"'Tis naught," Beauty replied in a sleepy voice. "I just wanted to say M'lord."

"'Tis well," the Beast muttered.

Chapter Seven

Shortly after the day that Beauty's brother Tom came upon the Beast spanking Beauty in the barn, the Beast came up with an idea. He'd long realized that he needed more men to train as his guards but knew not where to find the right men. One day as he walked through the barn he stopped and watched Tom working with a young horse, a yearling colt that was already very large and extremely strong, having been bred to be a warhorse powerful enough to carry a knight in full armour.

For the first time the Beast really looked at Tom. Beauty's brother appeared to be in his early twenties. He had dark blond hair that reached just past the nape of his neck. His shirt was off, and the Beast could see the play in his arms and chest muscles as he struggled to control the scared yearling without causing the animal any injury. The Beast noticed that Tom seemed to be very strong and fit, with an impressive set of muscles. From the many reports he had received as well as his own observations, the Beast knew that Tom was also an extremely hardworking young man.

The Beast was no fool though, as he remembered well the story of the lass, Molly, and knew that Tom probably still blamed him for her death. He also knew full well that Tom held a grudge against him for taking Beauty away from her family and into his bed, especially without any marriage vows between the two of them. Of course there was also the matter of the time he had ordered Tom to be whipped and nearly had him hung. He realized that Tom had to hold some anger and resentment, possibly even a real hatred for him.

The Beast also knew that, for Beauty's sake, he needed to try to bridge the chasm that divided himself and Beauty's brother. Not even to himself would he stop to consider why it was suddenly so important for him to please Beauty. After much soul searching and consideration, the Beast decided to offer Beauty's brother an opportunity to join the ranks of his guards.

The Beast approached Tom as he worked in the stables and said gruffly, "Tom, I want a word with you."

Tom felt a flash of the familiar resentment and a trace of fear that he struggled to keep hidden as he cautiously answered the Beast, "Yea, M'lord, is there something amiss?"

"I am in need of some more guards," the Beast said without fanfare. "It requires constant combat training. Guards need good horsemanship and hand to hand combat, along with skill in the use of the long bow and broadsword. Would you be willing to work hard?"

Tom hesitated. He was so surprised that his guard slipped and some of the fear and hatred he still felt around the Beast showed in his eyes.

"What's the problem, man?" The Beast's voice had an ominous ring, and only Beauty would have noted the sardonic humour hidden in the words. "I've never done you any harm, have I?"

"M'lord, with all respect, you have indeed." Startled, Tom couldn't stop his words. "You sentenced me to be whipped and also hung for a crime I did not commit. My young sister wanted only to save me and you took her to your castle and into your bed. She was a virgin, an innocent, gently reared lass. To this day, you use her as if she were nothing but your whore and you keep her from seeing her family. The only time I've seen her since you stole her from us, you were beating her, right here where we're standing."

"That was no beating, not really. It was just a little spanking. It was more in jest than serious, and you know that's all it was. Anyway I didn't hang you, did I? And one more thing, your sister is no whore and I have never thought of her or treated her as one." The Beast's temper threatened to explode even though on one level he secretly admired the man's nerve. "Go on man, what other grievances do you have against me?"

"I might as well have my say, for if I've angered you, I'm already dead," Tom smiled wryly. He took a deep breath before continuing,

"Ever since your King invaded our land, things have not been right for the peasants. There is no law or justice anymore, just blind force. My family has suffered greatly under your rule, just as others have. Even if you do not consider Beauty as a whore, how do you think the villagers see her? What will become of her once you tire of her? And another thing, the lass I would have married, Molly, was beaten so badly she was crippled for life. Now she's dead because of you. Many girls have been found brutally murdered after having been taken to the castle. Taken by your orders and against their will."

Tom knew the risk he was taking but the words had been held in check for far too long. They now flew from his mouth, heedless of the danger.

"In God's truth, Tom, I swear I did not beat or cripple the lass Molly. I did not murder any of the women. I have never done that kind of injury to any woman," the Beast avowed, still reining in his temper. "As for the lass Molly, God's truth, I don't even remember if I took her to my bed or not."

Tom looked the Beast in the eye and saw the truth there. Not the whole truth, some of the answers Tom wanted were missing, so it wasn't all he needed to know, but he believed the Beast when he claimed not to have crippled Molly.

"And about your family's suffering, I know naught about it but I do know this: joining the guards will bring more income to your family and give them some security. It would make things much easier for them." The Beast paused before adding smugly, "I will reassure you on one thing Tom: I give you my word of honour, here and now, that what ever happens between Beauty and myself, she will never suffer from my neglect. I will make sure she is always well cared for and that she always has everything she needs. God's truth, Tom, I think your sister's got precious few complaints with her situation."

"Excuse me, M'lord, but would she tell you if she had?" Tom countered brusquely.

Deep inside, he was both shaken and touched by the Beast's reassurance that Beauty would always be well cared for. For some reason, as yet unknown even to himself, he believed the Beast.

"Trust me, Tom. If your sister was unhappy or upset with me, she'd let me know," the Beast laughed, "in thousands of ways."

Reluctantly, Tom joined the Beast in his laughter. "Knowing Beauty, I'm sure she would."

"So you'll begin the training?" the Beast asked again. "I know you have no loyalty to me but if you give your word to serve me, I know you'll keep it. At least you will if you are anything at all like your sister. Could you swear fealty to me?"

"Yea, M'lord. You honour me," Tom replied. "I'll join the guards, if not out of loyalty to you, then to get a chance to see Beauty sometimes. I swear I will strive to live up to the honour you do me."

The Beast thought aloud, "Now all I need to do is to find another stable boy. Someone as hardworking as you are."

"M'lord, if I might venture, my brother Nate is young and mischievous but he's also strong and hardworking. He might be good for the job." Tom volunteered the lad before he thought.

"Mischievous is he? It must run in your family," the Beast mused aloud. He then asked, "How old is the lad?"

"Thirteen, nay, fourteen now." Tom hesitated then thought of something. "It wouldn't work though, he needs to be home to tend to our mother. She's been in poor health for several years."

"That's too bad," the Beast said slowly, trying to ignore that last bit of information. "Still, I'll think on it, mayhap I can find a workable solution."

What the Beast was thinking of however, when he made his way back to the castle, was that Beauty had a young brother and a very ill mother that she hadn't seen in a long time because of him. He tried to remember his reasons for disallowing Beauty any contact with her family, but his mind refused to come up with any.

A softer man might feel guilty for denying her the right to visit her family, he mused, so it's a good thing I'm not a weakling like that. Still, deep inside him there was an uncomfortable feeling; it felt uncommonly like guilt.

During the evening meal, a feast of roasted boar and venison, Beauty asked him casually how fared his day.

"Things went well today," the Beast told her. "I hired a new man to begin training as one of my guards. Perhaps you know him from the village."

"Perhaps. Who is he?" Beauty asked, without much interest, as there were few men in the village that she'd had very much contact with.

"One of the men from my stables," the Beast said straight-faced. "Tom."

Not daring to even think it, Beauty asked, "Tom? The man we call Tom Two? I mean, the man you almost hung with my brother?"

"Nay, lass," the Beast said with a straight face, "the other man I almost hung that day."

"You gave Tom, my brother Tom, a position in the guards?" Beauty was shocked to her soul.

"Why not?" the Beast said off-handed. "He's a good, strong man and hard working."

"M'lord, I'm loathe to say this but he hates you," Beauty pointed out gently. "I doubt that he'll ever lose his hatred of you."

"Why ever not? You have," the Beast stated with a trace of arrogance, rising to pace around the room before he turned to face Beauty. "Besides, we talked for a long time today. We've come to an understanding, Tom and I. It seems that we have something of a bond between us."

"Really?" Beauty asked puzzled and surprised. "What bond could there possibly be between you and Tom?"

"You." The Beast looked her in the eyes and said simply, "We both care for you."

This admission shook Beauty to the core. She flashed a brilliant smile at the Beast as she walked around the table to stand in front of him. "Thank you, M'lord."

She stood on her toes to give him a kiss. It was the not first time she had ever approached him for a kiss but it was the first time she approached him with a kiss so full of joy and passion. Usually the Beast initiated the lovemaking, but not this time. This time the rest of the dinner was pushed aside by Beauty. Plates and goblets hit the floor with a clang and were quickly forgotten as the Beast found himself being pulled down onto the wooden table.

He soon learned that it did not make a man either soft or foolish to do small things to please a woman. To the contrary, pleasing a woman made a man very hard indeed, at least certain parts of him. It was a lesson that continued as the pair staggered up the long staircase on weak legs and together fell onto the soft bed. The lesson Beauty gave the Beast on a woman's gratitude continued long into the night. The Beast barely crawled out of bed the next day and dragged himself to the training field.

Tom began his training the next day. From the first he seemed to be almost hopeless and totally inept. He was clumsy with the sword and could hardly aim an arrow. His one and only strength was his horsemanship.

Although he was exceedingly tired, the Beast trained Tom personally and he worked him very hard, sometimes taunting him without mercy for his lack of skills. The Beast may just have given up on Tom but for one thing: Even from the first day, on a few occasions, when the Beast worked him real hard and jeered at him enough to loosen his temper, Tom would respond with flashes of brilliance. Once, he came very close to defeating the Beast at archery.

The Beast was not a stupid man; he knew what he saw but kept it to himself. Although he was trying to keep it hidden, sometime in the past Tom had been highly trained in the use of weapons and fighting skills. The Beast pondered this and added it to the puzzle surrounding Beauty.

On the first day of the second week of Tom's training, after a particularly nasty taunt from the Beast, Tom's temper exploded and the Beast soon found himself flat on his back with the point of Tom's sword at his throat.

Looking up into the irate face of the young man holding the sword, the Beast quietly said, "Tom, you do remember your oath of loyalty to me, don't you?"

Tom grinned unexpectedly and laughed aloud, "Aye, M'lord, most unfortunately I do."

"Tom, you aren't fooling me." The Beast looked the young man in the eyes. "I won't ask you where you trained or who trained you. If you want me to know these things you'll tell them to me, but I do know you are well trained as a warrior. You have had much more training than any other peasant to be found in this village. Use your skills wisely."

Tom looked down at the Beast and realized how much he'd given away. There was no way for him to know if the Beast fully appreciated the import of his discovery. He extended a hand to the Beast and helped him to his feet. The training session continued and Tom dropped his pretence completely, letting his true skill show through. The Beast made no further comments on Tom's newfound abilities.

One day during the third week of Tom's training, Nate showed up at the castle. The lad begged admittance and asked to see Beauty. When his request was refused, he pleaded to see Tom instead. Through sheer stubbornness, his request was granted.

He was directed to the training fields. There he saw Tom and another man duelling furiously. As he approached, he saw it was the Beast.

"Don't you hurt my brother!" the lad yelled, running to hurl himself at the Beast. "Don't you dare! I'll kill you!"

He started pummelling the fierce warrior with all the strength in his slender body. The Beast was startled and beginning to get angry but Tom quickly stepped in to grab Nate, pulling the boy away.

"Sorry M'lord!" Tom hurried to get the words out, fearing reprisals on the lad. "This is my younger brother Nate. He must have thought our practice fight was in earnest. Forgive him, I pray, he did but seek to defend me."

"I'm sorry, M'lord," Nate muttered, his eyes downcast as he realized just what he had done. "I wasn't thinking. I just wanted to defend Tom."

It was a long, tense moment waiting for the Beast's reaction. The Beast looked at the pair, weighing the affection between the two, and knowing that their obvious bond included Beauty. The boy, Nate, was slender with Beauty's colouring of golden blond hair and bright blue eyes. His face and body were just beginning to show traces of manhood.

Tom still held the boy, his hands resting on the boy's shoulders.

He could feel a faint shiver travel through the boy's body as they waited. Finally the Beast's nearly dormant sense of humour broke through and he met Tom's eyes and laughed aloud.

"Mayhap I should have hired him for my guard," the Beast teased Tom. "He might even be better at hand to hand combat than you are."

"It's possible, M'lord," Tom laughed too, in relief.

"What brings you here, Nate?" Tom asked turning his attention to his brother.

"It's our mother," Nate blurted, trying to prevent tears from coming to his eyes in front of this fierce warrior. "She's much worse. She feels hot to the touch and she's coughing all the time. She keeps asking for Beauty. I'm scared, Tom. I think she may be dying." At this last his voice lowered and threatened to break. "I don't know what to do for her."

"M'lord, can I please take Beauty to see her? She's quite gifted in the healing arts," Tom asked quietly. "I give you my oath to return Beauty to you as soon as it's possible."

"Nay, Tom. Go saddle four horses and bring them to the castle. Quickly," the Beast ordered. "I'll fetch Beauty."

"You'll be coming with us, M'lord?" Tom asked quickly, surprised. His question went unanswered as the Beast had already left in a hurry to get Beauty.

Striding back to the castle, the Beast finally felt the true weight of his thoughtless cruelty as he realized for the first time what it meant to keep Beauty from her mother. Please God, he thought, don't let the old woman die before I can get Beauty to her. He knew instantly that Beauty would be lost to him forever if that happened.

The Beast stormed into the great hall and bellowed with all his might, "Beauty!"

She appeared instantly, pale and fearful at his tone. "M'lord, What's wrong? Have I angered you?"

The Beast reined himself in and spoke tenderly, "Nay, never fear my love."

Beauty's eyes widened with pleasure at the Beast's rare use of the endearment as the Beast continued, "I want to take you to the village.

Your mother is very ill. She's been asking for you and Tom said you're skilled as a healer."

Beauty was surprised to find Tom and Nate mounted and waiting outside the castle door. Her joy at seeing her younger brother again was quickly tempered by the news of her mother's illness. Still, she managed, somehow, to lean over from the back of her horse and hug the lad tightly and enthusiastically, almost unseating him.

"Beauty!" The lad blushed at being hugged by a mere woman in front of the legendary Beast.

"Don't worry, lad," the Beast told the boy, before kicking his great horse into a gallop. "'Tis better to have a woman hug you than hit you, and your sister's done both to me many times."

"You've struck the Beast?" Nate looked over at Beauty, his eyes wide with astonishment.

Beauty merely shrugged, "He's not so fierce."

After that, the group rode to the village quickly and silently. They pulled their horses up at the small hut. Entering, they found it almost bare. There were almost no furnishings and very little food was to be seen. Beauty ran to her mother's side but her joy at seeing her was tempered by the sight that greeted her. Her mother was indeed very ill, feverish, coughing and painfully thin.

"Why does no one make sure she has enough food?" the Beast asked in a loud voice.

"How am I to do that, M'lord?" Beauty pointed out. "I've been forbidden to come here."

"What about Tom?" The Beast fought to ignore a quick surge of guilt by accusing others.

"M'lord fool, Tom was almost hung when he was falsely accused of stealing a small amount of grain. What chance would he have if he really did steal food from you?" Beauty raged before Tom could utter a word.

"Women!" The Beast shook his head. "I did not mean to suggest that either you or Tom should steal from me. You could have asked me for some food for your brother and mother, Beauty. I'm not a monster."

"I'm truly sorry, M'lord," Beauty apologized softly, realizing that she'd actually hurt this proud man's feelings. Then she requested softly, "M'lord, I beg you to let me stay with her a few days. I feel mayhap I can nurse her back to some health."

"Nay woman," the Beast paused then continued quietly before she could protest, "we'll take her to the castle and care for her there. Gwyneth can help you as she's good at these things too. Bundle up anything she might need. Nate, gather your things too."

The Beast turned to Tom, "I guess Nate will get the job in the stables after all."

"What about our hut? And the fields?" Nate demanded, puzzled at this turn of events.

"Ease your mind, lad," the Beast told the boy. "You won't be coming back here."

"You're taking my whole family in? To care for them?" Beauty was astonished. "I'll be able to see Nate and my mother whenever I want to?"

"Tis naught," the Beast replied off-handed, "it's a big castle. I don't know why you never suggested it before."

"Tis a great deal, it means the world to me. Thank you, M'lord," Beauty whispered, kissing his cheek. "But you know well why I never suggested it to you. You forbid me to see my family. My promise, remember?"

The Beast grinned wickedly and leaned over to whisper in her ear. "You can thank me later, mayhap tonight in bed."

The group rode back to the castle, the Beast carrying Beauty's mother in his arms. Nate and Tom both had their hands full trying to ride while holding onto their meagre possessions. Beauty had stuffed her mother's collection of herbs and healing medicines into a rough bag and carried them herself.

Back at the castle, the Beast had Tom help Nate get his things settled into the shed in the barn before joining them in the castle. The Beast carried the older woman up the stairs to a small sleeping chamber in the castle. He sent for Seth and had him help Beauty and Gwyneth while they quickly readied the room, lit a fire, made up the bed with fresh linens and placed Beauty's mother into it.

The three of them, Beauty, Gwyneth and Seth, tended to Beauty's mother. Beauty quickly brewed a foul smelling herbal tea and forced it down her mother's throat. By then, Tom and Nate joined them in the small room. Beauty then made a poultice, and put cool, damp cloths on her mother's head. Only then did she feel free to turn her attentions to Nate.

"I love you Nate." Beauty hugged the lad, tears freely streaming down her face. "I've missed you so much. I'm glad you'll be living here so that I can see you."

"I'm glad we'll be here too, Beauty." Nate hugged her back, whispering, "But I swear I will never like that man."

"Give it time, Nate," Beauty smiled. "He's truly a better man than even he knows."

She sat by the bed with Gwyneth and the servant, Seth. She stroked her mother's forehead, talking softly to her without even knowing if her words were being heard. She kept changing the damp, cool cloths when they began to warm up. Soon one of the other servants brought her a tray with clear broth for her mother and a dinner of roast pork, savoury vegetables and warm bread for herself, Seth and Gwyneth.

Beauty was exhausted but unwilling to leave her mother's side until the Beast reminded her that the servants, Seth and Gwyneth, would be glad to keep watch through the night and tend to the woman. They promised to call Beauty if she was needed.

Seth took Beauty aside, out of Gwyneth's hearing. "I'll take good care of your mother, Beauty, and you well know it. I feel very sorry that she ever got into such poor condition. It is as if I've let your father down."

"Nay, Seth, my old friend," Beauty told him, "tis my fault."

"Does it matter?" Seth asked her gently. "We just have to make her well and strong again. I'll help any way I can."

"I know you will Seth," Beauty told him gently.

"I care for her, Milady," Seth admitted softly. "Even though I have no right to."

"I'm glad you do," Beauty said, kissing the man's cheek. "And as far as I'm concerned, you have as much right as any man to care for whom you will. Things have changed greatly around here in the last few years. Watch her tonight and I will see you in the morning."

Beauty got into bed beside the Beast and looked over, almost shyly at him. "Thank you, M'lord, for helping us today."

"'Twas nothing, lass." Gently, he drew her into his arms, showing her a tenderness that was rare but very real before gently teasing her. "You'll thank me properly when you're not so exhausted though."

"Nay, sir," Beauty whispered in his ear, smiling slyly, "I'll thank you most improperly. But later, much later." She dozed off instantly.

For several days, Beauty used all her skills and energy fighting for her mother's life, and ever so slowly the older woman's health began to get better. Finally the older woman regained her senses enough to have a joyous and tearful reunion with Beauty.

"Mother, I love you so much. I've missed you awfully." Beauty hugged her mother gently. "I'm so glad you're here and that you're healing."

"I've missed you too, Beauty. I've been so worried for you," her mother sobbed in her arms. "How goes it for you? How do you fare with that dreadful man? How did I get here? Am I now a prisoner too?"

"Of course you're not a prisoner here. The Beast heard you were ill and brought you here so that I could take care of you. And to please me. He's a hard man, fast-tempered, stern and strong-willed, nay, stubborn really, but he has a good soul in spite of his reputation. He can be warm and good natured. He has never hurt me," Beauty grinned wryly, "Well, not too much."

"You sound like you're in love with him," her mother pointed out sharply. "Do you forget who he is? Who you are?"

"Nay, Mother," Beauty replied, "I forget nothing, but I have come to care a great deal for this man. Tis not unlike a maid being given in marriage to a man she fears and loathes at first and slowly comes to care for him."

"But this is no marriage, Beauty," her mother said softly.

"To me, it is," Beauty told her mother. "I think of him as my husband. Tis the only way I can keep my self respect. The Beast is the only man I will ever give myself to, whether he keeps me or not. I will never know another man's touch."

Beauty's mother listened and pondered what she heard but kept her thoughts to herself. As her faint energy drained, she slept again. Her progress was slow, and by the time there was any real improvement in her condition, Beauty, Gwyneth and Seth were all exhausted but relieved and very happy. They hadn't been at all sure the older woman would ever recuperate from her illness.

It was a mixed blessing however, for as soon as Beauty's mother felt the least bit better, she started to make known to the Beast exactly what she thought of him. She began to tell the Beast constantly and in painfully explicit detail what she thought of his looks, his life, his treatment of Tom, Nate and Beauty. It was not a flattering assessment for the Beast or pleasant for him to hear, to put it mildly.

She harangued him for keeping Beauty as a hostage and sleeping with her without a thought about her chances for a good marriage, the future, her good name or the possibility of bastard children. She insisted that he used Beauty only for sex without any tenderness or care about her feelings, and insinuated that he was a selfish and inadequate lover. She also berated him for his care of the castle and the village. She insulted him and defamed his character in front of Claire. She complained of the food and the servants, and then loudly assailed his character when he attempted to discipline them.

"God's blood!" the Beast raged when he had a moment alone with Beauty. "Tis well we're not in our chamber, else I'd beat you half to death this time!"

"M'lord! Calm yourself." Beauty tried to soothe him. "How have I wronged you this time?"

"Why didn't you warn me that your mother was such a shrew!" he angrily complained after a long day of being harangued for his sins. "I need a drink, a lot of drinks."

The Beast drank deeply from a tankard of ale. "Did you have to feed her all that muck? About how I'm so cruel and thoughtless. Did you have to tell her I was so inadequate as a lover? She tells me you find me much too fast, too clumsy and even too short to please any woman. Too short! Hah! What comparison have you had, woman?"

"M'lord! Please believe that I never said those things to her! I would not tell her the private things that happen between us." Beauty was shocked but she protested, "Why would I tell my mother that you were inadequate or too short? You're on me every spare moment we can find, riding me as well and as often as you ride your charger. As for short, I don't know how to compare your endowments with other men for I've never seen any other man naked, but you fill me almost to the point of pain. I simply cannot imagine how you could be any larger, how any more of you could possibly fit inside me. And as for telling her you fail to pleasure me, how could I? You know exactly when you pleasure me; indeed, the whole castle hears my screams at the moment I reach the peak of my pleasure."

"So I do give you pleasure when I mount you?" the Beast asked, slightly drunk.

"M'lord fool." Beauty didn't answer; she merely shook her head and smiled. "Men!"

Beauty was truly shocked and puzzled by her mother's uncharacteristic behaviour but she tried to defend her mother to the Beast. If she could smooth this over, she thought to herself ruefully, she could become a diplomat and help bring peace to warring counties.

"Remember, M'lord," Beauty soothed him, "she doesn't really know about your recent kindness. All she remembers is that you took me from her. She'll soon see you as I do and come to lo... "

"Come to what?" the Beast demanded. Could he have heard what he thought he'd heard?

"I'm sorry, M'lord, I've lost all sense and order to my thoughts." Fearing her loose tongue would betray her, Beauty quickly fled the room leaving the Beast standing there with a silly grin on his face.

Chapter Eight

As the summer slowly passed into autumn, there was a great deal of uneasiness amongst the small group living in the castle. Although the Beast had learned how to show some of his tender feelings and he had slowly begun to extend small courtesies both to Beauty and her family, all was still far from well.

The lass, Claire, still clung to Beauty, following her everywhere as Beauty worked to keep the castle and its grounds running smoothly. Part of this dependency on Beauty was based on her fear of the Beast and Beauty well knew it, but part of it was based on sheer loneliness. It also was the natural fear and despair of a young girl suddenly and brutally cut off from the only family she had ever known, and the suffering of the victim of an extraordinarily vicious attack and rape.

Beauty used the time she spent with Claire as an opportunity to try to teach the girl some of the tasks she did and the principles behind the management of such a large estate. She tried to show her the various methods of maintaining the castle and its grounds, along with teaching her the basics of reading, writing and math. She also worked, gently, on the girl's comportment, grammar and manners.

The girl wanted very much to be like Beauty. She admired Beauty's style and manners and she tried very hard to learn, but deep inside she was still a very disturbed girl, barely recovering from the ordeal of her grandmother's murder and her own rape. Her concentration seemed apt to wander and she was prone to breaking into tears for no apparent reason.

The presence of Margaret, Beauty's mother, also proved to be an irritation for the people living in the castle. She freely ordered the staff and servants about as if it were her castle, frequently countermanding the Beast's orders. The servants were getting nervous and edgy just from having too many conflicting voices to listen to.

To make matters worse, whenever the Beast tried to be alone with Beauty, at least during the day, either Claire was underfoot or Beauty's mother was in the way. The older woman and the girl proved to be very effective barriers to the frequent, rowdy and spontaneous sex the Beast and Beauty had come to enjoy sharing. It was very frustrating for both of them.

For months, the couple had made love, had sex or just plain fucked in every room of the castle at any and all hours of the day or night. They had copulated in every position imaginable, from standing and slamming into the castle walls, to stretching out on the great dining table, or lying on soft furs piled high in front of the great stone fireplace. They made love slowly, playfully, tenderly, furiously and always passionately.

Arguments turned to love play, tender moments to passion, dinner was apt to become a feast of a different kind entirely, and even tickling, wrestling matches and the playful spankings would soon turn amorous.

The servants had long since learned to knock before entering a room as they went about their daily duties, but those same servants were also more relaxed than they had ever been since the Beast's arrival. They had even begun to smile indulgently at the loving couple. Suddenly because of the presence of Margaret and Claire, that all seemed to have ended forever.

To make matters even worse, Claire was still completely terrified of the Beast. While he fully sympathized with the girl's plight, the Beast was quickly growing weary of the girl's practice of giving a small scream and bursting into tears whenever he happened to come near her. Beauty quizzed the girl about her excessive fear of the Beast but she never received an intelligible answer.

Then, one day, Beauty's brother Tom was injured by the Beast during training. While practicing with broadswords, the Beast accidentally caught him with the edge of his blade. Tom was brought into the castle and once again Beauty and Gwyneth were pressed into work as healers, this time along with Margaret, Beauty's mother.

It was not a deep or very serious wound but it gave Margaret yet another sin to lay at the Beast's feet, one more thing to complain about incessantly. It also strained the tenuous truce between the Beast and Tom; not because Tom blamed the Beast for his injury, but because Tom was simply a restless and demanding patient, ill used to lying about idle.

Margaret continued to harbour ill feelings towards the young lord and she wasted no chance to make him aware of it. The injury to Tom gave her fodder for complaining even longer and louder. She had found confederates, it seemed, both in Claire and to the Beast's surprise, Gwyneth, not to mention his own manservant, Seth.

The Beast often found the four of them huddled together, seemingly conspiring against him. Was he going crazy he wondered?

He could understand Seth joining the group. The man hadn't been with him long. In fact, he was the only servant of any status to have come with the castle. He had once been the personal manservant to the old lord. His service to the Beast was impeccable, but his loyalty to the Beast was recent and still tenuous.

The Beast was very surprised however that even his long time servant, Gwyneth, was seen whispering with the small group. Gwyneth had been the only source of support in his life long before he'd met Beauty. She'd been with him since he was fostered as a boy, first as his governess, then as his personal maid.

Thus, things in general, as well as the lack of freedom or privacy, in particular the privacy to indulge in frequent sex, seemed to cause tension between everyone in the castle, especially between Beauty and the Beast. Beauty was grateful for his care of her family and of the girl, but was also strained and hindered by the very presence of the group. Every time she held the Beast in her arms, a picture formed in her brain of her mother's disapproving glare and the wide, frightened eyes of the young girl, Claire.

With her family present, Beauty also began to realize that she'd been fooling herself by treating this arrangement between herself and the Beast almost as a marriage and acting as the lady of the castle. In truth, she was simply ruined and living in disgrace, and because of that, doomed never to marry any man and never to know the joys of having children. It was no longer possible to think of her promises to the Beast as her own form of wedding vows. She had to admit, finally, that she had simply and completely sold herself like a common whore. It mattered naught that her price had been high indeed, for the price of her decency had been the life of her brother. She had still willingly sold herself into a life of depravity and sin. Needless to say, Beauty heard all of this from her mother, repeatedly. This realization contributed to the tension between the pair because Beauty suddenly felt too ashamed and inhibited to fully express her passions. Of late, the very presence of these passions, which she still felt strongly and very frequently, caused her to feel a conflict deep within herself.

Even at night, the bedchamber had ceased to be a refuge and a place of pleasure for the pair. Now it was a place to finish the arguments begun earlier in the day. The pleasure had become hurried sex. Sex that did little to please either participant and certainly failed to bring the sense of peace and sharing that it once had. Now the sexual act was simply a release of tension and pent up frustrations.

Because of the tension in the castle, the Beast and Beauty now frequently quarrelled. They could be seen and heard throughout the castle exchanging harsh words, throwing and breaking things and slamming doors. There was one promising note, although no one seemed to realize it at the time. Through all the stress and turmoil the Beast never spanked Beauty in anger, not even in play. Indeed he raised his voice to her often but he never raised a hand to her or to any of the castle's other inhabitants.

Beauty's brother, young Nate, was yet another cause of the Beast's irritation. The boy had settled into life at the castle well enough. He was a good hand in the stables and a hard worker, but he was also a very energetic young lad whose mischievous nature had been long denied in the sheer toil of trying to help support his family, to care for a weak and ailing mother, and to survive.

Nate began to feel safe and secure with life in the castle and soon began getting very bold and disrespectful around the Beast. He felt like his sister's situation gave him some protection from the Beast's wrath. He was also the only one to notice the new control the Beast held on his temper. The boy grew wild and became prone to pulling mischievous pranks on the Beast and some of his guards.

Unbeknownst to Nate, the Beast had not mastered his temper completely. It was all the Beast could do not to take a switch to the lad. He secretly wondered what Beauty would say about it if he did though. Knowing Beauty, he realized that she would not hesitate to make her feelings well known. Knowing that he feared the reaction of a woman increased his inner rage. The lad's days were numbered, whether he realized it or not.

To add a final touch to his problems, one of the kitchen helpers was caught smuggling a bundle of food and some silver out of the castle.

The Beast was pondering what to do about the thief when Beauty, alone for once, found him likewise alone in the great hall.

"You seem uneasy. Is there aught that troubles you, M'lord?" she asked gently as she stood before him.

"Many things trouble me of late, Beauty." The Beast looked at her, still awe-struck by her beauty.

"Mayhap I can help?" Beauty sat by him and looked at him softly. "Or at least listen. Tell me what bothers you. Please, M'lord."

"First, let's get some food together and have some horses saddled. We need to get away from the castle and have a few moments alone," the Beast suggested.

As an answer, Beauty sent for a servant to fetch the cook and then to go to the stables and have the horses saddled. The Beast shouted after the servant, "Tell them to make sure Tom Two saddles both mounts and not the lad, Nate. Tis very important."

Beauty looked at him quizzically but remained silent at the strange order. A bundle of food was brought to them and hand in hand they left the castle. Mounting their horses, they rode into the woods. They came to a small meadow near the stream and dismounted. They removed their boots and sat with their feet dangling in the cold water. They ate the cold chicken, bread and cheese packed by the cook, and of course they drank the wine.

"Why is there so much tension between us of late, my Beauty?" the Beast asked softly. "Why do you no longer enjoy being with me?"

"Things are unsettled at the castle now," Beauty replied evasively. "That's all."

"No it's not. What's wrong, my love?" the Beast persisted.

The endearment softened her and Beauty replied honestly, "Tis that the presence of my family has made a truth clear to me. A truth that I have long denied even to myself." She lowered her eyes. "I live with you without any marriage vows spoken between us. I am disgraced and shamed like a common slut."

"Tis not so! You are no slut, my Beauty," the Beast replied forcefully. "Answer me truthfully, did you not feel right and natural with me before your mother came to the castle? Was not your passion real?"

"Yea, M'lord," Beauty blushed, "as you well know."

"And did you ever feel that I thought of you as a slut or a whore?" the Beast actually blushed. "Well, after the first day or so."

"No, M'lord. You have always treated me as if I was your honoured lady," Beauty replied.

"I once asked you if you would leave me if I ever released you from the bargain and you said you would, for decency's sake. Now I ask you another question. Would you want to go, to leave me if I released you from the bargain? Are you here with me because it's where you want to be?" The Beast held her eyes as he asked her the question.

"Nay, M'lord," Beauty whispered softly, "I would not want to leave you even if I could. I truly want to be by your side."

"Then don't let others turn you from me, I beg of you." The Beast met her lips in a soft, gentle kiss and Beauty's passions flared.

They made slow, satisfying love on the riverbank. Afterwards they lay entwined in each other's arms.

"Now tell me what else is troubling you, M'lord," Beauty gently prompted.

"Well, actually there are three things that trouble me. The least of which is your family, especially your mother. She hates me and she causes my own servants to treat me with a large degree of disrespect. Beauty, how can I get her to hold her tongue and stop her ceaseless haranguing?" The Beast looked bewildered. "I think the girl, Claire, would mayhap have grown to know me by now were it not for your mother."

"Poor man, to be so harshly put upon by a mere woman," Beauty teased gently. "Take ease, mighty beast. I pray that she'll soon cease her nagging when she learns what a fine man you really are and how caring you've become. So will Claire when her mind recovers from the horrors she's seen. Right now you are tied, in her mind, to the awful death of her grandmother and the brutal attack upon herself. One day soon, I promise, she'll learn to trust you and come to realize that it was indeed you who saved her. Simply be patient, mighty beast. I will also talk to them of course, and try to show them what a fine man you have become. What's your next trouble?"

"Nate!" the Beast snarled. "He's constantly underfoot and causing trouble. He fixed a bucket of water so that it fell on my head as I entered the stables." He glanced over and saw that Beauty was struggling not to laugh. "The water did no harm, but the bucket almost knocked me unconscious. He pushed straw from the loft down on me and almost hit me with his pitchfork. Harmless but annoying pranks, but then he put a burr under my saddle the other day. If I were a lesser rider I might have been killed."

"He's a boy," Beauty pointed out calmly. "You're a man and lord of the castle. Can you not control one small lad?"

"How?" the Beast shouted.

"Were I you, I'd give him a quick tour of the dungeon, M'lord, followed by taking off your belt and giving him a good harsh strapping. That ought to put some fear and respect for you back into him!" Beauty told him sternly, before asking, "Or does M'lord only like to use the strap on helpless women?"

"Helpless hah! It seems I've not used it on you in a good long while, my Beauty," the Beast muttered as he stared at her with his eyes narrowed.

When she shivered he continued, "I held my temper because I thought you'd be angry with me if I beat your brother."

"I'd be angrier still if he killed you, my fine idiot," she snapped at him. "I never told you to stop all forms of discipline. Regardless of what you seem to think, I've never wanted you to be overly soft or weak. I only begged you to be fair, to show some compassion and wisdom in your judgments. If the lad is truly guilty of wrongdoing, then take care of it. If you feel he needs to be punished, do it. Now, what's the third problem?"

"I caught one of the kitchen lads stealing food and some silver." The Beast paused. "There's no mistake this time, lass, I caught him myself."

Beauty paled, "Will you hang him?"

"I should," the Beast said wearily. "Else there will be others."

"Do you know why he stole the things?" Beauty asked. "Was he too lazy to work hard enough to feed his family? Or was there another reason?"

"He works here, and his wife and four children try to work the fields. His wife was ill and the children had to work the fields without any supervision. Although they tried hard, they did a poor job of it. With the crops so low this year there was not enough food to keep his family alive," the Beast smiled sadly at Beauty. "I knew you'd ask."

Beauty thought long and hard. Finally she spoke softly, "You can't let him off without any punishment, that's obvious. Were I you, I'd have him publicly whipped, with enough force that no one watching would want to be treated likewise, then I'd send him away to tend his fields and find another man to work in the kitchen. Someone with less mouths to feed waiting at home."

"Beauty, you shock me," the Beast gaped at her. "You want me to whip not only your young brother but also some poor, starving thief?"

"It's not what I want, you know that, as the very idea sickens me," Beauty said sadly while inside she reflected on how much humanity this warrior had gained. "It's the least you can do without losing the respect of my brother, the villagers and even the men who must follow you into battle. You must exercise your right of judgment to keep their respect and to remain effective as a leader."

"However, I do have another idea, if M'lord wishes to hear it." Beauty gazed at him and seeing his silent nod continued, "I know you have a fine herd of young warhorses, many ready to train; in fact, some of them have already been started. Soon you and your guards will have many new mounts and you will even have several spare horses to sell to other knights. The villagers have no horses in the village at all, M'lord. Couldn't you spare an old mount or two? To help them in their ploughing and mayhap pull an old wagon?"

"Yea, mayhap I could," the Beast muttered. "I'll think about it."

Mustering her courage, Beauty continued, "And is there any way you could make sure the villagers had enough seed to plant?" she grinned. "Without seeming too soft?"

"Yea." The Beast's reply was without force and sounding very noncommittal. He seemed preoccupied but still she pressed on.

"Also, I've heard that in the land where you were born, they have methods to bring water to thirsty fields and also to drain off the excess if there is too much rain," Beauty smiled at him. "Think, M'lord, how much more food there would be for all of us, the serfs, the guards and even yourself if you were to share that secret with the people of the village."

"You mean to have me dig in the dirt like a commoner?" the Beast snarled. "Now you go too far, woman!"

"Nay, of course not, M'lord dolt. I mean you to teach the commoners how to dig in the dirt with more success," Beauty shook her head, smiling.

"I'll think on it later. Stop pestering me, woman." The Beast rose. "First I have to deal with a thief and a young prankster."

"Beast?" Beauty said softly. "Take care my mother doesn't hear of how you deal with the prankster, else you'll never hear the end of it."

"I'll take that warning to heart. Beauty, will you stand by my side whilst I deal with the thief? I know you're tender-hearted and with your gentle nature it would be hard for you to view the whipping of the peasant, but it would show your support for me before the rest of the people." The Beast made his request with quiet dignity.

Beauty's stomach roiled at the very idea but she kept her head high and her smile calm. "Yea, M'lord."

Then she gave a small smile. "But it would make it easier to watch if I knew that after you finished punishing this thief, you were also going to try some of the things I mentioned to help the rest of the vassals earn a better living."

"Okay, beautiful nag, it's a bargain." The Beast kissed her quickly but with passion. "Let's finish this."

They mounted their horses and returned to the castle. Beauty was true to her word. She stood near him on a high platform; her face impassive while the Beast himself whipped the thief for all to see. When he stopped, the man's back was a mass of bloody stripes.

"Did you have to do that yourself?" Beauty whispered aside to him, her hands still clenched into tight fists.

"Either myself or Gerrin, my chief guard," the Beast replied, stroking her hands and coaxing her fingers apart. "And Gerrin would have enjoyed beating the man to death."

"Gerrin! I hate the man, he's nothing but a brute," Beauty snarled forcefully.

"Isn't that what you once thought of me?" the Beast asked softly. "Once upon a time?"

"Mayhap I was wrong in your case, I've yet to decide." She teased before asking, "M'lord? If I can do it without making you seem too weak or soft-hearted, may I get someone to tend this man's wounds? I could mayhap send my mother to the village to tend the man."

"Yea," the Beast relied softly, "it would be a good idea to send your mother. 'Twould give me plenty of time to deal with the prankster."

Beauty paled even more at the reminder of the impending punishment of her unsuspecting brother, but she trusted the Beast to handle the matter well. She knew the lad would be more scared than injured by the Beast's punishment.

A short time later Beauty's mother slipped out of the castle and into town accompanied by Seth. Margaret thought her departure was unnoticed and in defiance of the Beast's wishes. She knew not that he had planned the mission of mercy she was on. With her she carried the herbs and potions that she had taught Beauty to use so well. While she was gone, the Beast took her youngest son into the dungeon.

Nate was very scared and trying very hard not to show it as the Beast took him on a bizarre tour of some of the more macabre places in the castle. The boy showed his defiance at the opening to the dungeon, covering his fear with his usual bravado, "You wouldn't dare put me in there, M'lord. Beauty would take your head from your shoulders."

"Beauty would be angered but soon she would bend to my will," the Beast told him coldly, "as she always has before."

"Funny, M'lord, I thought you had bent to hers," the boy muttered before a glare from the Beast convinced him to hold his tongue.

Finally the Beast took him into the dungeon itself and showed him the various implements of punishment and torture kept there. The lad tried to maintain his show of defiance but it was a losing battle. The Beast made the boy place himself on the rack, in the iron maiden, and then in the chains and shackles mounted in the dungeon wall.

The boy was afraid but stoic almost until the end of the tour. He finally broke down completely and burst into tears when the Beast pointed without a word to the chopping block while he casually hefted a headman's axe,

"I don't like burrs under my saddle, lad," the Beast said coldly.

"I... I'm sorry, M'lord. Please... " Nate blubbered, falling to the straw floor.

"Bend over the block, boy. I don't want to hear it." The Beast was implacable.

Putting down the axe, the Beast dragged the petrified boy to the block and strapped him down tightly.

"Comfortable, lad?" he asked almost gently, ruffling the lad's hair as the boy cried openly.

The Beast considered touching the blade to the boy's neck as if measuring his stroke but deemed it unnecessary and overly harsh.

Standing behind the boy so that he couldn't be seen or heard, he removed his belt. He jerked down the boy's pants and began to beat the lad with the belt. In truth, it wasn't really a very fierce beating. It didn't need to be harsh. The boy was already broken without the Beast being excessively severe. Besides, at that point, the lad realized that for now his head was safe on his shoulders. He was happy to be able to feel anything at all, even the sharp kiss of the belt on his backside.

The Beast left the boy still sobbing and wearing a few welts, but relatively uninjured, tied to the block. He walked away and stood in the shadows to give the lad time to compose himself and think about his future behaviour.

The guard, Gerrin, had been looking all over the castle grounds for the Beast. He was told by one of the guardsmen to check the dungeon. He came into the dungeon and saw the lad tied over the block. He noted the few bruises and dark welts on the boy's bare buttocks and the tears in the lad's eyes. A dark thought came to him.

"Trussed you up all helpless and left you here all alone, didn't he, me lad?" Gerrin whispered crudely into the boy's ear. "Don't seem like he beat you half enough though. Not half enough for a pest like you. I've felt the effects of your pranks meself."

Gerrin moved around to the boy's face and grinned a malevolent grin before whispering, "Maybe I should take advantage of having you trussed up like this. There's ways I could take some pleasure of you even though you're a lad. Hell's fire, you're almost pretty enough to be a lass anyway. Your face resembles that slut of a sister of yours. I could use you like a lass then I could take your head and everyone would blame the Beast."

"No one would believe you!" Nate cried, filled with terror. "The Beast would have your head!"

"But it'd be too late to save you, wouldn't it lad? Besides, they all know the Beast brought you down here so they'll think he did the deed. Some of them might even approve, you being such a pest and all, and if they don't there will be a revolt. I don't care a whit which side I'd be on. I just love a good fight. I'd really enjoy killing a few mangy peasants." Gerrin still spoke softly and his words were a mystery to the Beast as he watched from the dark shadows. "Almost as much as I'd enjoy killing the Beast and that whore sister of yours."

Nate screamed, "No!"

The guard moved to pick up the axe. "I'd best skip my pleasure and just take your head."

The Beast emerged from the shadows in a terrible rage. He shouted, "Gerrin, damn your black traitorous soul to hell! Don't you dare touch the boy. He's a part of my family and I'll see you drawn and quartered if you don't put that blade down and leave now."

"Do you really think you can stop me, M'lord?" Gerrin roared back. "Without your guards to save you? You're alone and unarmed. I'll kill the boy and lay the blame at your feet. You think you're better than anyone else because you are so high born, but lately you've turned weak."

In a blind fury, the Beast attacked Gerrin. Ignoring the blade Gerrin held, he charged the man so fast and hard that Gerrin was slammed into the wall. Gerrin was stunned but he still reacted instantly, swinging the blade with all his might. Gerrin was a well-trained and highly experienced warrior and he outweighed the Beast by quite a bit, all of it muscle. Worst of all he had a horrible, deadly weapon in his hands.

The battle was long and furious. Tied down as he was, Nate couldn't really see the action but the sounds of battle filled the ears of the terrified boy. He heard grunts and groans, the thump of fists hitting flesh, the whistle of the axe blade cutting through the air and the clash of the axe hitting the stone walls and castle floor. Several times he felt the swish of the blade in the air around him. Once the blade hit the edge of the block, barely missing his head.

The Beast finally forced the guard to run for his life, defeating the man by the sheer weight of his wrath, but not without sustaining a serious cut to his side from the axe blade.

As Gerrin ran from the dungeon the Beast untied a shaking, white-faced Nate. Nate quickly pulled on his pants, then tore his shirt into a makeshift bandage to stem the blood flowing much too freely from the wound on the Beast's side.

Slowly, Nate supported the Beast as much as he could, and the two of them made their way out of the dungeon. Together they negotiated the winding stairs and made their way into the great hall of the castle before the Beast, weakened from the loss of blood, finally collapsed on the hard, stone floor.

Chapter Nine

"Beauty!" Nate shouted at the top of his lungs, sobbing at the same time. "Beauty! Guards! Somebody! Anybody! Come quick! Help! The Beast is injured!"

Suddenly Beauty appeared at the top of the stone stairs. She looked down and saw the Beast lying on the cold stone floor, a pool of blood surrounding him with her brother by his side. Her heart seemed to stop at the sight. A servant appeared behind her.

"What happened?" Beauty gasped as she went pale, shocked at the sight of the Beast prone in a slowly spreading pool of blood.

"That guard, the mean one, attacked me." Nate knelt on the stone floor and cradled the Beast's head and shoulders in his arms, tears streaming freely down his face.

His voice was strained and choked, "The Beast was injured defending me. Beauty, you have to save him."

"You mean Gerrin?" Beauty blanched even as she called for the servant to fetch more help. She couldn't help remembering her doubts about the head guard's character. "The Beast's own head guard did this to him?"

"He attacked me with an axe while I was tied down across the chopping block. I was totally helpless." Nate swallowed several times before he continued, his eyes red from his tears of fright. "The Beast saved me. He attacked Gerrin barehanded but the guard had an axe, the headsman's axe. After all the trouble I've caused the Beast, he risks his life and gets hurt defending me. Please, Beauty, don't let him die."

Gwyneth and Margaret had arrived in time to hear Nate's brief account of the attack. Gwyneth was instantly ready to do anything she could, to move heaven and earth to save her master. Margaret took a little longer to come to the aid of the Beast. Finally two things helped her to put aside the fierce antagonism she normally felt towards the Beast, at least temporarily, to help Beauty and Gwyneth save his life: That the Beast had been injured defending her boy, Nate, and the look of despair on Beauty's face.

There was no mistaking that look. It was the look of a woman in love, facing the death of her lover and determined to do anything possible to save him. Fortunes had been squandered, men's souls had been lost, and wars had been fought over just that look of love on a woman's face. The strange thing was, Margaret was sure Beauty had not yet realized how much she loved the Beast.

Margaret silently admitted defeat. With a great deal of willpower she put her resentments firmly behind her. She was simply and completely outnumbered. Her oldest son, Tom, respected the Beast. He had not completely overcome all his old resentments of the Beast yet, but he had begun to sing the young lord's praises on many matters. Her youngest son, Nate, now owed his very life to the Beast. Her only daughter loved the man with all the depth and passion a loving mother could pray her whole life for her daughter to find.

The manservant, Seth, and the girl, Claire, stood off to one side. Seth had come to a grudging respect for the young lord, and though he would rather die than admit it, he would fight to the death to defend him. Claire was a different matter altogether; she was there more because she hated to be alone than because she was worried over the Beast. She still felt adrift and clung to Beauty. She was curious, both about how the mighty warrior came to be injured and about Beauty's knowledge of healing.

Claire still feared all men to some extent but she was even more terrified of one so strong-willed who could be so loud, so demanding and full of bluster. She had learned well what there was to fear from the harsh brutality of men but had yet to learn what tenderness could be hidden inside a strong, rough man like the Beast.

Seth ordered two of the servants to help him place the Beast on the long table, then to boil water with which to cleanse the lord's wounds. The bleeding was terrible and seemed unstoppable. Beauty could see a vessel deep inside the wound spewing blood. All three women fought desperately to figure out a way to stem the steady flow of blood.

"Seth, bring me some silk thread from my sewing kit!" Beauty commanded, inspired by a distant memory.

When the manservant quickly returned, she threaded the needle and then, without fully knowing her reasons behind her actions, she ordered the nearest servant to pour some of the steaming water over the needle, thread and her hands. She grimaced as she washed her hands with the scalding water.

At Margaret's quizzical look Beauty shrugged, "There has to be a reason I learned to sew, something more important than making countless tapestries. I think I can patch that vessel with some good stitching. Cleanliness might not help, but it can't hurt. There's no other possible way to save him."

"The barber... " Gwyneth began, protesting.

"The barber always wants to open a vein and bleed a wounded man," Beauty said curtly. "It makes no sense to me. It never has. It seems to me like it's the loss of blood that's likely to kill him. And a dirty wound seems to me to heal slower than one that is kept clean, contrary to what the healers and barbers believe."

Quickly, she stitched the vessel deep in the wound and then, using a new piece of silken thread, she put a few long stitches in the Beast's skin to hold the wound closed. The women mixed a poultice of hot water and mouldy bread. They kneaded it into a thick paste and applied it to the wound before binding it with strips of clean white linen. Finally, they had some of the servants carefully move the Beast up to his bed in the master bedroom.

For the next few days, the three women kept a constant vigil by the Beast's bedside. They spent the long days continually putting cool cloths on the Beast's forehead only to change them as soon as his hot skin warmed them again. They were kept busy ceaselessly changing bandages and striving to revive him enough to force a little bitter herbal tea, cool water and clear broth down his throat. They held his hand and talked softly to him when he seemed delirious.

Sometimes, in his delirium, he talked about Beauty. She smiled sadly at his words though, for while they were alternately passionate and tender ramblings praising her beauty, her warmth, passion in bed and even her fire and temper, the Beast never spoke of love. Surely if he did harbour some trace of love for her he'd mention it in the throws of his delirium while his guard is down, she thought ruefully. It didn't help matters that her mother heard these ramblings, some of which were very personal and sensuous.

Nate stayed close by ready to help Beauty much of the time since he felt responsible for the Beast's injuries. Tom, nearly recovered from his own injury, sat on a chair in the Beast's room watching the women and Seth while they tended to the Beast.

A tiny miracle happened in that room although no one noticed it at the time. The small group began to grow together, to almost become a family. Tenuous bonds were forming even as they fought together to save the wounded warrior.

Even the girl, Claire, began to lose her fear of the Beast. She saw him for the first time as a man, not a monster; a man who could be wounded just like anyone else. And for the first time she fully realized that just like he had saved Nate from Gerrin, he was the one who had saved her from the murderous band of thieves. Slowly she began to help the others take care of the Beast.

She would take turns with them, forcing liquids down his throat and wiping his forehead. She even helped Beauty with bathing him and changing his sheets. She saw some of the wounds, both new and old on his body, and began to realize the extent of the perils he had faced and the battles he had fought before coming to rule these lands. The scars that horrified her also served to remind her that he was very human and very courageous. They gave her a glimpse of the reason behind his cold, rough facade. Hearing him speak so tenderly about Beauty, even in the throes of delirium, also gave her a hint as to the true nature of the man inside the armour.

Finally she opened up enough to discuss her fears with Beauty. Slowly, as they sat alone by the Beast's bedside, the source of her fears came out. It seems she had known of the Beast's reputation long before she received her injuries. When she had been raped by the thieves after witnessing the murder of her grandmother, she had partly feared that the Beast himself was behind the attack. He was always rumoured to be behind anything bad that happened in the village. He was a convenient scapegoat for the villagers' complaints. That he had rescued her and brought her to the castle had mattered not one whit to the girl. She had simply assumed he would wait until she was stronger before he forced her into his bed. Due to his reputation, in her mind, he was a vicious monster.

Even though he never made a move towards her or even said an unkind word to her, she had been deathly afraid and still suspicious of him. She was fearful, unwilling to believe in the real motive behind his kindness to her.

Now, seeing him injured and perhaps dying, she finally came to see the Beast as a man. She finally knew he had saved not only her life but also Nate's.

Sometimes when they were both caring for the Beast, her small hands and Nate's would meet and they would look shyly into one another's eyes. If anyone watching had beheld those gazes they would have seen how touching and innocent those gazes were, but everyone who could have seen was too busy or too preoccupied to notice.

Once, standing side by side at the Beast's bedside, as their hands brushed not completely by accident, they locked their little fingers together. For long minutes they stood there, silently, with only their little fingers entwined. With his heart beating fast, Nate gently slid the palm of his hand over hers until she turned her hand palm up in his and their fingers interlaced. They stood there, still side by side and silent, but now they were looking at each other and smiling.

Seth, too, seemed to be overcome by some long repressed emotion. The servant, a man of just fifty years, walked over and stood firmly by Margaret's side. Much closer than he'd ever dare come to her before. He fixed a steady gaze on her, watching her every movement with what seemed like a calm resignation. She noticed and flushed, but she said nothing. However she often looked into his patient, dignified face and smiled softly and sadly.

Sometime during one of the long nights when Beauty was alone with Nate, she asked the lad, "Nate, why is it so important to you to save the Beast? I know he took you to the dungeon to punish you. I worried that you'd come to hate or resent him."

"So? You knew what he had planned for me." Nate hung his head but grinned ruefully. "I deserved it."

"You were playing some dangerous pranks and I knew he was going to punish you," Beauty replied quietly. "And I must admit that I had some idea how he would go about it. I thought perhaps he would use his belt on you."

"You knew?" Nate blushed. "How did you know?"

"Let's just say that I had given him some suggestions on how to deal with you," Beauty told her brother with a small shrug of her shoulders.

"Beauty! You suggested to the Beast that he tie me down to the chopping block?" Nate was shocked.

"Heavens! That must have been frightening. I know well how terrifying M'lord Beast can be when he acts so fearsome," Beauty smiled. "But the block was his idea, I just suggested a tour of the dungeon and... "

"And the belt," Nate finished for her. "Did you have to be so blessed helpful, Beauty? The strange thing is he didn't really hurt me with it. Not very much. I'll admit it was no more than I deserved. Everything was fine, at least until that guard, Gerrin, attacked me. The Beast punished me using my mind, my own fears, much more severely than he punished me by using the belt on my body." The lad paused, and then blurted out, "Beauty, he could have let me be killed by Gerrin and he probably should have. I've been nothing but trouble to him since I came to the castle, yet the Beast defended me. He even told the guard that I was part of his family. He risked his own life defending mine. Now I owe him my life and my loyalty."

"As do I, Nate," Beauty said gently, hugging the lad. "He saved my life today also, for I could not bear to lose you."

"Beauty, what do you think he meant when he said I was part of his family?" Nate asked her quietly.

"I'm not sure, Nate," Beauty said softly. "I think he's beginning to regard you as a younger brother. I think he cares very much for you in spite of your pranks, mayhap even because of them. He'd never admit it though because he doesn't want to seem soft or weak. That's part of the secret of the Beast, Nate. His one fear, from what I can tell, is to be seen as cowardly or overly weak and tender hearted."

"How could that be? His ferocity is legendary." Nate was surprised. "As is his courage."

"It goes far back to his childhood," Beauty smiled softly. "If indeed you'd call what he had a childhood. That's part of why your pranks intrigued him so much."

"How do you mean that? That's what you said before wasn't it? Mayhap because of my pranks? And I'm not really his brother," Nate said. "I wouldn't really be his brother unless you married him."

"I imagine it's because you're the only one who's ever been bold enough to play pranks on the Beast. I think it showed him a piece of the childhood he missed. I also think it made him feel a certain admiration for you and your nerve. It might even have made him feel like you had seen the real man inside the warrior and accepted him as a man and not a beast or a monster. As for marriage between us, I fear that it's never going to happen, Nate," Beauty sighed. "Even if I do want it to with all my heart."

"He's not a beast at all, is he Beauty?" Nate asked softly.

"No, love. He's no beast at all, just a very strong, obstinate man with a great heart buried deep inside a fierce exterior." Beauty hugged her brother.

She laughed in sheer relief as the Beast stirred on the bed beside them and groaned loudly, finally showing signs of awakening. "He does growl a bit like a beast though doesn't he, Nate?"

"Sometimes, but usually only when he's awake." Nate hugged her back.

Later that night, with Nate finally in bed, Margaret came to stand bedside watch with Beauty. It was a quiet, private time for the two women; a rare thing ever since Margaret had arrived at the castle.

Margaret met Beauty's gaze directly and spoke her mind without equivocation. "You love him very much, don't you daughter?"

Beauty stood still and silent for a long time before she answered softly, "I do, Mother. It's strange, I've fought so long against admitting my love for him, even to myself, that it's hard for me to say the words, hard to even think them, but yea, I do love him."

"He's not an easy man to love, is he?" Margaret asked. But she continued without waiting for Beauty to answer, "He is a good man though, deep inside."

"Yes, he is, Mother," Beauty replied. She then asked curiously, "Then why do you treat him so poorly? He oft says he'll have to take to wearing his armour inside the castle if you sharpen that tongue of yours any more."

"For several reasons: First, to see if he really has learned to control his temper. Also, there's still some resentment at seeing any man reign as lord of the manor. Then again, I begrudged him any happiness for not allowing you to visit with me for so long." Margaret paused before continuing, "Finally, I held him in great disfavour for destroying your chances at making a decent, worthy marriage, and giving me lots of grandchildren."

"I see," Beauty said softly, "'tis truly a host of sins and grievances you've laid at M'lord's feet. Some of them, nay, most of them are even deserved. It matters not, Mother, I love him."

"Will you two ever marry?" Margaret asked.

Beauty smiled sadly, "I doubt it. He once told me he would marry me, that one woman was as good a wife as another, so as long as that woman had a title and a dowry."

"And?" her mother almost shouted. "Beauty... "

"And I have decided that I want to be married to a man who cares not if I have a title or a dowry," Beauty told her mother. "A man who cares only for me."

"You... " her mother started again.

"Nay, Mother. Do not even suggest it. I have some pride," Beauty said with quiet dignity.

"Doest your pride warm your bed at night? Comfort you? Give you pleasure and love? Children? I urge you, tell the man all your secrets," Margaret argued.

"Nay, Mother. I will not, at least not yet." Beauty firmly ended the conversation, although she knew her mother would never let the matter drop so easily.

Beauty sat down on the bed beside the Beast, slumping against a feather pillow she had leaned up against the carved wooden headboard. Margaret decided to bide her time. She kissed Beauty's forehead and left the room without another word. She had a plan forming in the back of her mind though, and a new goal firmly planted in her thoughts.

It was a long time before anyone realized that as he drifted in and out of consciousness, the Beast heard pieces of the conversations going on around him. He heard Beauty's admission of love for him, but there was something at the edge of his consciousness that told him to keep the information to himself. He was strangely pleased to hear it though. A rare contentment filled him and he drifted off again into a peaceful slumber. By the morning after Beauty had the conversation with her mother, he was awake and slowly becoming more fully aware of his surroundings. He sat up for the first time and even managed to eat some of his morning meal. He was still very weak but already showing definite signs of improvement.

By chance, the first person the Beast saw when he was fully awake that morning was Claire. The girl was sitting on a chair by his bed, frowning over some stitches on the small piece of tapestry she was sewing. It seems Beauty was still very determined to teach the girl some genteel skills. Claire looked up and saw the Beast watching her and gave him a wide smile.

"Oh good, you're awake, M'lord," the young girl gushed. "We've been so worried. I'll fetch Beauty."

The girl threw her arms around the Beast's neck, hugging him briefly and quickly kissing his cheek before she ran from the room. It was a shocked and bemused Beast that Beauty found when she reached the warrior's bedside.

"M'lord, I must admit, I'm very pleased to see you awake. How do you feel?" Beauty fussed over him.

She felt his forehead, checking for signs of fever, before fluffing his pillow and smoothing and straightening his sheets. Then she lightly but lovingly kissed him on his lips. It was one of the few times she had ever initiated a kiss on the Beast's mouth, and both of them realized it but neither of them made any comment on it.

"I feel like someone almost cut me into pieces. I'm weak and sore but I'll live I think," the Beast muttered wryly. "I fear for my sanity though, for I could swear Claire kissed my cheek before she went to fetch you."

"Weak?" Beauty teased gently as she changed the bandage on his wound. "M'lord actually admits to being weak? It only took an axe to his side to force the admission from him."

"How's Nate?" The Beast worried in his fever that Gerrin had injured the lad.

"He's fine. I expect he'll be here shortly," Beauty said. Adding in a whisper, "It seems there are now two people he tries to stay close to."

At Beast's questioning look Beauty continued, still whispering, "You, M'lord, and the girl, Claire."

"What do you mean?" the Beast questioned, his mind a little slow still.

"He wants to stay near you because you saved his life," Beauty smiled as she drew up a chair and sat by the Beast. "And he wants to say near Claire because he's smitten with her. I think a romance is brewing. It's really sweet. It's a good thing the girl's finally decided she can stand to be near you. Now Nate doesn't have to try to split himself in half between the two of you."

The Beast snorted, "Women!"

"Nate said something to me while you were unconscious, M'lord, something that touched me deeply." She took a deep breath and met his eyes full on before she continued, "He said that you claimed him as part of your family."

"Part of our family you mean, Beauty," the Beast gently corrected, reaching out and taking her hand.

For her answer she only smiled, not wanting to trust her voice. Soon Margaret came in with some hot broth, milk and a small portion of roasted chicken for the Beast.

"Well, it looks like you'll live, more's the pity. I guess you'd better eat then and get your strength back," she snarled at him, showing no sign of her recent acceptance of him.

"Mother!" Beauty exclaimed shocked. "You keep a civil tongue in your head or I'll tell the Beast that you stayed by his side fretting over him most of the nights just like the rest of us."

"I was but worried for you." Margaret may have changed her opinion of the Beast but she wasn't ready to admit it to the man yet. However she couldn't hide the flush that crept up her neck. "I'd best go find Seth."

"Tis strange, Mother. He's usually right behind you," Beauty muttered solemnly, but her eyes danced with mischief.

After her mother left the room Beauty looked over at the Beast and said wryly, "There's another small romance, it seems. If the pair of them ever admits it, for I fear Seth is afraid to admit his feelings. Of course, as with many men, he is exceedingly stubborn."

"Tis very strange," the Beast commented slowly, not quite looking Beauty straight in the eyes. "I'd always heard that he was in love, from afar, with the former lady of the castle. That she never knew of his affection because his love and respect for the old lord kept him silent, and surely her own love and respect for her husband was well known. Tis good that he's finally gotten over her."

Ignoring Beauty's look of blank astonishment, the Beast ate slowly, content to look at Beauty. He decided not to mention some of the things he'd heard while they thought he was too ill to hear their talk. The small piece of private conversation between Beauty and her mother puzzled him the most. From what he could make out, the words they'd left unsaid seemed more important than the words they'd actually said.

Shortly after he ate, the Beast drifted off to sleep once more. His dreams were confused and troubled until Beauty appeared in them. Even in his dreams, she calmed everything down and eased his way. When he awoke again he lay there silently, just watching her with strange longings and even stranger feelings wandering through his head. For the first time in his life he thought the word "marriage" without a shiver of revulsion.

In a couple of days the Beast moved down to the great hall to recover. He was a poor patient, always restless and grumbling. Luckily there were more things in the hall to occupy him. His guards and soldiers visited with him often, sharing war stories. Other servants brought him news of the village and the castle itself. Beauty made sure musicians played most of the day, lutes, flutes and harps mostly. A balladeer sang sometimes, and jugglers and acrobats performed in the evenings. Still the Beast grew ever more and more restive. He wanted to get up and search for Gerrin. He wanted Gerrin dead.

Tom was now completely healed. He began to train again and acted as a liaison between the Beast and the guards, reporting to the Beast on the hunt for Gerrin and on the progress of the guards' training sessions. Claire and Nate sat and talked with the Beast for short periods before they disappeared together. Off to play or to cause mischief, the Beast wondered wryly as he watched them go?

Seth hovered over the Beast as much as he could without straying too far from Margaret's side. That was quite a trick as Margaret's softening attitude towards the Beast seemed to have disappeared as if it had never occurred. In fact, she avoided him as much as possible.

At his question, Beauty reluctantly explained her mother's attitude, "She admits that you're a good man, M'lord, but she still refuses to accept our living together without being wed. Don't be alarmed, for I explained to her that you required certain things of a potential wife."

"I do?" The Beast pretended not to remember.

"You told me once that you required your future bride to have a title and a dowry, M'lord, but that else wise you had no preference for one woman over another," Beauty reminded him coolly. "You once said you cared not to get married except to produce an heir so it mattered not whom you were married to."

The Beast feigned fatigue, muttering a single phrase as he seemed to drift off to sleep, "Mayhap I once was a fool."

Beauty briefly considered smothering him with his own pillow. "Men!"

The next day the Beast sent for Tom. "I want you to go fetch the other Tom from the stables. I recently promised Beauty to implement some things to help the peasants grow more and better crops. I've decided to give the other Tom the responsibility of handling those matters for me. It'll give him a chance to earn a little extra money and show him that I still have trust in him after... "

"After almost hanging him?" Tom smiled. "Admit it, M'lord, you're trying, without giving him an apology, to make things up to him, like you did for me."

"Yes," the Beast muttered. "Am I that easily read, then?"

"Nay, M'lord. Tis a good plan," Tom said, "and it's a good plan to have me fetch him. If anyone else told him you wanted to see him in the great hall, he'd probably fear for his life. He's still deathly afraid of you."

"I'm glad someone around here is," the Beast muttered ruefully. "These women around here pester me constantly without the slightest fear of reprisal."

"Even Beauty?" Tom asked.

"Especially Beauty, she wants my head on a platter," the Beast muttered sardonically.

"Nay, M'lord, she really wants your hand in marriage," Tom grinned but he left the room rather quickly after that remark.

When the other Tom, who came to be called Tom Two by most of the castle inhabitants, appeared in the great hall, the Beast bade him to sit by the fire with him so they could talk. The Beast described to Tom exactly what he wanted of him. He made arrangements with the young man for helping the peasants with their crops. A more astonished young man the Beast hoped never to meet, but as Tom Two's bewilderment faded he began to show a surprisingly agile mind. He slowly lost some of his fear of the Beast. Finally, he spoke up and began to exchange ideas with the lord.

The Beast also sent a rider to a nearby fiefdom to bring a travelling carnival to the village for a harvest festival. Beauty helped him make the plans.

At night, Beauty and the Beast retired together to his bedchamber. As the Beast's health improved he began to turn to Beauty in the night. He and Beauty made love, at first cautiously and tenderly, but soon passionately and endlessly.

It was a rather idyllic time for all the castle's inhabitants. Too idyllic to last for long. When the Beast could pleasure her fully with all the fierce passion and strength in his soul, Beauty almost wept, for she knew he would now leave her to search for Gerrin. The Beast, knowing his strength had returned, ordered his horse to be saddled. He went to head the search for Gerrin.

Chapter Ten

Before he left, Beauty was standing in front of the castle. She smiled bravely and kissed the Beast in front of his men with no small degree of passion. She stood there watching as the Beast and his knights rode away and his foot soldiers marched out the castle gate. She stayed watching until the men were all completely out of sight until even there dust from their passing had died down. Few noticed the tears welling in her eyes.

Once the group of men were gone she wandered about the castle grounds aimlessly. Her bravado faded and the crushing fear and loneliness hovered over her like a black cloud. She was brooding and restless. The castle inhabitants, including Sir Gregory, the knight assigned by the Beast to protect her, worried greatly about her. Beauty seemed wrapped in her own thoughts. Although she was normally aware of people's feelings around her, she failed to realize just how frustrated Sir Gregory was to be left behind.

He was a warrior, not a Lady's maid! The knight went about the task of guarding Beauty with diligence and courtesy however, as it was his nature to do whatever tasks his liege assigned him to the best of his ability. He was well read and intelligent, a fitting companion to Beauty.

Margaret stepped in and took charge of the day to day running of the castle with the help of Seth, Gwyneth and Claire. With most of the horses gone from the stables, Nate had some spare time to spend with Beauty, but even he couldn't lift her spirits. She felt cut off and alone.

The Beast sent frequent messengers, but most of the messages were disquieting. The bad news they received almost constantly from the Beast's messengers did nothing to help ease Beauty's state of mind. However much she hoped for one, there were no private, more intimate messages from the Beast.

It seemed that while the Beast was recuperating and idle, lying in bed and healing from his wounds, Gerrin had used his time very well. He had roamed the countryside stirring up the unhappy peasants and collecting the most vicious men he could find. He had soon surrounded himself with a small army of nefarious followers. Peasant malcontents, roaming thieves, more than a few rebellious guards and some bloodthirsty mercenaries all joined his growing band of renegades. Before long he had a small but truly formidable army of miscreants.

Reports of Gerrin and his treacherous band came to the castle from all over. Tales of burning villages, wild plundering raids, looting, cruel rapes and vicious murders abounded. Some reports had the band headed back towards the castle where they thought the Beast was still recuperating and his soldiers were not fully prepared to defend the castle. As the band of thieves approached, they were said to be raiding small villages and plundering other castles along the way. Nothing left behind in their wake had been untouched.

Messengers were sent out to warn the surrounding shires and even to the nearest castles. Another messenger was sent to warn the local villagers, telling them to come to the castle for the safety to be found inside the great walls.

Beauty, Seth, Gwyneth and Margaret worked hard along with the rest of the servants to provide some small comfort to the villagers who crowded inside the castle courtyard. Village women and the castle servants laboured long and hard together, cooking almost continuously to feed the extra mouths.

The village men hunted for game, with Beauty's permission. Others worked long hours with the blacksmiths to make weapons: Arrowheads, lances and swords. The few soldiers remaining at the castle and the village men banded together to shore up the castle's defences. Even the villagers' children worked, running errands and gathering firewood and water under the watchful eyes of the few remaining guards.

The Beast and his men caught up with the outlaw group several times, attacking them and engaging them in small skirmishes. The thieves were too elusive however; they always seemed to have an escape route planned. Gerrin commanded his band with absolute authority and did not hesitate to kill anyone who disobeyed his orders. His right hand man was a callous former guard named Wolford.

Gerrin and Wolford were both skilled and masterful at strategy, and they knew the Beast and his tactics well. Gerrin also knew the local forest as well as the Beast.

In each of the skirmishes, the Beast's men succeeded in capturing and killing some of the rebels, but Gerrin, Wolford and the fiercest of the murderous scum evaded the Beast time after time.

At the castle, Beauty waited and prayed. She was afraid for both the Beast and her brother Tom, but she was also strangely restless. To make matters worse, since the Beast left she hadn't had a spare moment to herself. Hardly even enough time to pray. The crowd of serfs camped out in the castle courtyard had questions and demands for her constantly, and the incessant smell of cooking food was making her feel out of sorts, almost queasy. Once or twice she had the strange thought that the sight or smell of even one more roasting chicken would cause her to vomit.

Time dragged by slowly. Gwyneth and Margaret stayed by her side, both noticing the strain Beauty was under and the unusual pallor to her skin. They wondered about her and worried for her health.

Nate and Claire were inseparable. They worked with the servants, keeping the food supplied and the castle clean. Nate also had his work in the stables and had begun to spend his few spare moments training with the small group of remaining guards. The older men took the boy under their protection and enjoyed helping him as he learned to be fairly proficient in the use of various weapons. Sir Gregory spent time with the boy whenever he could be away from Beauty.

Two weeks after the Beast left to head the hunt for the outlaw guard, a horrifying report came in. Another young woman from the village had been found raped and murdered, but this time the body was found within sight of the castle walls. Looking at the mangled body, Beauty was so shocked she almost fainted. She had seen the woman before. It was the woman who had been tied up in the Beast's bedchamber on the day she'd slapped the Beast. Several of the villagers knew the woman had been taken to the castle. In spite of his present absence and his recent wounds, some of the peasants blamed the Beast for the woman's murder.

Still seeking Gerrin and his band, the Beast knew naught of this new outrage. Following reports of raids, the Beast and his army of guards found themselves backtracking a bit. The more they searched for Gerrin and the pillagers, the closer the trail led them back to the castle. Finally, they took advantage of the nearness of the castle to replenish their food and supplies and get some fresh horses.

The Beast and his men decided to spend the night at the castle before going out once more to search for Gerrin and his knaves. It was the wrong night to be home.

The tense situation came to a head, exploding suddenly and unexpectedly. The anger and anxieties of the peasants erupted into a mob of murderous rage against whoever was looting and plundering the land, and against whoever was brutally raping and murdering the young village girls.

In the villagers' eyes, it was the same person to blame for both the looting, robberies and the murders. In spite of the fervent protests and denials from the castle inhabitants, the Beast was being blamed, especially for the murders. The word among the peasants was that if he himself wasn't the one committing the vicious acts, then he was turning a blind eye and letting it happen. His quest to bring in Gerrin was seen as a sham.

His past habit of taking the village women at will worked against him. His reputation was his own worst enemy. His ferocity and ruthlessness were legend, while his recently acquired humanity was virtually unknown.

One of the village spokesmen, a man secretly in contact with Gerrin, sought to raise the ire of the rest of the villagers against the Beast. He was very loud and vocal as he accused the Beast of the barbaric murders of the young girls. The army following the Beast defended him, decrying the violent murders and insisting that the

Beast had no part in the atrocities.

For a while, it seemed there would be bloodshed between the villagers and the Beast's men. It soon appeared that but for his guards, the Beast was in mortal danger of being killed by a mob of the very people he was working to defend. His own words didn't help in his defence. He had been feared and hated too long. His recent softening and the changes within him had not been seen or even acknowledged outside the castle walls.

Beauty stood in front of the crowd and added her voice to the Beast's defenders of course, but her words went unheard. Although she was generally well liked by the villagers, she was also relatively unknown to them for she had always kept slightly to herself. There were a few vocal serfs loyal to Gerrin or to some of his men who worked to turn the crowds against her.

She was accused by some of them of loving the Beast to the point of blindness. Others decried her, calling her a slut and accusing her of being nothing but the Beast's whore. For the most part those few who would raise their voices to defend her were silent, and whether they were too fearful to speak or just knew not what to say was unclear.

To her dismay, the villagers whom she'd always thought of as her friends, that she'd fought so hard to defend to the Beast, failed her utterly. Her months of working quietly with the Beast to improve living conditions for the serfs counted for nothing. Months of trying to get the Beast to think of them as real people just like himself, to consider their feelings and the struggles in their daily lives, and to deal with them more fairly, all that effort to aid the peasants was for naught.

Her loud, fervent protests of the Beast's innocence were ignored, for the mob was simply too angry and much too enraged and irrational to listen. Without knowing it, they had turned on their one true defender. Beauty knew well their reasoning, but she was deeply hurt as well as afraid for the Beast. The worst part for Beauty was that they destroyed the image she still held deep in her heart, the image of herself as the Beast's honoured wife, and not his whore.

Some of the crowd openly wanted both Gerrin and the Beast

ousted or killed. The castle inhabitants feared they would have to use the Beast's own guards to defend him against the irate villagers.

Surprisingly, it was the other Tom, the one known in the castle as Tom Two, who managed to defuse what was building up to a full blown riot. He gathered a rare piece of courage and stood at the castle gates in front of the crowd.

"You don't know the real Beast! He lives in the castle surrounded by mystery with a fearful reputation and a name destined to bring dread to all to hear it," Tom Two shouted. "But you all know me very well. You know that I have had no reason to have any love for the new lord. He ordered me to be hung for a crime I didn't commit."

Tom Two paused as the crowd roared, then continued as they fell silent again, "But lately, the Beast has truly changed. He's grown much wiser and more patient than he was when he first came to us. Partly, I think because he's learned to love, thanks to Beauty." Tom Two gazed over at her as the crowd settled slightly.

"Partly, mayhap because he's no longer constantly at war, fighting for his King. Anyway, he's offered me a position. A chance to help him to make your lives a little bit better. He has plans to help you in many ways, plans that you have yet to hear. I now know better than anyone else present that he has grown to be a worthy, wise and caring lord."

"He plans to supply the village with plow horses for the planting, and wagons for the harvest. Before this band of thieves caused so much turmoil, he had his blacksmiths hard at work making us some new ploughs. They're ready for next spring's planting. Unbeknownst to you, he's even added more seed to that which you have stored and set aside to be planted. He's even arranged to bring in more cattle, chickens, ducks, geese and goats from the neighbouring village so that we will have more food to eat and still have enough livestock to supply our eggs and milk. He wasn't going to tell you any of this; I was just supposed to slip the extra birds, goats and lambs in with those you already have. He didn't want you to know of his gifts to you. Is that the way a tyrant rules?"

"He has a festival and a feast planned to celebrate our harvest.

Later, he's arranging to have skilled engineers travel from the north to study our water supply with an eye to improving it so that we don't suffer so badly from droughts or floods. Is that the way a despot rules?"

Tom Two continued, "There have been no more hangings since Tom and I were freed. Indeed, the last man to be caught stealing was let off with only a whipping, even though he was proven guilty of stealing much more than we were ever accused of taking. Is that the way an oppressor rules?"

Gradually, the mood of the crowd began to change. The loud outcry and protests faded to a murmuring as the villagers began to realize the recent changes in the Beast.

Encouraged, Beauty once again spoke up. "I've been with the Beast when he was so angry, so enraged really, that I marvelled at how he could keep any last vestige of control, but he did. He's not a gentle man, tis true, and he is often harsh with me but never has he been brutal, and believe me, I've given him reason often enough." She smiled in spite of herself and a chuckle ran through the crowd. "I know he did not murder those girls. It's just simply not in his nature, else I'd be long since dead. This woman was at the castle, 'tis true, but the Beast never touched her. She was sent away unharmed. I know for I was there. I also know that the former guard, Gerrin, is both brutal and vicious, filled with a dark bloodlust. He thrives on the pain of others and enjoys the savagery and wanton destruction of battle. He would stop at nothing to feed the anger of this crowd. He would use any means to cause you to revolt. He would do these things just to cause a fight, for the sheer love of bloodshed. He's a vicious animal without any scruples or morals. Once, he even tried to kill my brother Nate."

Hearing this, the crowd slowly turned against Gerrin and his men. Nate was well liked in the village in spite of his youth and constant pranks. The Beast once again stepped forward. This time he spoke quietly and wisely, ignoring his close brush with death at the peasants' hands.

"My men and I go on the morrow to capture Gerrin and to wipe out any trace of his murderous band. I blame myself that I did not see him for the barbarian he is sooner. It's to my eternal shame that I ever trusted him, but I did." The Beast paused. "I thought a fierce warrior would serve me well as a good second-in-command but I was wrong. Looking back, I understand that he was evil and savage all along. I never realized that he was so bloodthirsty. He was the one I sent to fetch maidens to pleasure me and he was the one who was ordered to return them to you uninjured. I never knew they were not being returned alive. You, the subjects in my own village, did not trust me or respect me enough to report the girls' deaths and that also is to my blame. I will carry the weight of their wasted lives with me always in my heart. I grieve for their loss even more because I now know what it means to love."

Beside him, Beauty gasped aloud as the Beast continued, "So at dawn I must leave the one I love to go avenge those whom you've lost and to make our land safe again. Protect Beauty for me and honour her while I'm gone."

The crowd shouted their approval as the Beast drew a stunned Beauty into his arms and kissed her in front of them with all the passion in his soul. He caught her up in his arms and carried her into the castle and up the long stairs. He made love to her with a passion, almost a desperation that left her breathless and weak long into the night, and again as dawn began to lighten the sky.

The Beast was stunned to see almost all the villagers standing along the road and in front of the castle. They cheered and called out encouragement to him, wishing him luck on his search. He had never gone on a quest with so many people cheering him on before, and something deep inside him was truly touched.

He kissed Beauty again and waved to the crowd before mounting his great black warhorse and giving his men the order to mount theirs. The mounted warriors and foot soldiers went out to hunt Gerrin and his men. This time they vowed they would not return until the deed was done. This time they were cheered on by the villagers. This time Beauty's fears were tempered by the joy she felt at the Beast's public admission. This time she had more help from the villagers. She had more peace, yet still she was restless and filled with dread.

Several days later, Beauty was kidnapped. Desperate for some time to herself, she took her guard, Sir Gregory, and went into the forest to search for moss and medicinal herbs. Both Margaret and Gwyneth protested loudly about her going off by herself but she failed to heed their warnings, only agreeing not to go very far. She also promised to keep her guard, Sir Gregory, at her side. Besides, she pointed out, their stocks were low on these herbs and they needed replenishing against the chance of injuries to the soldiers. She also needed herbs for the ailments that would accompany the coming winter.

She had gathered various herbs and moss and was ready to return to the castle when the attack happened. Suddenly, a noise in the thick forest brush caught her attention, but before she even had time to look around at the source, she saw her guard, Sir Gregory, fall from his horse, an arrow sticking out of his side.

She turned her mount to go to his aid but he urged her to run for her life. The sight of another arrow appearing on the ground next to Sir Gregory convinced her that her only chance to save either one of them was to reach the castle and the other guards. She turned her horse and kicked the mare into a full gallop.

She had not gotten far when she heard noises behind her that sickened her: It was the telltale swish of a sword through the air and the moan of a dying man. They've killed Gregory, she thought, and it's my fault. I have to get to the castle. She urged her mount on but in seconds she was surrounded by the small band of thieves.

They formed a tight circle around her, and she watched them in silent horror as one of them dismounted and approached her. It was Wolford. Escape was impossible. Wolford quickly grabbed her. He tied her hands tightly together and roughly put her back on her own mount, but this time with one of the thieves controlling the reins. They set out at a rough gallop as she struggled to remain upright on her mount.

She turned her head as they passed the fallen body of her guard, Sir Gregory. Guilt ate at her since held herself responsible for his death by insisting that he take her into the woods and ignoring the danger from the band of thieves. She knew the death of that good man would haunt her always.

143

Chapter Eleven

Beauty found it extremely awkward to hang on to her mare with her hands tied together but she clung on desperately as the thieves rode for hours at a fast pace. She wanted to stop to relieve herself, but refused to ask for even that boon. In spite of the danger on her fleeing horse, she felt safer than she would be if these men stopped and let her dismount. She knew all too well what they had planned for her. It was impossible for her not to. They taunted her cruelly with lewd remarks and graphic descriptions of the fate in store for her when they reached Gerrin.

Beauty was stricken with horror and desperation but, as fate would have it, there was something she didn't know. Something that would have given her some hope. She never realized that Sir Gregory, her guard, was not dead. The moan she'd heard, the sound of a man's death, wasn't from Sir Gregory but from one of her attackers. Even bleeding as he was and fallen to the ground, Sir Gregory had managed to kill one of the thieves. The slain thief lay on the ground next to him, the knight's sword still sticking through the man's chest.

Sir Gregory had run the man through, then fallen still beside him. He kept his head and played dead until the band of thieves left. Once they were gone, bloody and badly injured, he dragged himself to his horse and struggled to mount. He grasped the stirrup and tried to pull himself up. Because he was so weakened by his injuries, he failed as he struggled to make it onto his horse. The animal ran off, heading towards the castle. Gregory sank back to the ground and lay there hoping that help would come from the castle and find him soon.

It was only a matter of a few minutes before some of castle guards found him, weak but hanging onto a thread of life. Margaret had alerted the few remaining guards when Beauty and Sir Gregory failed to return for the midday meal. Sir Gregory's horse, running into the barn without him, caused the guards to mount up and ride out in search of Beauty and Sir Gregory. Margaret rode out with them.

Luckily Margaret knew well Beauty's favourite spots for finding the moss and herbs she used in her medicines, so she was able to direct the guards to the right area. The guards carefully carried Sir Gregory back to the castle and sent a messenger to tell the Beast what had happened.

Fate was with them for once and the messenger found the Beast and his men the next day. The Beast's men were closing in on Gerrin and nearly ready to spring a trap. Although the news of Beauty's capture left the Beast more terrified than he'd ever been in his life before, he had to keep his wits about him. Because of Beauty's kidnapping, the Beast had to plan his strategy very carefully indeed.

Beauty had been dragged over the countryside almost continuously since her capture. When she was finally brought before Gerrin, she was weak with hunger and sick with fear. Her clothing was torn and filthy and her hair hung in a tangled mess. She turned her head and refused to look at Gerrin or even acknowledge his presence as he taunted her cruelly.

"So this bedraggled slut thinks she's too good for the rest of us. Well I'll show her what she's good enough for," he grabbed his crotch in a vulgar gesture, "before I kill her."

He approached Beauty and began to reach for her. It was too much for Beauty; she felt sickened by hunger, fear and even the smell of Gerrin. As soon as his hands touched her skin she lost complete control and vomited all over him, completely voiding the contents of her stomach. Gerrin was enraged. He backhanded Beauty, sending her sprawling to the ground, and then backed off to remove his smelly, offensive tunic. Realizing that Gerrin was a coward at heart, Beauty decided to play on his ignorance and try to instil some fear into the villainous warrior.

"I'm sorry." She faked a cough. "I cannot keep my food down lately."

"You're probably breeding the Beast's bastard child," Gerrin dismissed her. "That won't stop me from having my pleasure of you. My greatest pleasure is the fear you sluts show when I begin marking you with my dagger."

"Do I look like I'm breeding?" Beauty snapped, covering her fear with anger. "I've longed to give the Beast a child for 'twould make my position with him ever more secure, 'twould be my chance to become lady of the castle. I've been unsuccessful. Lately, I've been very ill, coughing and vomiting, a fever that comes and goes, terrible headaches. I fear the... "

Beauty's voice trailed off as she sank back weakly onto the hard ground. It was the hardest pretence of her life but she worked hard to keep up the illusion of a dreaded illness. Gerrin wasn't fooled, but he also wasn't sure. Rumours of plague and death had long since spread throughout the countryside and the illness was greatly feared.

For a while it was enough as Gerrin's uncertainty and fear kept him off Beauty. She huddled into a tight ball, torn between shivering and fits of wracking coughs. Every time Gerrin came near her she vomited, aided partly by some of the very herbs she had gathered that morning. The repulsion of having her vomit on him every time he came within a foot of her certainly helped cool his perverted ardour. The fear that she may really be ill also stayed his hand. Disgusted with his prize captive he ordered her tied to the nearest tree, which made her feel somewhat relieved, at least temporarily. Beauty used the time well, praying and longing for the Beast, but also thinking and planning on how to save herself.

For countless days, the Beast and his men had been steadily closing in on the thieves. The news that Gerrin had taken Beauty roused them to even greater effort. The Beast's men finally trapped Gerrin and his ragged band of followers in a place that left no chance of escape. The thieves had a swift river at their backs and a high stone cliff alongside them.

The Beast moved quickly and silently through the trees to find where Gerrin had Beauty. He went to his men and told them where she was tied.

"I need the archers to be very cautious. I want only my top archers to send their arrows to the right side of the camp, by the horses, where Beauty is tied up. The rest of you aim for the men as they come out of the tents." The Beast was grim. "Watch that they do not move my lady closer to the fray. Beauty must be protected."

At the Beast's order, the archers let fly their arrows. Over and over, they notched their arrows and let them fly. Gerrin, Wolford and his men ran for cover, grabbing their swords and bows as they began to fight the Beast's men. After countless arrows had downed many of Gerrin's band of men, the Beast and his men approached the clearing, swords in hand. Gerrin stirred himself into action. He managed to avoid the rain of arrows and made his way over to where he had Beauty tied, knowing that was the safest place in camp to be. He grabbed Beauty and untied her from the tree they had her tethered to. He dragged her into the middle of the fray, holding a dagger to her throat.

Gerrin held Beauty with the dagger, just barely slicing her tender throat. He called out to the Beast, "Look lively, me fine lord! Hold your arrows lest ye wound yer slut! I'll slice her throat if ye attack!"

When the Beast saw this he froze, his heart seemed to stop within his chest. "I know you, Gerrin!" he called back. "You will do many things to her, the least of which is slicing her throat if I let you live!"

"Then I will kill her now, just to get her off my hands so that I can kill you," Gerrin growled. "Or let me get to a horse."

Swallowing his pride, the Beast appeared to back down. He faced Gerrin and slowly, deliberately put down his sword. He cleared a path to the horses tied nearby; pushing his men and Gerrin's out of the way even as the two factions fought relentlessly. His eyes never left Beauty's face as he watched Gerrin practically toss her onto a mount with her hands still bound. He stood silently, waiting for that moment when Gerrin tried to mount, hoping that Beauty would be able to control her horse and get away. He wanted to signal Beauty but was unable to do more than meet her eyes.

Beauty landed on the horse on her stomach with an audible thud. Somehow she understood what the Beast was willing her to do. Struggling and manoeuvring, she managed to get herself astride the horse.

Around her the battle raged, and it was a fight to the death for all involved. The Beast's mounted soldiers fought the thieves with either an axe, mace or broadsword. The sounds of battle filled the air. The terrible screaming of wounded and dying men and injured horses mingled with the clash and clang of weapons, sword against sword and sword against armour. Most of Gerrin's men were killed in the long and bloodthirsty fight that followed.

Gerrin loosened his grip on Beauty for a mere instant. He was keeping an eye on the Beast while mounting his own steed. That was all it took. The Beast gave Beauty's horse a mighty whack with the side of his sword and the mare jumped and began to run.

Feeling the horse beneath her tense, Beauty had also reacted instinctively. At the same time the Beast whacked the mare, she kicked the startled horse with all her might causing her to rear and kick at Gerrin who still held the reins. Gerrin fell back, the reins pulled from his grasp, and the Beast was on him in a second.

The poor horse bolted with Beauty struggling to stay astride him despite her bound hands. As the horse galloped through the thick brush and trees, Beauty felt the slap of branches against her face and the sharp sting as some of those same branches scratched her. She ducked her head and desperately held on as tightly as she could while her mount continued its frenzied run. The poor mare stumbled a few times but kept to her feet. She ran at breakneck pace, only slowing slightly for the stream. The mare jumped the very log where the Beast had used his belt on Beauty. Still Beauty hung on, grasping a handful of the mare's mane even with her hands bound.

Summoning all her courage, she leaned forward along the horse's neck and tried to speak slowly and calmly in the horse's ear. It had little effect on the steed's mad panic. 'Twas only luck that kept her mount from falling, killing them both.

Behind her, in the clearing, the Beast and Gerrin fought desperately and viciously. Both men were fairly equally skilled and both managed to hold off the other. Gerrin lost his sword yet fought on armed with only his dagger. As they fought, Gerrin managed to grab a sword from the ground near a fallen man. Soon he managed to disarm the Beast, sending his sword flying.

Desperate to defeat Gerrin and go to the rescue of Beauty, the

Beast managed to find another fallen thief and do the same as Gerrin had, wrenching the sword from the thief's dead hand.

The battle continued in earnest. It was almost as if the two were alone in the clearing while around them the soldiers and thieves fought a vicious battle. The thieves were fighting for their lives, but with fewer weapons and less training, they were slowly being beaten down.

The Beast had his full attention trained on Gerrin until he heard the clash of a sword very close to his head. He soon became aware that Tom had stepped in and prevented one of Gerrin's men from stabbing him in the back. The Beast almost tripped over the wounded and fallen thief but Tom quickly attacked Gerrin. He distracted the former guard while the Beast regained his footing. The Beast recovered his balance and once again engaged Gerrin, this time with Tom guarding his back.

One by one the thieves died, felled beneath the arrows and swords of the Beast's men. As the battle waned, several of the Beast's soldiers raced to their horses and gave chase to Beauty's horse. Although she was helpless to stop her horse's deadly run with her hands still tied, eventually the horse tired and slowed enough for one of the Beast's men to catch the mare and rescue Beauty.

The guards gently untied her hands and helped her from the panting horse. Although they wanted to take Beauty straight back to the safety of the castle, she insisted on being taken forthwith to the Beast. One of the guards held her small, trembling body in front of him as he rode slowly back to the clearing where the battle still raged.

Finally, only two men were still fighting, a fight that was terrible in its intensity. Gerrin faced the Beast with the knowledge that only one of them would survive. Gerrin fought as if he were possessed by demons. The clash of the two men's broadswords continued long after the rest of the sounds of battle faded. The two men had to stumble over the bodies of the fallen and injured men as they battled each other.

It took all the skill and fury the Beast possessed but finally Gerrin was captured, badly injured, but still alive. The guards reached the clearing in time to see Gerrin's capture. They got there just as Gerrin dropped to the ground. He was unconscious and bleeding from the head. In spite of her ordeal, Beauty jumped from her horse and flung herself into the Beast's arms, kissing him passionately and joyfully, heedless of the watching men.

The Beast and his men searched through the bodies, quickly and efficiently killing the injured thieves and binding the wounds of their own wounded. They helped the wounded soldiers mount.

Tom looked through the dead and dying searching for a face he had not seen. "Beast!" he called out sharply. "I cannot find Wolford. I think he may have escaped."

"He always was a bit of a coward," the Beast replied. "He always looks for a way out for himself. He is still a danger, as long as he lives."

"We will have to hunt him down then," Tom said, "or Beauty will never be safe."

"We will," the Beast agreed, "but I doubt he will be found. I think he will leave the area and never return."

"Are you sure, M'lord?" Tom asked.

"Nay, and we will search for him," the Beast sighed, "but the main danger is done. Wolford will never be able to raise a force like this. Gerrin had a rough charm, as he could pull people into his plans. Wolford is a follower. A vicious scum but a follower, not a leader like Gerrin."

The Beast had wanted to capture Gerrin alive to be taken back to face the angry villagers. He well knew and respected their thirst for revenge. He tied Gerrin's unconscious body to a horse and they rode back to the castle. Along the way, the former guard regained a semblance of consciousness. He was tossed into a dungeon for the short time he had left to live.

Beauty's mother took care of her, tending to the myriad scratches and bruises that covered her face and body. She moaned over each injury but rejoiced that there was nothing worse. No broken bones, no rape. Gently she and Gwyneth helped Beauty bathe and dress. Gwyneth took her time, gently combing out the worst of the tangles in Beauty's hair and pulling the rest into a snood at the nape of her neck.

By the time Gerrin was held in front of the angry mob, he was dazed but aware of his surroundings. He wavered but stood in front of the crowd while the Beast pronounced his sentence for murder and treason. Hearing his sentence, Gerrin broke down and begged for the mercy of the axe, but the Beast denied him that mercy. He coldly ordered the doomed man to be drawn and quartered. Beauty stood by his side, her battered face impassive as the Beast gave the command.

Before the terrible sentence could be carried out, Gerrin managed to wrench himself free from the guards holding him and tried to throw himself to his death from the castle wall. His cowardice was apparent to all who witnessed it. It was to no avail, as he was quickly recaptured and led to the gallows. As he was hanged, Beauty felt slightly ill but she watched the execution without flinching. No one but the Beast knew that she closed her eyes as he was taken down from the gallows, still barely alive, to be hacked into quarters. The bloody pieces of his body were left hanging from the castle walls, his head on a spike. Seeing how pale the sight made Beauty, the Beast vowed to have them removed as soon as possible. The remains would be fed to the pigs; there would be no decent funeral for Gerrin.

After Gerrin died his gruesome death, the mob slowly thinned out and the villagers and soldiers gradually went back to their everyday lives. Beauty, Nate, Tom and her mother sat in the great room and had a tearful reunion.

Beauty was greatly relieved to learn that the guard, Sir Gregory, had survived his injuries. She apologized to him for her stubbornness in going to the woods and putting him at risk.

The guards were sent to catch the few remaining thieves, a pitiful few who had managed to get away. Gradually peace was restored to the castle.

Things in the village also returned to normal. Most of the villagers' thoughts soon turned to the upcoming harvest and fair. Many of them had never been to a fair, although the elder villagers vaguely remembered having regular fairs when the old lord held the castle. All the villagers looked forward to the event, as it would be a momentous break in their dreary routines.

Many times during the following days Beauty wanted to get a private moment with the Beast to discuss the pronouncement he'd made before the crowd, but her efforts seemed to be thwarted.

The Beast was always busy, trying to restore things to normal at the castle. Beauty herself was busy with the running of the household. She was also recovering from the various scratches and bruises she had accumulated during her ordeal, but luckily none were severe enough to cause any scarring. By the time they reached their bedchamber every night, they were both too exhausted for any discussion.

Beauty longed to have that private discussion with the Beast. She was overjoyed and overwhelmed by his declaration of love, yet she wanted something more. Public announcements were one thing, and she loved hearing the words from the Beast, but she greatly desired a more private and intimate conversation with him.

She was ready to admit her love for the Beast, to herself, to him and to the world at large, but the Beast seemed to be avoiding her, almost as if he regretted what he'd said to the mob. She was happy to hear him shout his love for her aloud, but for the first time in a long time she felt a deep craving for something more. Something much more personal and romantic. At the same time, she also wanted the open and public relationship to be made permanent, to be sanctioned by the law, the King and the church. Damned be it, she thought to herself, what I want is a real marriage.

Beauty went to her mother and Gwyneth separately to discuss this but neither of the two women were much help. Gwyneth, busy as always helping the cook prepare the evening meal, just advised her to be patient. It was not the answer Beauty wanted as her patience was already wearing much too thin.

Beauty spoke with Margaret in the garden the next day. It was her mother's favourite spot. Margaret wanted Beauty to scheme to catch the Beast. She suggested several plans but none of the schemes were agreeable to Beauty, her nature being much more open and honest.

"Then if you're so open and honest, Beauty, tell him the truth!" Margaret raved, never at a loss for words. "Tell him everything!"

"I want him to marry me for who I am, not a worthless title and dowry," Beauty replied. "I want him to marry me for love."

"So? Who marries for love anyway? Love comes later, if it comes at all. I never met your father before the wedding. I never even saw him. It was just through God's mercy that I ever came to truly love him." Margaret took a deep breath. "So? You won't trick the Beast and you won't tell him the truth, what else is there? Your pride gets in your way, Beauty. Would you rather have the Beast as a husband warming your bed, or your pride? Think on it. Patience hasn't worked. You refuse to tell him the truth and you don't want to trick him. What's left? You could try to make him jealous but there's no one around who would make a worthy rival."

"I wouldn't resort to such a petty trick anyway," Beauty grinned ruefully, remembering. "Besides, as I recall, every time he gets jealous, I wind up face down across his knees getting spanked like a child. Then I'm unable to sit down for a very long time."

"At least he can control your wayward nature," her mother murmured.

"Thank you so much for the kind thought, Mother!" Beauty murmured with a trace of sarcasm but she smiled openly at the memory. "Although he gets very passionate afterwards. He almost makes the spanking worth it."

"So he has been jealous before?" Margaret tried to put the picture of an extraordinarily passionate Beast firmly out of her mind. "There's one last way, Beauty, one last thing to try. You could give him a child."

"Let's turn the talk to you, Mother. What's this between you and Seth?" Beauty quickly distracted her mother, wanting to avoid this topic. "He's always at your side these days and you always seem to be smiling at him."

"He's just an old friend," Margaret pointed out, "as you well know, that's all it can be. He has no station and no rank. How can I marry him after the love I had for your father?"

"Who mentioned marriage?" Beauty asked surprised as she studied her mother, seeing her blush like a young girl.

Castle life had well agreed with Margaret. The melancholia that had held her in its grip for years had disappeared and her health was now fully restored. Gone completely was the haggard and frail woman who had first come to the castle. The peace she felt now that life was more secure again was reflected in her entire being. The joy she received from being near her children and the pleasure she received from nagging the Beast now shone in her face.

The woman standing next to Beauty was now a beauty herself. She had the same colouring as Beauty, although her eyes were a little paler shade of blue and there was a touch of grey in her blond hair. In spite of the fact that her eldest child had reached his twentieth year, she was still shy of forty. She was dressed in a satin gown of sky blue, with a low cut neck. Her figure was still good, although just a little thicker than Beauty's. Her gown was trimmed with seed pearls and dark blue velvet ribbons, ecru lace and an ecru linen under slip completed the outfit. She looked stunning, Beauty thought, and in love.

"I mean... " Margaret was flustered and blushed like a young maiden.

She turned her face away and pretended to study a rose bush.

"Do you love him?" Beauty probed.

"I'm too old for such nonsense," Margaret answered slowly, evasively. "I guess you think I'm a just silly old woman."

Beauty gave a rather unladylike snort. "You are neither silly nor old! And that did not answer my question. Do you love Seth?"

"Yea," Margaret admitted, still blushing shyly as she picked up a pink rosebud. "Of course not with the fire and passion I felt for your father, but I do love him with a different passion."

"Then marry him, with the blessing of all your children. I know our father would have approved." Beauty hugged her mother. "He always wanted you to have whatever made you happy, did he not?"

"There's a small problem though," Margaret told her daughter, hugging her back. "He's afraid to admit his love for me because of my rank."

"Men!" Beauty exclaimed. "How can they be so stupid?"

"I'll tell you what, my daughter," Margaret said laughing and hugging her daughter, "I'll work on getting my stubborn, stupid man to the altar and you do the same with your stupid, stubborn man."

"And then we'll go to work on Tom," Beauty laughed.

"And then we'll work on Tom," Margaret agreed, "who might turn out to be the stupidest and most stubborn man of them all."

"At least Nate looks like he's not going to be so difficult," Beauty sighed. "He already knows how to love."

"Nate has a good heart under all that bluster and fooling around," Margaret said softly hugging her daughter. "He's a lot like you in that respect."

Chapter Twelve

One day, about a week after Gerrin's capture and execution, a royal messenger arrived at the castle, having been sent there by the King. The messenger was a well-known knight named Sir Richard. He travelled with the full complement of squires, guards and retainers, all clad in matching tunics with his emblem emblazoned on them and carrying colourful pennants. Their mounts were groomed to perfection and the metal from their bridles and the soldier's shields all gleamed in the bright sun. It was an impressive and stirring sight. His arrival caused quite a bustle in the castle. Rooms were aired out and beds prepared. Servants, who had barely recovered from the recent events and stress of trying to take care of the villagers, were once again running about trying to cook, clean and care for the knight, his men at arms and his other followers.

When Sir Richard was first brought before Beauty, she was startled. She had to admit to herself that he was one of the most extremely handsome men she had ever seen. He was quite young, several years younger than the Beast, and he had golden blond hair just long enough to reach his collar. He was trim with a firm, taut build and he had warm, brown eyes. His manner was polite and refined, and he had a warm sense of humour. In short, he was everything she had dreamed about when she was an innocent young girl. He embodied the man who had been her romantic fantasy long before she ever met the Beast. He was handsome, courteous, rich, titled and intelligent, with a warm sense of humour and famed for his valour. She liked him as a man and as a friend, but romantically he left her unmoved. She looked to the Beast and smiled with secret amusement.

Sir Richard was unaware of her reaction. He was instantly smitten with Beauty. Everything about her, her face, figure, hair and eyes fit

156

his ideal of the perfect woman. Her personality intrigued him. He admired her warmth, patience and gentle humour while realizing that she possessed intelligence rare in a woman, or a man for that matter. To Sir Richard, Beauty was a perfect jewel with the heart of a woman. He took one look at the Beast's manner with Beauty, how he stood nearby her, how he seemed to be aware of everything about her even when he was talking to someone else, his air of protectiveness and even almost ownership, and sighed to himself. This woman would have to be a valued friend, and only a friend.

The Beast and Sir Richard had a long, private meeting. It seemed the King not only had several messages for the Beast, but he was checking up on him in a rare sign of concern. In a seemingly casual manner, Sir Richard examined the castle and grounds, questioned the staff and met with Margaret, Gwyneth and Seth. He even talked long and hard with Nate, Claire and Tom.

He seemed very interested in how well the Beast handled his dealings with the people with whom he was in daily contact. Sir Richard was particularly interested in how the Beast had grown into his role as the ruler of the castle and the surrounding lands and village. Sir Richard even rode through the village and countryside and spoke with several of the peasants, including Tom Two.

He gave the Beast several messages from the King, but following instructions, he held one special letter back to be delivered at a later date. A unique and very personal missive from the King.

After Sir Richard delivered his initial messages to the Beast and had finished his many conversations with the rest of the castle inhabitants, he began to follow Beauty around the castle. To the Beast's consternation, the knight seemed to be constantly trying to get Beauty alone, away from the Beast, and even away from the castle's many servants. It was an effort of which the Beast most assuredly did not approve.

From the Beast's observations, Beauty certainly didn't seem to mind the attention either. To the contrary, she seemed to fully enjoy Sir Richard's companionship. The two were often seen talking and laughing with each other. A fact that Margaret took great delight in pointing out to the Beast. Beauty's mother deliberately nurtured the

Beast's already budding jealousy, bringing it into full bloom.

Finally the Beast was so enraged that he went to the training field where Sir Richard's men were practicing along with his own soldiers and began to practice his swordsmanship, working long and hard to the point of exhaustion. Finally, when his angry energy was spent and the edge was off his temper, he left the practice fields. He wanted to find Sir Richard and Beauty. God help the knight if he was alone with Beauty, the Beast fumed storming up to the castle. He vaguely wondered why Sir Richard himself wasn't training with his men. He thought sourly to himself, didn't knights have an obligation to keep in shape, to be battle ready?

After a fruitless search through the castle and the grounds, the Beast headed back to the training field where his guards were still fencing with Sir Richard's men.

Tom was engaged in swordplay with one of Sir Richard's guards. The young guard fighting Tom was of fairly short stature with a slender frame. The smaller guard was wearing a helmet and metal breastplate. The guard made up for his smaller size by displaying a very fierce and relentless fighting spirit.

When the Beast came over, Tom broke away from the short guard. He saw the look on the Beast's face and took pity on the man. He told the Beast that Beauty and Sir Richard had gone for a ride in the forest several hours earlier. The Beast instantly had his horse saddled and went in search of the pair.

The Beast never looked at the guard with whom Tom had been practicing. He never noticed that the small guard stared after him as he rode away, stared long and hard. Indeed, he had taken no notice at all of the small, slender guard. He should have. He would have been shocked to his bones if he had.

The Beast's fiery temper faded while he searched in vain for Beauty and the knight, but deep inside a spark of fear remained. A tiny trace of fear that he refused to admit or examine. The fear that he held Beauty only by force and by her vow to him and not by her own true choice. The fear that he would not be the one she would have freely picked to be with. He only knew that he desperately wanted to find Beauty and Sir Richard.

He found the pair of horses tied to a tree, so he dismounted and tied up his own horse nearby. It seemed the couple had gone for a walk in the woods. It was easy to follow their path since they had walked along the deer trail. There were signs of their passing: footprints and bent branches.

It so happened that the Beast caught up with them at a small stream just as Beauty slipped on a wet stone. The Beast saw Sir Richard take Beauty's hand with one of his and slide his other arm around her waist to steady her. He saw Beauty smile back over her shoulder at Sir Richard as she whispered something with a small laugh. His temper returned as a blind rage enveloped him.

He was upon the pair with a roar. "What in God's name are you doing with this man, Beauty? Do you play me for a fool? I thought you promised to be the one person in my life I could trust."

"You can trust me, M'lord. I was doing you no dishonour," Beauty said proudly. "I was merely walking and speaking with Sir Richard, and you well know it, if you'd but used your head before letting loose your temper."

"I am not a fool. I know Sir Richard's been trying to get you to himself, just the two of you alone, for days now. Why do you think it was so necessary to this knight, this man, to get you alone?" the Beast raged. "He is enamoured with you. He was holding your hand when I rode up. I saw him."

"M'lord, I can explain... " Beauty started.

"The lady's done nothing to deserve your anger, sir," Sir Richard protested. "Nor have I. If you would but think, you know neither one of us would do anything to hurt you. You know us both well. We are two of the few people you know you can trust."

The Beast heard the truth in the knight's words but the fire was raging in his blood. It demanded release.

"Leave us," the Beast coldly ordered Beauty.

He drew his sword. Sir Richard, in defence, did likewise. The two men began fighting with deadly ferocity, the swords clashing loudly and gleaming brightly in the afternoon sun. The two knights were evenly matched and the fight seemed to go on forever without either of them inflicting serious damage on the other. Beauty was horrified at the thought of these two men fighting over her, particularly since neither of them wore any armour. Finally she could stand it no longer.

"Nay!" Beauty shouted. Fearing bloodshed she jumped between the two men. "Stop this madness!"

Turning to the visiting knight she said, "Sir Richard, please, I beg you to return to the castle."

"I cannot leave you here with him," Sir Richard protested. "I fear for you. He'll kill you."

"Nay, I'll be fine," Beauty assured him calmly. "Truly, on my word of honour, I will be fine. Again, I must ask you to return to the castle."

"She will be all right." At the muttered words, Sir Richard turned and looked at the Beast in amazement. The Beast nodded at him and continued ruefully, "But I may not be."

"I don't think the lady will hurt you too badly." Sir Richard smiled, bowed and with a trace of defiance, kissed Beauty's hand before he quickly left the couple alone.

As soon as Sir Richard left, Beauty flung herself at the Beast, kissing him as she slammed into him, knocking his sword to the ground.

"You were jealous, you big fool!" she laughed joyously, kissing him.

It was hardly the reaction the Beast had expected but he managed to adjust to it. He lifted her up so that she could wrap her slender legs around his waist but her long skirts were tangled up and got in the way. They both tumbled to the ground. He slid his hands up under her skirts, rolling her over so that she lay panting under him. He teased and stroked her moist femininity before entering her in a joyous celebration of their love. They moved together on the forest floor for a long time. By the time the Beast rolled off of her, Beauty's beautiful peach silk gown was torn and covered with dead leaves and stained from the grass. She was very satisfied, very satisfied, indeed.

After making love, as they lay together in the woods, Beauty finally got her chance to have the little discussion she'd been wanting. She took advantage of her chance and spoke.

"M'lord, I've been wanting to speak to you for a long time," Beauty began softly. "There is something I need to know. Did you mean what you said to the crowd? When you said that you loved me?"

"Yea, Beauty, I did." The Beast was almost shy for once in his life. "I do admit, I love you more than my own life."

He leaned over to give her a quick, tender kiss and grasp one of her small hands. He planted another gentle kiss on the back of her hand.

"Tis good, for I truly love you too," she told him, smiling widely before she pulled him over to her for another kiss.

"I know," the Beast grinned, "I heard you tell your mother you loved me when you thought I was still unconscious."

"M'lord!" Beauty laughed, cuffing him smartly on the shoulder with her fist. "I have to ask you something. Why did you shout your love to the crowd but never say aught of it privately to me?"

"Why did you tell your mother of your love, but not me?" the Beast countered.

"Mayhap we're both fools, I know well I am," Beauty sighed kissing him passionately. "After all, I love a man and I know not his real name."

"Nor I yours," the Beast reminded her.

"My given name is Isabella, M'lord," Beauty told him shyly.

"It's a beautiful name," the Beast told her solemnly, "but I think I still prefer to call you Beauty."

"And who do I have the pleasure of addressing? What is your real name, M'lord Beast?" Beauty questioned him in return.

The Beast winced and covered his face with his large hand. He looked through his fingers and said wryly, "Sir Sebastian, at your service."

Beauty laughed, "Sir Sebastian? That's not so bad. How came you by such a name as the Beast? Was it because of your fierce nature?"

"Not really. My younger brother couldn't say Sebastian aright; he kept calling me Bast," the Beast laughed openly. "I guess it was a stroke of luck I became known as the Beast instead of the Bastard."

"My younger brother also had his hand in my name," Beauty explained, laughing. "Isabella got shortened to Belle when he was young. Belle is French for Beauty, so... " she shrugged. "Anyway, I think I prefer to call you the Beast, or even Sir Beast."

The Beast groaned and rolled onto his back, pulling her atop him. His mouth hovered just a breath from hers as he asked, "Is our discussion over?"

"Nay!" she laughed, kissing him quickly before turning serious. "I want to repeat a question I asked you months ago, to see if by any chance your answer has since changed."

"What question?" The Beast was wary.

"If I were to get with child, what would you do?" Beauty was serious.

"Truly, I know not, for I know not what M'lord, the King, wishes of me." The Beast tilted her face up with a gentle finger. "But I can tell you that I will protect and care for you and any children that God gives us. I can also swear I will never willingly marry another for I do love you with all my heart and all my being. I was going to wait for an answer from the King to tell you this but I'll tell you now: When Sir Richard reports back to the King, he'll carry a petition from me asking the King's permission for us to marry."

"M'lord, you astound me," Beauty whispered.

"But do I please you?" the Beast asked, a little anxiously.

"You know you do," she smiled at him, the truth of her love shining brightly in her eyes. "As you keep telling me, you're no fool."

She kissed him willingly and they made love yet again, this time with less frenzy and a more tender passion. It was a long time before they arrived back at the castle. Sir Richard greeted the couple warmly, his worry for Beauty's safety long since dispelled by Beauty's mother and her brother Tom.

"I take it she still doesn't know?" Sir Richard asked the Beast, taking him aside.

"Nay, I'll tell her my secret when she tells me hers," the Beast replied.

"But you already know her secret," Sir Richard pointed out gently.

"Not by her words. She still hasn't told me." The Beast was stubborn.

"I see," Sir Richard said, "'tis naught but a fool's pride that holds your tongue."

"Fool's pride? Fool's pride is what you show when you persist in trying to best me in the joust," the Beast challenged, "or with bow and arrow or the broadsword."

"We'll have to settle that after the fair. We'll have a small tournament, just the two of us." Sir Richard met the Beast's challenge. "And some contests for the guards."

That night everyone was in good spirits. The Beast and Beauty seemed to have reached a new understanding and both of them openly expressed their love without regard for anyone else in the room.

"When I first saw her, I was going to ask you for her hand," Sir Richard said sadly to the Beast over dinner. "I'd marry the girl gladly, even if you won't, and the King be damned, but I could see at a glance that she truly loves you though and I have no desire to be second to you."

"In a few days, at the games, you will indeed be second to me," the Beast replied arrogantly. "Bet on it."

"Wouldst you bet the Lady Beauty?" Sir Richard asked teasing. "Because if not, why bet? 'Twould be no pleasure at all to win naught but mere money from you."

"Well, money's all I'm wagering," the Beast said firmly, then winked and laughed. "It's most unwise to wager a woman, they have minds of their own and the strangest things can put them in a terrible temper."

"As M'lord Beast is about to find out," Beauty laughed, teasing, "yet again."

"See what I mean?" the Beast laughed and shrugged.

As planned, Beauty left the table so that the two men could speak privately again. She went and checked on the kitchen staff, deciding to go over the details of the morrow's menu with the cook. She was surprised and delighted to find Gwyneth and the cook locked together in an embrace.

"Sorry, Milady." Henry, the cook, lowered his head and backed away from a blushing Gwyneth. "Was there aught I could do for you?"

"Nay, Henry," Beauty smiled gently, "I was but thinking about the

163

menu for tomorrow."

"We can go over it now," the cook offered.

"Beauty?" Gwyneth spoke up softly. "About what you just saw. I promise you it will never happen again."

"Why not?" Beauty was astonished. "If you and Henry care for each other what's the harm in that?"

"You don't think such behaviour is improper?" Gwyneth asked.

"I make no judgments," Beauty said with a gentle smile before continuing, "I only know that I want you both to be happy."

"What about the Beast?" Henry asked quietly. "How would he feel if Gwyneth and I asked him for permission to marry?"

"I think he'd be very pleased and happy to grant your request," Beauty smiled, "but I think he'd threaten you with dire consequences if you failed to make Gwyneth happy. He feels a great deal for her."

"He does?" Gwyneth asked, surprised.

"He tells me you were the only real source of love and support during his childhood. That you were the only one to try to see the boy inside the young warrior," she told Gwyneth. "He worries that you gave up any chance for a life of your own to stay by his side throughout the years. He feels he owes you a great deal."

"'Twas naught. I was but loyal to the master I served," Gwyneth said humbly.

"He knows that," Beauty told her, "and he is loyal to you."

"What?" Gwyneth was astonished.

"Don't mistake me," Beauty said, "the Beast has never said such a thing to me but he has spoken of you in ways that make his feelings obvious. The rooms each of you has over the kitchen could be made over for your living chambers if you were to marry."

"I assure you, Milady, that our service to you and his lordship would never lessen," the cook said.

"It had better," Beauty thought aloud. "You and Gwyneth are always ready for our summons. You deserve more time to yourselves. There must be a maid who can answer our summons if we need anything at night. Gwyneth, pick one of the younger maids and train her to take over for you at night and Henry, pick one of your assistants and do the same. I will see to the Beast. He will give you permission to marry."

"Are you sure?" Gwyneth asked.

"I am most sure. I can handle him, at least sometimes." Beauty smiled as she left the kitchen, leaving the happy couple behind her.

Still restless but happy for the couple she'd just left behind her, Beauty went out the side door and walked alone into a small garden. She sat for a while on a stone bench, relaxing and breathing in the fragrant night air. Impatient, she then strolled over to the fountain, letting the cool night air wash over her. Soon she noticed she wasn't the only person in the garden. Passing a large bush, she came upon her mother and Seth embracing. The older couple jumped apart like naughty children, flushed and flustered.

"I hope this means there's going to be a wedding," she said eyeing the pair with mock severity.

"As soon as we can arrange it, Milady," Seth replied, smiling broadly. "I hope you approve?"

"I do, most certainly," Beauty kissed his cheek, "and your old lord would too."

Beauty hugged her mother, genuinely touched for her, before leaving the garden to the lovers. Romance must be in the air, she mused.

She strolled into the stables to visit her favourite mare who was due to foal soon. She stroked the mare's soft head and fed her a handful of grain. Speaking softly to the mare, she stroked her sides and looked at her carefully. The mare was due soon as her bags were filling with milk. Still, Beauty did not expect the foal for a day or two yet.

Soon Beauty became aware she was not alone in the barn. She found Nate and Claire sitting on a pile of straw in the last stall. Before they realized she was there, Beauty saw their lips meet in a tender kiss. It was so sweet and innocent that she sighed aloud. The two kids heard her and quickly jumped apart.

"Beauty!" Nate exclaimed, coming over to Beauty. "Claire and I were just... "

"I know what you were just doing, Nate. I do have eyes," Beauty smiled. "You just be sure that you don't do anything to hurt that girl."

I won't Beauty," Nate said earnestly. "I love her."

"Tis good," Beauty told her brother, "but you are both so young."

"Not so young, Beauty, many couples are married at our age," Nate replied softly but with a new hint of maturity.

"I know, but it still seems far too young." Beauty asked Nate, "Are you planning to marry Claire?"

"Claire is not ready for marriage as she was hurt far too badly by the thieves," Nate answered, showing a maturity and wisdom that made Beauty proud. "But I do love her. Someday, perhaps we will marry."

Beauty hugged her brother. "Nate, I'm glad I found you for another reason. I have news. I hope it makes you happy. Mother and Seth are getting married."

"That's great! When did you learn this?" Nate asked.

"Tonight. I just found them in the garden, embracing. It was just after I found Gwyneth kissing the cook and just before I came in here and found you and Claire embracing." Beauty mused, "It makes me wonder who I'll find together on the training field at the games."

"You'll probably just find Tom and one of Sir Richard's guards," Nate teased. "That smallish guard most likely."

"Nate!" Beauty gasped, wondering if he knew what he was suggesting.

"Wrestling, probably. He trains with them constantly," Nate pointed out wide-eyed, seeming completely innocent and unaware of the train of Beauty's thoughts.

"You had better get back to Claire," Beauty said, quietly, "before she gets mad at me for taking you away from her."

"Claire would never get mad at you," Nate told her, "she considers you her ideal of what a woman should be."

"Then Heaven help her," Beauty laughed heartily, "for I am truly very far from ideal."

"That is what I told her," Nate teased his older sister, "but she persists in her strange beliefs."

Back in the great hall, Sir Richard and the Beast were still having their meeting. Sir Richard had one more message for the Beast. It seemed that the King, worried about holding these lands, now wanted all his knights and lords to marry and produce heirs. The Beast was one of the most important to the King, and he was one of the few who was still single. The King stopped just short of a direct order but strongly suggested that the Beast marry. He had even gone so far as to make out a list of possible wives for the Beast. He had listed several worthy ladies, all with noble blood.

At the end of the list the King had added a personal note:

> *There is one lass who was daughter to the old lord of your castle. He ruled your land before we took this country and I gifted you his castle. He is dead. She and her family have disappeared, I know not where or what became of them. I did not wish them to come to harm but the old lord would not surrender. His name was Sir Thomas, and his wife's was Lady Margarite. There were three children as I recall but I do not know the girl's name. She was an extraordinarily lovely child. If you could find her and marry her, I would approve. I know long ago I promised never to ask such a thing of you, so this is by your choice but if you did decide to marry the girl it would go a long way to securing the loyalty of the serfs. Her sire was a noble warrior. I defeated him but I wouldst honour him enough to see his family well and the girl would make you a fine wife.*

> *With God's grace, as always,*
> *Your King*

Reading this, the Beast's heart soared. Without any hesitation or doubts he knew who that girl was, the lass that the King desired him to marry, and he realized that he wanted it too, more than he had ever dreamed possible. He hurried to his chambers to seek out Beauty.

"I'm sorry I was so busy with Sir Richard," the Beast said as he entered the bedchamber. "I hope you weren't bored without me."

"M'lord, although I always prefer to have you at my side, you would be truly astonished at how interesting my night was without you," Beauty grinned happily.

She was already waiting for him dressed in a soft shift as she sat on the edge of the great bed. The Beast began to remove his clothes. A bath was waiting for him.

"How so?" The Beast was curious.

"Well, it seems that love is in the air," Beauty smiled as she watched him undress. "I saw no less than three couples in the throes of an embrace."

"Three couples? Who were they?" The Beast was not really interested in women's gossip but he knew well the consequences of ignoring something Beauty had on her mind.

"I'll tell you all about it later. Right now I'm too curious. What was the final message from the King?" Beauty asked inquisitively as she readied herself for bed, brushing her long hair. "Sir Richard made it sound very important."

"'Twas nothing much," the Beast replied off-handed. "The King said he will come visit next summer if he can. Oh, and he requests that I marry soon and produce an heir. He even sent a list of acceptable women for me to consider."

"Marry?" Beauty's heart felt like a stone in her chest; she dropped the brush and turned to him in alarm. "At his request?"

"Yea. Mayhap it's time. I've sent for the priest but he won't be able to get here for at least a fortnight. That gives me time to find a lady from the King's list and ask her." The Beast pretended to read the list again, frowning over the names listed there.

"List?" Beauty fought to keep the tears from her eyes. "The King sent you a list of women to marry? What about the things you said today in the forest?"

"I said I would follow the King's orders and that I would try to get his approval for us to marry. I didn't know he had already made a list of maidens for me to consider. There is one he recommends above the others," the Beast said. "She is young and pretty, according to the King. He speaks of her skills at managing the household and the lands. He even praises her handwriting, but I do not believe that. Real ladies are not educated in such things. She is also known to be skilled at healing and with horses. But there is a mystery."

"How so?" Beauty managed to say, but she was stunned.

Could he be talking about her? No, it was impossible. Still, she had all the skills the King had listed, Beauty thought, and whether the Beast knew it or not, she was of nobility. Finally, she made her mind up to use all the weapons at her disposal to fight for this man, including her true birthright.

"She was the daughter to the old lord and she has disappeared," the Beast continued speaking as though he didn't know well the fevered workings of Beauty's mind, "along with her family. I don't know why there is no record of her name, except that the knight who led the invasion of this castle burned all the records and papers he could find, even the old knight's family Bible. It makes no sense to me. To top it off, the old lord and his lady kept the children much to themselves until they were of an age. The villagers had rarely even seen the girl."

The Beast looked her over with a gleam in his eye before he continued with just a bit too much nonchalance. "'Tis too bad we can't pass you off as the girl but she was very well bred and known to be a very gently reared child and so is sure to be a refined and beautiful lady."

His too carefully controlled voice gave him away.

"Oh you monster!" She launched herself at the Beast in a fury knocking him back onto the bed, pummelling and slapping him.

Laughing, he caught her easily and rolled her over onto her belly. Still laughing, he spanked her with vigour in spite of her squirming and struggling. When her bottom was warm and glowing pink all over, he stopped. Still holding her face down, he gently kissed, nipped and stroked her pink bottom. Then he rolled her over and entered her in a smooth motion, moving ever so slowly within her as his hands explored her soft body. His thumbs brushed her breasts, teasing and hardening her nipples. Gradually he built up the speed and intensity of his thrusts. She was with him at every thrust, matching him perfectly.

When she felt about ready to spin off the edge of the world, soaring off into space, he slowed down. Again and again they built towards a peak, only to have the Beast slow things down, prolonging their pleasure until it was almost unbearable. Finally, both exhausted and dripping with sweat from their exertions, they reached their peaks together. They cuddled without words for a long time, basking in the afterglow of a truly memorable climax.

Eventually, when their breathing returned to normal, they had to talk.

"Don't ever think to keep a secret like that from me again," he growled with mock ferocity.

"Nay, M'lord," Beauty replied with feigned meekness. "How long have you known, M'lord?"

"Almost from the first, Beauty." The Beast stroked her hair. "You are much too refined and educated to be a serf. You are everything the nobility is supposed to be but seldom truly is."

The Beast raised himself up on one shoulder and looked at her with all his love and respect for her shining in his eyes.

In a voice almost choked with emotion, he asked her softly, "Will you marry me, Milady?"

"Just to please the King?" she asked, eyes wide, covering her emotion with a glib rejoinder.

"The devil take the King," the Beast snorted, "to please me. I love you, Beauty."

"I must admit, I love you too, M'lord Beast," Beauty replied.

"So will you marry me?"

"Yes, M'lord Beast. I've wanted to marry you for a long time," Beauty replied, almost whispering, as this moment was far too important for loud words. "In truth, I've felt married to you for a long time."

"As have I. Beauty, I once told you I would have to marry a woman with noble blood and a dowry. Why didn't you tell me you were the daughter of the old lord?" the Beast questioned. "At least you had the title."

"I had my pride too. As you do," Beauty pointed out. "I wanted to marry someone who wanted me without a care as to my birthright or dowry."

"Do you think I care a whit about your title?" The Beast kissed her soundly. "Or that I care that you have no dowry? I love you, Beauty."

"But I do have a dowry, M'lord." She got out of bed and went into a corner of the room.

Pressing a small, hidden latch in the wooden floor, she revealed a secret hiding place just big enough to hold a small leather bag. She pulled out the bag and took it to him.

"My dowry, M'lord." She poured the contents of the pouch onto the table beside the bed.

There was a collection of fine jewels, necklaces, bracelets and earrings with set precious stones. There was also a vast quantity of loose gems, along with an old document that proved to be the title to another castle. The deed had been her mother's dowry.

"So you will marry me?" The Beast was unconcerned with the small fortune in gems.

"In a fortnight, you said?" Beauty asked, joining him once again on the bed.

"Yea, or sooner if we can arrange it. Mayhap Sir Richard has a priest with his retainers, but I cannot fathom any reason why he would. Is there any problem? Would that be too soon for you to make your preparations?" The Beast wanted an answer.

"Nay, a fortnight is good," Beauty smiled, pulling him closer. "Any longer and the baby would be showing."

The Beast was momentarily stunned, stuck both motionless and speechless. Before too long he recovered enough to move, then hugged Beauty in a joy that seemed too great for mere words. She knew she would carry the memory of the rapture in his face at that moment in her heart for the rest of her life.

The Beast held her with a tenderness she could scarcely believe before kissing her with so much reverence that it was almost as if he were worshipping her. It was an intimacy too precious for lovemaking, although joyous lovemaking would certainly follow, and soon. This was a time for sharing their emotions with heart and soul, and not with the voice or even the body.

The silent celebration continued for a long time before they did turn into gentle, sweet lovemaking. Even the gentle loving slowly turned into something else: a fierce need, a passion that threatened to consume them both. When they climaxed, they were both out of breath, speechless. It took a long time but eventually the Beast recovered his composure enough to speak.

"Baby? Was that another secret?" the Beast growled with mock severity. "Do I have to spank you yet again?"

"Anything M'lord wishes," Beauty mumbled even as she drifted off to sleep, "as long as he thinks he has the energy for making up afterwards."

"Maybe in the morning." The Beast's own exhaustion hit him and he cradled her in his arms as he, too, fell into a deep, contented slumber.

Chapter Thirteen

The next day, while the servants started making all the preparations for the guards' contests and the tournament, Beauty and the Beast, along with Sir Richard, Nate and Claire visited the peasants' fair.

Beauty was dressed in a soft blue dress, simply adorned with white lace and a golden girdle circling her hips. Claire wore a soft pink dress that was also simple and showed her youth to her advantage. All three men wore dark woollen hose, white shirts and brightly coloured tunics. The group was well dressed and they were all strikingly attractive, but there was nothing so ornate or fancy about their dress that it would make the peasants feel awkward or ill at ease. They wanted to enjoy themselves amongst the serfs and have fun at the fair.

They stood as a group among the crowd of villagers as they watched the jugglers and acrobats perform, and they ignored the stares of the villagers as they listened to strolling musicians. They even bought some of the peasants' food, meat and vegetable pies, crisp red apples and fresh, cold milk. They sat at a long table and ate as they happily watched the happenings all around them.

When they saw a peasant woman with several children tagging along with her looking for a place to sit and feed her children, Beauty called out.

"Come, sit here, there's plenty of room at our table," she invited.

The woman was stunned and very pleased but too far shy and afraid to accept the invitation. "I wouldn't want to bother your lordships. My children can be very energetic."

"There's no bother," Beauty smiled, "please, sit with us."

"Of course, you and your children are welcome to sit with us," the Beast said with a welcoming smile. "'Twould make Beauty very happy for she loves children very much."

Shortly after that, Sir Richard disappeared along with Nate and Claire, leaving Beauty and the Beast to wander around the fair alone. Strolling hand in hand they stopped to watch a puppet show. The puppets depicted a ferocious warrior and a beautiful woman. He kissed her soundly. By the end of the skit, she was bossing him around shamelessly. Beauty wondered a bit at the Beast's reaction to the story when all of a sudden, he laughed so hard he almost fell off the bench. Relieved, she joined him in his laughter. They were still laughing at the antics of the puppets when suddenly a small boy, maybe six years of age, who was running around without looking where he was going because he was overly excited by the colourful sights and sounds, ran into the Beast's hard legs. The boy ran into the Beast hard enough to cause the lad to fall to the ground. The poor lad landed with a thud on his little behind then sat there and cried aloud until the mighty warrior bent down and gingerly helped him to his feet.

"Are you all right, my lad?" the Beast asked gently.

"I'm fine, M'lord," the boy sniffled, but tried to be brave as he looked up in awe and a little fear at the lord.

"You're a brave lad," the Beast told the boy.

The boy's mother, a young, fresh-faced village lass hurried over to gather up her young son. "I'm most sorry if my boy is disturbing your lordship." She curtsied quickly, horrified at the sight of the Beast holding her son. "It won't happen again, M'lord."

"'Tis naught. He just fell down. He's not disturbing me at all," the Beast smiled at the nervous young woman. "He's a very brave lad, isn't he?"

"Thank you, M'lord." The young woman smiled back at the Beast, pleased at his compliment and dazzled by his smile.

"He's a very good looking little fellow too," Beauty added, meeting the woman's eyes.

"Thank you, M'lord, Milady." The young mother, pleased and flustered, quickly hustled her son off.

Beauty smiled at the Beast, a secret woman's smile, and whispered, "It won't be such a bad thing, will it, to have a son of our own?"

174

"I want several sons and some daughters too," the Beast whispered back. "Most of all I want pretty little girls who look just like you, but without your temper of course."

"My temper, indeed!" Beauty fumed. "I'm not the one with a temper so ferocious that legends have sprung from it."

"Nay, lass, you are the one whose temper is too furious even for legends," he shot back.

He laughed and ducked as she cuffed him on the arm. Grabbing her hand, they stood to the side and watched some of the peasants' games. Soon Sir Richard joined them again, but Nate and Claire were nowhere to be found.

The trio cheered and bet with each other about a foot race. Then they did the same during the contest to see who could jump the highest. They laughed aloud as several peasant boys tried to catch a greased piglet. Soon they noticed that Nate was one of the pig chasers. When the tug o' war began they cheered openly for both sides.

The tug o' war turned out to be one of the highlights of the day. Every time one side seemed to have an advantage, one of the soldiers or guards would grab the rope for the other side, thereby evening the odds. Soon it seemed as if all the Beast's guards were on one side, and all of Sir Richard's men were on the other. At the end, the Beast and Sir Richard joined their men on the ropes to the delight and surprise of the villagers.

The contest was lost however, when one of Sir Richard's guards lost his concentration for a moment. The unfortunate guard's attention wandered from the rope he was pulling on to the peasant girl pulling right next to him. It seemed that in the girl's exertions, her shift had slipped and her full breasts were in eminent danger of popping right out of the plunging neckline of her dress. The young guard, upon noticing this, was so distracted that he suddenly let go of the rope altogether. His side lost the contest but he was seen later strolling with the young maiden, holding hands and laughing.

Surprisingly, the Beast didn't seem to see the day as a waste of his time. As he sat in some deep grass under a shady tree, he finally realized that these were his people to live with and to rule and protect, and that it was important for them to have small fairs and celebrations. The most important thing that happened all day was that he and his lady mingled freely with the villagers. For the first time he met some of them person to person. He encouraged several of the serfs to sit with him.

Soon he was surrounded by a small group of his villagers. They spoke of their daily lives as he listened and learned. Beauty was very proud of him and very happy to see the proof of the changes in him. Her heart swelled with her love for him.

The Beast noticed how many of the women had babes in their arms and small children at their sides. He truly enjoyed watching the small children running about and playing with each other. It seemed strange that he had never taken note of babes and small children before.

The chance to talk to the Beast was just as important for the peasants as it was for him. For once, the Beast was finally seen as a real man, not just some mythical figure from the castle on the hill.

As the evening approached, Beauty and the Beast joined the peasants in some simple country folk dances. These were not the courtly dances which the Beast personally thought were boring. These dances were lively jigs, dances that could leave a body breathless and thirsty. The Beast sent some men to the castle to fetch and open a barrel of ale for everyone. The peasants were shocked by his actions but also very pleased.

Beauty loved every minute of the day, every minute of seeing the Beast relaxing, enjoying himself and at one with the people he ruled.

That night over a simple dinner of crusty bread and roasted chicken, Beauty and the Beast laughed about the day they'd had, mingling with the serfs and enjoying the fair. Sir Richard told them about a lass he'd spent the afternoon talking to.

"Just talking?" the Beast teased.

"Well, maybe there was a little more than simple talking going on," Sir Richard said smiling. "But of course, as a knight, I'm far too polite and dignified to say anything more."

"Sure you are," the Beast laughed.

Beauty said nothing but smiled as she ate her chicken.

"Claire and I had fun at the fair," Nate said.

"We saw you trying to catch the greased piglet," Beauty told him. "What else did you do?"

"We ate lots of food, saw some puppets and I ran in the race against other boys my age," Nate said.

"I just sat on the sidelines and watched Nate," Claire said. "There were too many people milling around, but I enjoyed my day very much."

"That settles it then, we'll have to make it an annual fair." The Beast smiled at the girl who smiled back.

"And the games tomorrow, between us, will you make those an annual event also?" Sir Richard jested. "I'll be glad to come back once a year to beat you in the joust."

"Mayhap you will win," the Beast said calmly, "once in every five years or so."

"This may be my year then," Sir Richard laughed. "I'll beat you and my guards will win their games, beating yours. Bet on it."

"All right, name your stakes," the Beast replied.

The two men dickered long and hard over the wagers and the odds before they finally came to an agreement. The final wager was for a new armour, sword and shield for the Beast if he were to win; or a pair of young warhorses for Sir Richard if he were the one to emerge victorious.

That night Beauty and the Beast made love long into the night with tenderness and simple joy, content with the day and with each other.

The next day, at the other part of the fair and festival, the Beast's men and Sir Richard's men met on the training field in a series of contests at arms including a small tournament between the two knights themselves. Both knights had their men march onto the field in a colourful procession with trumpets blaring and banners flying. All the men wore coloured tunics over their chainmail. The tunics matched the colours of the knight they represented. Both knights had on their best chainmail and armour, covered by silk tunics, with their shields highly polished and shining in the sun. Both men had large colourful tents set up well away from the action to rest and change in. People from the village watched from the sidelines and cheered whenever they saw a worthwhile competitor.

The two men's soldiers were all very well trained and fully armed so the opposing forces were fairly well matched. Of the Beast's men, Beauty's brother, Tom, proved to be the best at various events, including lance and swords, while Sir Richard's short, slight guard proved to be good with the mace and at archery. Other events included a footrace, a horserace and contests to see who could jump the highest and the farthest.

There was to be a final combat to decide the victor between the top guardsmen from both sides. Wrestling was to decide who would be named the best soldier.

The first day, the Beast and Sir Richard competed with each other with the broadsword and bow and arrow. They did so without adding their scores to those of their teams. At the end of the first day, the teams were evenly matched.

As the Beast and Sir Richard stood together away from Beauty, Sir Richard asked the Beast a seemingly casual question. "What do you know of the character of Beauty's brother Tom?"

Tom had already removed his helmet and chainmail in preparation for the wrestling to come. He stood impassive, watching as the small soldier from Sir Richard's guards rode over to one of the grooms standing nearby.

"He's a good man, hard-headed and hardworking. He's trustworthy and surprisingly loyal to me. We had some trouble once between us but he recently saved my life. I like the man. Why do you ask?" the Beast replied, idly watching Sir Richard's small soldier dismount.

"Because the soldier he's about to wrestle, the one who's tied with him after a full day of games, is my sister, Lady Althea," Sir Richard winked and looked around briefly before adding, "and yours."

"That's Althea!" the Beast was astonished. "But she was just a child when last I saw her, and a girl child, as I seem to recall. How comes she to be one of your warriors?"

"She's grown up. She's also inherited our father's hard head and iron will, that be how. She refuses to be relegated to what she calls women's work. She craves the excitement and travel of following me."

"She also seems to like Tom well enough," the Beast commented wryly. "Mayhap too well."

"He thinks she's a man and he treats her as an equal, as just another soldier," Sir Richard pointed out. "That's about to come to a sudden end when she dismounts and removes her helmet and armour."

Almost at the moment he said it, she did indeed remove her helmet and some of her armour in preparation for the wrestling match. To the great surprise of both the knights watching, Tom gave no indication of shock at all. Instead, he pulled the girl into his arms and kissed her soundly and with no small amount of passion before continuing to prepare himself for the hand to hand combat. As the kiss went on there were catcalls and whistles from the watching peasants and the guards on either side. It was apparent to all who saw it that this was no probing, tentative, first kiss either. This was a kiss of full passion and promise. Many onlookers were stunned but none more so than Beauty.

"Did you know that the soldier was a woman?" Beauty rushed over to ask the Beast and Sir Richard. "Do you know who she is?"

"I did not know it was a woman until Sir Richard told me just now, but now that I do know, I also know who she is. Her name is Lady Althea and she is Sir Richard's sister," the Beast paused before adding softly, "and mine."

"Your sister? So that means Sir Richard's your brother? Why didn't you tell me?" Beauty asked quizzically. "And why didn't you tell me your sister was here?"

"About Lady Althea? I just said I didn't know she was here myself. Not until just now when she removed her helmet. I haven't yet greeted her or even had a word with her myself," the Beast explained.

"No, M'lord, dolt. Why didn't you say ere now that you and Sir Richard were brothers?" Beauty smiled tensely. "Or were you ashamed to introduce me to your brother? After all, I'm not your wife, am I?"

"Beauty, I'm not ashamed of you. I love you and I'm very proud and honoured that you care for me. Remember, you have been introduced to Sir Richard. I just didn't want to tell you that he was my brother until all our business was finished. I wanted to concentrate on having my brother get to know my intended bride without worrying about the King's affairs. That's all, I was getting around to it." The Beast seemed sheepish.

"Sure you were." Beauty was strangely hurt, but she shrugged it off as she watched her brother wrestle with Lady Althea.

The wrestling match lasted longer than anyone watching would have suspected. Although Tom's strength was clearly superior, he held back. Also, Lady Althea was skilled and practiced at wrestling men much stronger and larger than herself. She knew some rather unorthodox wrestling techniques and tricks that were designed specifically to make up for her lack of size and brute strength, and she wasn't shy about using them. Tom was also hindered quite a bit by his interest in her slender body and his desire not to cause her any injury.

After a while he did pin her though, winning the match and the guard's part of the tourney. He stood and reached down a hand to help the girl up from the ground. She glared up at him before reaching a hand up to his. When she was standing, he quickly swooped her up and threw her over his shoulder. He silenced her shrieking protests by swatting her hard on the buttocks with a large hand, and without breaking stride he carried her towards the barn.

The onlookers laughed aloud but Beauty was still feeling disappointed with the Beast. She had the feeling that he was, perhaps, ashamed of her and that there was a reason why he had been so slow to introduce her to his family.

"Mayhap after Sir Richard left, you would have told me who he really was," Beauty sighed.

"No really, Beauty." The Beast knew she was still hurt and angry but he couldn't fathom why. "Truly, I had planned to tell you tonight. Sir Richard just wanted to see how things went for me, if I was well and happy, before he said aught of our relationship."

The Beast could see that Beauty was still not entirely satisfied with his reply. He sighed. Who could hope to understand a woman anyway?

"Milady, we really had planned to surprise you tonight," Sir Richard told her gently. "In fact, Lady Althea was going to surprise both of you tonight. Mayhap we can even get her into a dress for the occasion. That would surprise even me." They all laughed.

Beauty's sense of whimsy returned. "Do you know what the strangest thing is? Last night when I went into the kitchen, I found Gwyneth and the cook kissing. By the by, I gave them your blessing and your permission to marry," she told the Beast.

"So? You presume to speak for me? Just like a woman." The Beast jested loudly before he continued softly, "Tis a good thing you were right. I am glad for her and very pleased with your news."

"That's not all. As I walked in the garden to take in the night fragrances, I found my mother and Seth embracing. They told me they planned to marry and asked my blessing," Beauty continued, smiling softly, "which I gave."

"Good, she can nag someone besides me," the Beast growled in mock severity. "Seth should be knighted; he has a lot of courage."

Beauty flashed him a warning look then she continued, "Next, I walked into the stables and found Nate kissing Claire."

Her voice trailed off as her mood sobered. "They're both so very young, I wonder if it will be a problem." Her humour returned. "I then wondered aloud as I spoke to Nate who I'd find together at the tournament. Nate suggested it would be Tom and one of Sir Richard's guards. At the time, I wasn't sure exactly what he meant. It sounded strangely like he was insinuating that Tom would, um, how do I say this, prefer the company of men to women, but he said it was just that I was sure to find Tom challenging the smallest of Sir Richard's guards at swords. He implied that Tom and the small guard greatly enjoyed practicing with each other."

"Apparently they have been practicing with something other than swords," Sir Richard said.

"In truth, let us hope Tom has kept his sword sheathed," the Beast remarked, cynically. "She is our sister, after all."

"His sword?" Beauty was puzzled, and then blushed, "Oh I see, you mean his... "

"You really are an innocent, aren't you? Or at least you were before I came along," the Beast grinned wickedly. "That imp, Nate, must have already known something we didn't. Let's find him and ask him what he knew."

When they found Nate, he was indeed a valuable source of information. He had seen Tom wrestling with the small guard alone in the barn where no one else could see. Something raised Nate's curiosity so he watched the two wrestle from a hiding place in the back stall.

"When Tom pinned the young guard to the ground and he stared deeply into the guard's eyes I was surprised," Nate told the trio. "But I was well and truly shocked when he leaned down and started kissing the youth with all his might. I've never seen kissing like that before, except for when I spied on you, Beauty, and the Beast."

Beauty's eyes narrowed. "You spied on us?"

The Beast said gruffly, "Remember lad, I still have the dungeon."

"I'm truly sorry, M'lord, Beauty, I meant no disrespect." Nate blushed before he continued, "Watching Tom with the guard, kissing, made me feel funny. I was so startled that I dropped the brush I had been using to groom your horse and gave meself away. Once I had revealed my presence, Tom introduced me to the young guard. I was sure surprised to find out that she was not only a woman, but also your sister, M'lord. I was glad too. After seeing the two of them kissing, I wanted to try it for meself. So I did. That's when Beauty found me kissing Claire."

"Did you like it?" the Beast asked with some of his own curiosity.

"Well, yea," Nate told him, "but it was different for Claire and me. She's afraid of men, you see, because of the men who raped her, so I had to be real slow and gentle with her. I couldn't do it like Tom did with Lady Althea, holding her so tight and pushing my tongue down deep into her throat. I had to be real careful not to scare Claire any worse than she's already been scared."

"Nate, what you've just said shows wisdom some men never seem to learn." Beauty gave the Beast an evil eye before she kissed Nate's cheek. "I'm truly proud of you right now. Remember you're still very young. If you're patient and gentle with Claire now, someday you will be greatly rewarded. I promise you that."

That night Tom joined them for dinner along with Lady Althea. In spite of living and training along with Sir Richard's men, Lady Althea was truly beautiful, slender and of average height for a woman. It was only when she posed as a man that she seemed to be short. She had the same green eyes as the Beast, but her hair was a shade lighter, with traces of fire in the colour. She wore a green velvet gown, trimmed in gold and white. The gown was cut low at the bodice and fit snugly at the waist before flaring out like a bell. The sleeves fit snugly at the shoulders and flared from the elbows to end in wide points at the wrists, so that the inner lining of gold was revealed as her hands moved. Her hair was covered with a green velvet band and pulled into a bun at the nape of her neck. Slippers made of green velvet and gold trim completed the outfit.

It was a joyous meal. The reunion between the Beast and his sister was both tearful and touching. He kissed Lady Althea's face and hugged her until she protested from the lack of air. Sir Richard was publicly acknowledged for the first time since his arrival at the castle as the brother of the Beast. The maid, Gwyneth, was in heaven. She was now free to fuss openly over Sir Richard and Lady Althea.

Even Margaret had taken her real name back now that it was known she was the wife of the old lord of the castle. She was introduced to the Beast's brother and sister as the Lady Margarite, and her sons were introduced as Thomas and Nathaniel. Even Beauty, resplendent in a red silk gown, took her real name for the evening, Lady Isabella.

The Lady Margarite sat proudly at the table with Seth, the man who was her former husband's manservant and now was her fiancé. Nate and Claire sat together, laughing like children one minute and gazing shyly at each other the next. Tom and Lady Althea argued and ate and argued some more, but the sparks flew through the air around them and all those watching felt the passion behind the heated words. Although Gwyneth was very glad to be with Sir Richard and Lady Althea once again, her real focus was on Henry, the cook she planned to marry.

Beauty and the Beast formally announced their plans to marry but they kept the joyful news about the coming child to themselves for the moment.

"I hope you can stay until the wedding," Beauty told the Beast's family. "M'Lord Sebastian said it would take about a fortnight to fetch a priest."

"We'd be honoured to stay," Sir Richard replied.

He then took the Beast aside. "But why wait so long to send away for a priest when we have a friar travelling with us?"

"Why did you add a friar to your entourage, my brother? Seems like a strange addition to your usual assortment of retainers," the Beast questioned. "Or is the King behind this?"

"You know our King," Sir Richard replied. "When he has an idea, he likes it to come to fruition quickly."

"I admit, I still have hard feelings for him." The Beast paused. "I truly hope that I can be a wise and loving father to my sons and daughters when the time comes."

"'Tis strange. You never saw the human side of our father, and I never saw his cruelty." Sir Richard paused. "'Tis the difference between us. His first wife, your mother, was a bitter, evil woman who gave him two sons and died having taught him only the harsh and cruel ways of the world. My mother followed her. She gave him a son and a daughter, and taught him how to truly love and to be loved in return. He's not the same father who raised you."

"Love can change a man, 'tis true." The Beast spoke slowly, then sighed, "I now know that better than anyone, so mayhap when I've had a chance to see him and talk to him I'll be able to forget the past and honour him for the man he is today, as I know I should."

The next day was the climax of the tournament, the joust between the two knights. They were both using practice lances, lighter and more easily broken than regular lances. Their goal was to unbalance or unseat the opponent, rather than kill or injure him. Both knights had on gleaning helmets and shields, along with chainmail covered with brightly coloured tunics and heavy metal gloves. Beauty, watching from the stands in a light green velvet dress, had given the Beast a ribbon to tie around his upper arm as a token of her love.

The two knights were both evenly matched, so it took several passes for a victor to emerge. On the first pass, Sir Richard manoeuvred his grey stallion at the last minute so that even as he scored a hit against the Beast's shield, he caused the Beast to miss him completely.

The Beast made up for it on the second pass, being ready for the other knight's manoeuvre. He scored a hit and Sir Richard missed. At the end of every pass, grooms stood ready to throw them new lances to replace any broken ones. The two warhorses, Sir Richard's grey and the Beast's black stallion, pranced with barely controlled power at the end of the lanes before each pass, tensed and waiting for the command to run. For several passes, the two knights either traded hits against each other or scored hits simultaneously on each other and the tournament continued.

Finally, his horse slipping at a critical moment, the Beast dropped his guard and was unseated. Beauty ran over to him as he lay flat on his back in the mud and stared up ruefully at his younger brother.

"M'lord! Are you injured?" Beauty asked.

"Only my pride, Beauty," the Beast replied, reaching up to take the hand of his brother who had dismounted and come over.

Sir Richard had reached out a hand to aid his brother in rising to his feet. He should have been more cautious though, as the Beast easily pulled him down into the mud and muck beside him, laughing heartily all the while. Hearing the mighty Beast laugh openly as he wrestled his brother in the mud, the soldiers and villagers began to laugh too. That was fine. It was when Beauty laughed that the Beast had heard enough. Beauty soon found herself being grasped by the ankle and pulled to the ground, down into the mud and being tickled by both warriors; all the pageantry and decorum of the day was forgotten.

Sir Richard got out of the way as the Beast kissed Beauty soundly before rising and picking her up and setting her on her feet. The villagers looked on laughing and cheering loudly.

Beauty struggled to retain her tattered dignity as she looked at the two knights. "Men!"

She gathered her wet, muddy skirts from her ruined gown and stormed back to the castle. Ducking into the kitchen she ordered a hot bath sent up to the bedchamber, and took a leisurely bath and spent a long time getting dressed for dinner.

That night she feigned anger and let the Beast take a long time persuading her to make love with him. It was not only fun but she got lots of extra attention, lots of extra fondling, and lots of gentle caresses as she was slowly coaxed out of her anger. Mayhap I'll get mad more often, she thought dreamily as his mouth loved her. His form of penance is exquisite.

Chapter Fourteen

Beauty and the Beast were just planning to have a quick, simple marriage ceremony to be held right after the fair but many little things seemed to keep happening to delay the nuptials. Things that all seemed to have their start with Sir Richard.

First, he told them that the friar was too ill to perform the ceremony. Beauty and her mother could find naught wrong with the man, except perhaps laziness and a complaining nature. They both thought it was strange that the holy man had been well enough to marry Gwyneth and Henry before being stricken with his mysterious malady.

Next, Beauty's most skilled seamstress was delayed getting just the right lace for Beauty's dress, even though Sir Richard was supposed to have sent one of his fastest riders to court to fetch it. When the man returned with the wrong lace, the seamstress flatly spurned it. The tiny woman stubbornly crossed her arms, shook her head, and refused to even pick up her needle and thread. She insisted that the dress would be ruined if she used any other lace than the one she and Beauty had agreed upon.

Of course, Sir Richard was the only one to notice that the small chapel was not only exceedingly dirty but also in desperate need of several small, but important, repairs. In seemed that some of the pews were broken and the ceiling leaked. In spite of the fair weather, Sir Richard insisted the ceremony be delayed until the chapel was fixed and completely cleaned from top to bottom.

The delays put a strain on both Beauty and the Beast. Not on their relationship, as their love was much too secure for that to happen, but on their temperaments. Neither one of them was known for their patience, in spite of Beauty's usually composed appearance.

Surprisingly, it was the Beast who held up better, who showed a calmer demeanour and behaved with more dignity at each delay. He did roar a bit though. Beauty was clearly the more impatient one; she paced around the castle snapping at servants and then apologizing to them, only to snap at them again moments later.

What made the Beast's patience even more remarkable was that they had moved into separate quarters until after the wedding. The Beast also withstood the short period of celibacy far better than Beauty. Every morn the maids found her bed a mess of tangled sheets and tossed pillows, a sure sign that she was having restless nights.

When questioned about his patience, the Beast said simply, "I'm getting a great deal of pleasure from the simple anticipation of our wedding and our lives together, and of course," he grinned wickedly and winked, "our wedding night."

Lady Margarite and Seth, whose ceremony was likewise delayed, were also impatient of course, but they used the time well. They fixed up a small cottage inside the castle grounds for their home. It would be a warm and comfortable place for them to have some privacy and still be near the rest of their family. Working with some of the servants, they cleaned the cottage thoroughly. Then they furnished it with beautifully carved wooden chairs and a table. They had a bed put in one of the bedrooms, with thick mattresses, crisp linens and fur blankets. They hung some tapestries and even found some dishes and cooking utensils. By the day before their wedding, the small cottage was complete. More than that, it was a real home.

The night before the wedding, there was a feast in the great hall of the castle. Everyone was in great spirits now that the waiting was almost at an end. There was a sumptuous meal of roasted venison in thick gravy, green vegetables, hard breads and cheese, sugared fruits, wine and ale. There were even some sweet pastries for dessert. Musicians played throughout the night.

The guards made laughing comments to the Beast, even some jesting remarks about how he was now truly tamed. These remarks failed to have the effect on him they would have had even a month before. Now he simply smiled heartily and agreed with them.

"You should all be so lucky as to be tamed by such a woman," he laughed.

The festivities became too much for Beauty. She strolled into the garden she loved so well, seeking a moment's privacy. She sat there absorbing the fragrance of the flowers on the cool night breeze. She closed her eyes and thought about the Beast.

She remembered how they'd met and how scared of him she was. She thought of their first night together and fully realized for the first time how he had tried very hard to be patient and tender with her, and how foreign to his nature that small bit of patience had been. She relived the details of their lives together so far, each small step leading up to this union. She recalled watching the Beast as he learned wisdom and mercy, and realized how she had also learned patience and persistence. She smiled softly in sweet anticipation as she thought of the wedding night ahead for she realized that she was truly lucky to be marrying for love. She was one of the few maidens she'd ever heard of who had actually had a choice in choosing their life's mate.

Her mother came in search of her. "Is there aught amiss Beauty?" Lady Margarite asked her with concern.

"Nay, Mother," Beauty smiled softly, "all's truly right with me, with the whole world. I just wanted a moment to myself. I was remembering how far we've come together, the Beast and I, and wondering how our future would be."

"It's a little frightening, isn't it? To think that tomorrow you are to be wed, to be a man's wife?" Lady Margarite asked gently.

"It's even more frightening to think of how life would be if I were not to be wed," Beauty said firmly. "Or were we talking about you?"

"I admit I'm nervous, my daughter, but I know I'll be very happy with Seth. Like you, tis the thought of life without him that's truly frightening." Lady Margarite smiled and slipped an arm around her daughter.

The two women hugged each other and talked for a while before they each went to their beds.

Finally, on the third Sunday following the fair and harvest festival, the wedding day arrived. The Beast and Beauty were to be wed in a short, beautiful ceremony in the old stone church. The wedding day was so clear and sunny it was as if the perfect weather was a gift from above.

The Beast wore simple clothes: soft, dove grey, woollen hose, a white linen shirt, a grey doublet, trimmed with gold and embroidered with gold threads, and a grey coat trimmed with soft grey furs. His hair was neatly tied back at the nape of his neck. He stood outside the church and watched his lady arrive.

Beauty was mounted on a pure white horse, with long flowing mane and tail, and refined conformation. She had an ornate tasselled bridle and wide, decorated reins. The saddle itself was a work of art, well made and lavishly decorated.

Beauty's brother, Tom, as the male head of her family, helped her dismount. He took her arm and led her over to present her formally to the Beast. Beauty was breathtaking in a deep rose silk gown, trimmed with white lace at the hem and at the ends of the long, loose sleeves. The gown had a long waist and was cut back in front to reveal a white lace under slip. Small jewels and pearls were sewn around the low, rounded neckline, catching the sun and subtly emphasizing the soft swell of her breasts. A small, gold girdle loosely circled her slender hips and a gold lace cap held her hair back, the ends flowing in a soft mane down her back. A silk scarf covered her hair and the golden cap.

The Beast took her arm from Tom and the pair stood momentarily and faced the crowd of villagers and castle inhabitants. They listened to the cheers of the crowd for a short time before they turned and entered the small church.

The couple stood in front of the friar and recited their marriage vows with only their family and personal servants as witnesses. The Beast's voice was firm and strong as he claimed Beauty for his bride. Beauty recited her vows in softer tones. She sounded loving and calm, but also something else. Awe struck, mayhap? Tom and Nate stood by Lady Margarite, and of course Seth stood nervously on her other side. Sir Richard and Lady Althea stood near the Beast, both of them happy for the brother they barely knew but still loved.

The air sizzled with the heated glances passing between Lady

Althea and Tom. The two barely noticed the ceremony as their eyes hardly ever left each other. Gwyneth and her new husband, Henry, held hands as they watched the wedding. No one in the wedding party noticed the heavily cloaked man watching quietly from the shadows at the side of the church. Sir Gregory, however, kept a close watch on the man.

The stranger had arrived at the church late, having travelled a good distance just to be there. He was still dressed for travel and covered with the dust and dirt of the road. His tired body was stiff and his breathing was still slightly laboured from his hard ride, and he ached for a hot bath and clean clothes but he knew he would not have these things any time soon. He noticed and frowned over the heated glances that passed between Lady Althea and a young man standing in the wedding group. Still, as he watched the friar led the couple through their vows, he was exceedingly happy. The man kept hidden and watched in approval as the marriage was sealed with a tender kiss.

Then the friar united Lady Margarite and Seth in marriage. Lady Margarite was clad in a sky blue gown of the softest velvet. She looked beautiful and radiant, and far too young to be Beauty's mother. Seth was in black hose with a white shirt and a gold tunic. His coat was forest green and set off the colour of his eyes. He looked exceedingly handsome and very proud. This second service was also very short and plain. It was all the couple needed. It was everything.

Both couples were greeted with loud cheers and well wishes from the crowd outside. Some of the well wishes from the plain spoken villagers were rather crude and graphic but obviously well-intentioned. It was only as they prepared to leave the church that the stranger's presence was finally noted. The Beast saw him first. His eyes widened with shock and he quickly knelt on one knee.

"Your Majesty, you honour me," he said humbly, "and please me greatly. I never expected you to be here for my wedding."

At his words, the rest of the wedding party had also dropped to one knee. The startled villagers did likewise.

"Did you not know I would come if I could, Sebastian?" the King gently chided. "Rise, please."

"I had hoped, M'lord, that you would so honour us," the Beast replied. "May I present my bride, Beauty? I mean, Lady Isabella."

"I think Beauty is the right name for her," the King said, smiling as he turned to Beauty. "Please rise, Lady Isabella."

"Your Majesty," Beauty murmured, rising.

"You have made Sir Sebastian, who is very important to me, very happy this day. I have oftentimes wondered if he would ever find true happiness," the King smiled at Beauty and kissed her gently on her cheek. "But now he has learned how to love and for that I am truly grateful to you."

"Thank you, your Majesty," Beauty smiled. "I despaired of ever teaching him how to love after the way he was raised, but gradually the walls surrounding his soul were lowered and I found the true man inside the harsh, bloodthirsty warrior. The man his parents never even knew existed. Tis their loss."

Beauty never heard the soft gasp beside her. She never noticed the slight tightening of the Beast's hand on her arm. She never saw the slight flush on the face of the King. She only heard his soft reply.

"You're very right, Beauty," the King said sadly, "tis their loss. I'm very glad Sir Sebastian has you now. Thank God, he will never be that soulless warrior again."

"Please, Your Majesty, join our wedding feast," Beauty invited, smiling and happy. "It would be a great honour."

"I cannot, Lady Beauty," the King said wearily, "there are many pressing matters at court just now. I just wanted to be at Sir Sebastian's wedding. I promise I'll return in the summer to see the babe." He ignored Beauty's gasp.

"How did you know, Sire?" the Beast asked surprised.

"I've had two wives and countless mistresses," the King smiled wearily. "I know the signs all too well, believe me, I always know."

"Not even my family knew," Beauty whispered.

"Beauty, daughter, doest thou take me for a fool?" Lady Margarite scolded. "Of course I knew. Why else did I work so hard to get you married to this man?"

"Mother, you fought me every step of the way," Beauty protested.

"You constantly harangued the Beast, nagging him in such a shrewish manner. And with me you were even worse, recounting his faults endlessly. How can you say you worked hard for this marriage?"

"That which is forbidden is ever sweeter," Lady Margarite smiled serenely. "Is that not true, Your Majesty? Have you ever seen a maiden who wanted to marry the man her mother and father picked for her? Or does she want the man her mother hates and her father disapproves of?"

"Lady Margarite, your devious nature delights me." The King ignored Beauty and the Beast, who were both speechless.

He turned to the Beast's brother. "Sir Richard, you did a good job in delaying the wedding until your messenger could fetch me for the ceremony," the King laughed. "I bet your brother was almost ready to throttle you."

"He always is, Majesty," Sir Richard pointed out. "Why should he be any different now?"

The King spoke briefly to Lady Margarite and Seth, wishing them a good life together. His eyes narrowed but he did not say a word as he observed the obvious sexual tension between Lady Althea and Tom, except to gently tease Lady Althea.

"I see you managed to get yourself into a dress for this occasion, Lady Althea," he prodded her. "I wonder if you would be so accommodating at your own wedding?"

"Twould depend on who my father picked for me to marry, M'lord," the lady replied tartly. "And how I felt about the man."

"And who is this man who accompanies you today?" the King asked with a seemingly casual tone.

"This is Thomas, Lady Isabella's brother." Lady Althea presented Tom. "Thomas, His Majesty, the King."

"Majesty." Tom knelt.

"Rise, Thomas." The King acknowledged the introduction briefly as his head squire brought over his horse.

Before he left, the King even turned his attention to Gwyneth and Henry.

"Gwyneth is more than a servant to me. She has served my family well for years." He whispered to Henry only halfway in jest, "The day you fail to make her happy is the day I'll have your head."

"Then my head is secure for a long, long time, Majesty, for I love her deeply," Henry told the King proudly.

The King mounted and he and his retainers left quickly. Only Henry knew that they carried a veritable feast with them as they rode away.

In celebration of his wedding, the Beast gifted each village family with a bushel of grain and half a dozen fat hens. There was feasting in the castle with fine rich foods, game meats, sugared fruits, French pastries, and fine wines and ales. In the village there was a more humble feast but they did have venison and plenty of strong, stout ale.

During the wedding feast, Beauty and the Beast were so caught up in their own happiness that they never noticed the absence of Gwyneth and Henry. The lesser servants were also not as silent or as efficient as usual, having been imbibing ale all day, but for once no one noticed or cared.

Soon after the first course of grilled fish, Lady Margarite and her new husband, Seth, vanished. The Beast noticed them slipping away and kissed Beauty's hand, lightly nipping her palm.

"Are ye really hungry, lass?" he growled in her ear. "I myself feel the need for a bed more than the need for mere food."

"I hope M'lord isn't too tired to perform his husbandly duties," Beauty said softly, sliding him a sideways glance. "I heard many a young bride is disappointed on her wedding night, if her groom is not, ahem, up to the task expected of him."

She shrieked joyously as the Beast gathered her up into his arms without a word and headed for the long, massive staircase.

"M'lord! My ladies are supposed to prepare me for you in our chamber," she protested, laughing.

"Your ladies are going to be disappointed," the Beast smiled, kissing her soundly. "Besides, the ones who would perform that service, Claire, Lady Althea, your lady mother and Gwyneth are all otherwise occupied. Wouldst you really want to summon them now?"

"Nay, M'lord. And the men who are waiting to help you?" Beauty asked him. "Nate, Tom, Seth and Sir Richard?"

"You know well where Nate, Tom and Seth are," the Beast replied, becoming slightly winded from carrying her up the long, steep stairs, "and Sir Richard was very taken with the maid serving him at dinner. The pretty, young one with the large bosom. I don't think he'll miss us."

"Since when did you notice the maid's bosom?" Beauty asked suspiciously.

"Since I followed his eyes and saw what he gazed upon," the Beast replied, dropping Beauty on the bed.

"'Tis a good answer, M'lord husband." Beauty reached up for him.

"I'm not a stupid man, Milady wife." He leaned over to kiss her soundly before joining her on the bed.

They rolled on the bed kissing with all the joy in their souls. Beauty's cap was discarded and her golden girdle soon hit the floor. The Beast's long silky hair was quickly freed from its confinement and his coat was quickly discarded. Beauty stood and the Beast helped her remove her gown and the shift she wore under it. She watched as he quickly shed his tunic and shirt. She was amused but also impatient as he had trouble removing the tights over his erection.

The Beast noted her amusement and remarked wryly, "Well, at least you know I'm well up to the task you expect from me."

There was a new bathtub waiting there, readied for their use. It was a wedding gift from the Beast to Beauty. The new tub was brass and had been especially made for Beauty and the Beast. The most interesting thing about the new tub was its size. It was much bigger than the regular bathtub. It was big enough to hold them both with a bit more comfort. It had been filled with steamy water, with fragrant herbs floating on top, undoubtedly meant for Beauty. On the small table beside the tub there was a bar of rich scented soap, a flask of wine and a tray of cheeses and fresh fruit. There was also a small jar with a tiny amount of a red liquid in it.

"Shall we bathe first, M'lord?" Beauty asked, suddenly quiet. "Before we go to bed?"

"If you wish, Milady. There are many pleasures to be found in bathing together," the Beast grinned wickedly, "as you well know."

They took a long bath together, gently soaping and exploring each other's bodies. They fed each other bites of the cheese and fruit, and shared a goblet of the wine. The Beast noted the small bottle and examined the contents. He laughed aloud.

"What is it?" Beauty asked curiously.

"One of the women put some blood for the sheets in here, just in case you're not a virgin." He laughed anew.

"Why would anyone do that?" Beauty missed the humour. "They all know I'm no virgin. The whole village knows."

"It's tradition," the Beast explained. "Contrary to what your mother probably told you, many brides are not virgins on their wedding nights. Thank God for chickens; they give their lives so that proud grooms can hang a bloody sheet out the window on the morning after a wedding. Of course, they are also invited to be a part of the wedding feast."

"You mean it's something everyone knows but no one admits to?" Beauty asked.

"Sure," the Beast nuzzled her neck, "but in my case, I know you were pure when I first took you. I know not why but I saved the bloody sheet from that night."

"So let's hang the old sheet out the window and shock the shire," Beauty giggled, putting aside the wine and taking up a cloth and the soap.

"And everyone will think it's just chicken blood," the Beast laughed. "If they only knew." Then he sobered, "I don't think I'll hang out a sheet at all. I'm more than satisfied with your purity. Tis no one else's concern."

The Beast was soon in ecstasy as Beauty soaped his chest, her slippery hands moving ever lower. He moaned aloud as she brought him to a climax with her hands alone. He wanted to do the same for her but she held him back until she had finished the sensual cleansing of every inch of his magnificent body. She soaped and rinsed his hair before she let him begin on her.

He started slowly, or so it seemed. He spent long minutes just soaping the fingers of her right hand. Just her fingers, she thought, amazed as she felt the arousal forming in her feminine parts. Heaven help me when he gets to my breasts. He moved slowly from her fingers to her wrist. She felt the pulse racing there under his gentle touch. Slowly he moved up her arm, her stomach quivering slightly as he gently soaped her elbow before moving further up her arm to her shoulder. She found it hard to believe there was another whole arm still to go. At this rate he'll kill me, she thought.

Luckily the cooling bathwater saved her. Not completely of course, as the Beast did soap every inch of her lovely body and wash her long hair. He did spend a short eternity with his fingers playing her, bringing her to a screaming climax.

It was just lucky that the water cooled enough to speed the process along a bit, otherwise she would never have lasted through the bath. They sat back to back from each other, naked, on the fur rug in front of the fire and dried each other's hair with the course cloth towels.

Once again, Beauty took the lead, something that still surprised and delighted the Beast. Turning around to face the Beast's back, she discarded her towel and leaned over to kiss his neck. He turned to face her as she continued, nibbling gently before trailing her mouth lower. She licked and suckled his nipples, traced his abdominal muscles with her tongue and laved his navel. Then she got sexy. Her damp, silken hair trailed across his stomach as she took him into her mouth and loved him. She used her lips, tongue and gently, her teeth to give him pleasure.

Every time she felt him approaching his satisfaction, she slowed her motions, prolonging his sweet agony just a bit longer. Finally, the inevitable could be delayed no longer and she kept licking him until the last of the shudders left his body. Then she rose up and kissed him and he tasted himself on her mouth.

When he could stand, he rose and pulled her to her feet and led her over to the bed. With Beauty still standing beside the bed, the Beast went down on his knees to kiss her as intimately as she had him. In his mind it was symbolic, this act of going down onto his knees before her. Before this he had knelt only in church, as a sign of respect for God, or in front of the King, as a sign of respect for him.

Now he knelt in front of his wife, giving her all the sensual love she could ever want but also giving her his personal sign of his highest respect.

After Beauty climaxed, he stood and kissed her. Then he explained why he had taken her that way, and what it had meant to him. That explanation and his simple statement of love were the best gift he had ever given her. Finally, they sank onto the bed and the real honeymoon began.

They slept very little that night. They made love over and over again. They made love reverently, passionately and tenderly; they even made love laughing together. They cuddled each other, tickled each other and wrestled with each other.

They tried every position they could think of and somehow wound up in a few positions they didn't know they could even get into. At one point, when the Beast dozed off, Beauty idly stroked his back and firm buttocks. Failing to get the response she desired, she pretended fury. She gave him a sharp slap on his taut buttocks, then another.

"Wake up knave and service me!" She spanked him playfully but smartly until with a low growl he rolled over and pulled her atop him.

"Vixen!" he roared in mock anger. "How dare you presume to spank me! I am your lord and master."

"M'lord was sleeping when I required his services," Beauty told him. "'Tis most unseemly for a man to sleep when his lady desires him so greatly."

"Milady is very greedy tonight. She has worn me out," the Beast teased, even as his body gave very solid evidence to the contrary. "Canst a man get some sleep?"

"M'lord Beast can have all the sleep he wants," Beauty replied as she straddled and rode him, "in another fifty or sixty years."

They awoke the next morning stiff and still tired, but very, very happy. They made love with exquisite tenderness before they dressed and went downstairs in search of food.

At breakfast they noticed that Lady Margarite and Seth, who had joined them in the great hall, seemed likewise to be somewhat the worse for wear except for their silly grins.

Gwyneth and Henry were nowhere to be seen at all, at least until it was time for Sir Richard and his retinue, including Althea, to leave. To be truthful, Sir Richard's departure was delayed from the scheduled time. Lady Althea was nowhere to be found. Eventually she came out of the castle, disconcerted and dishevelled, and hurried to mount her horse. There was no grin on her face. Her lips were pursed so tightly that they probably ached from the strain.

Beauty, the Beast and Sir Richard all noticed her tense mood but no one in the group had the nerve to ask her what was wrong. Tom never showed his face until the leave-taking was over and every last bit of dust from the horses' hooves raised by the departure of Sir Richard's great entourage had settled completely back down to the road. When he finally did come out of the castle his mood was as black as Lady Althea's.

The honeymoon continued long past the wedding night. Not just for Beauty and the Beast, but for all three of the newly married couples. Most of the time, Beauty and the Beast kept to themselves, content with making love endlessly and planning their future. They talked of the coming child and of other children they hoped to have. They made hopeful plans for their lives together. They even spoke at length of their plans for the village and the people who lived there. They had dinners with Lady Margarite and Seth fairly often and Beauty gently teased her mother because she and Seth always seemed to retire early.

"Are you so eager to go to bed because you're getting old, Mother?" Beauty asked with her eyes wide. "Or because you've learned you're not so old after all?"

"I'm not so very old, am I daughter?" Lady Margarite told Beauty smiling widely.

"You're not old at all, Mother, you have a beauty and youthfulness that's eternal." Beauty kissed her mother goodnight and watched her walk away with Seth.

She turned to the Beast with tears in her eyes. "I'm so happy for her. I thought she would never know joy or love again."

The Beast enfolded her in his arms. "Then I'm happy for her and for you too. Your happiness is very important to me."

"As is yours to me," Beauty whispered against his lips.

Beauty and the Beast even sat down to dinner once or twice with Gwyneth and Henry. It was a novel sensation for the two servants, to be waited on and treated as if they were valued guests, but they enjoyed it. That is, they tried to enjoy it but Henry kept jumping up and going into the kitchen to check on the progress of the meal. Gwyneth's eyes followed the servants around the room as they served the meal, and Beauty knew that those servants would soon get a long lecture about their manners and the quality of their service.

The Beast trained with the guards enough to stay in shape but most of the training sessions were held under the direction of Tom. It was very arduous training as Tom was well aware that the villain Wolford was still at large, even though he had not been spotted for some time. It did not help the other guards that he was also in a black mood.

The guards suffered from many aches and pains for it, but they were very well trained. Beauty's brother turned his foul temper into hard work and he trained furiously and made sure all the other guards trained hard too.

The only other time Beauty and the Beast were apart was when the Beast went into the village to speak with Tom Two, who had become both an overseer for the Beast and a spokesman for the villagers. Beauty usually spent her time away from the Beast wisely, sewing little baby clothes, dealing with the castle servants, walking in the garden, and talking quietly with her mother and Gwyneth.

Other than these meetings, the newlyweds frolicked with each other almost continuously. They rode into the woods and made love in the grass. They returned the horses to the barn and made love in the sweet smelling hay. They ate dinner in the great hall and made love on the dining table. Then they went to bed and made love all night long.

Chapter Fifteen

The brisk but pleasant fall weather soon turned into a bitterly cold winter. In spite of the extremely harsh weather, with its excessive cold and deep snow, there was a real sense of peace and contentment both in the village and the castle. The crops, although not overly abundant, had been sufficient to keep hunger and starvation at bay for both the serfs and the castle inhabitants.

There were still some problems with thieves, but the problems had decreased a great deal. Evidently most of the roaming bands of raiders had finally learned the harsh lesson that this was a village to avoid at all costs.

There was one lingering problem however; there were reports that Wolford was still alive, robbing and attacking both peasants and the nobility across the land. The Beast kept a watchful eye and had many men out searching for the bloodthirsty bastard, but his exact location remained elusive.

The Beast had a powerful reputation as a lord who ruled the village firmly but also guarded it very well and protected his villagers fiercely indeed. The villagers began to feel safe and were grateful to the Beast for his protection. They no longer felt any of the old resentment towards him.

The villagers not only had enough food, they even had plenty of firewood and peat moss for once. The Beast and his men had helped them repair their small huts and fix their roofs. For the first winter in many years, the serfs were able to keep themselves warm, to be moderately but adequately fed, and even to be relatively safe and happy.

The guards trained in the barn or main hall of the castle using straw targets mounted on the far wall as archery targets, and moved the tables to find room for fencing with each other. On any days that were even a little bit warmer, the guards trained outside, sometimes in deep snow.

After all, the Beast reminded them sternly, when they grumbled about the cold, not all battles were fought on warm, sunny days. Still, the castle frequently rang with the clash of swords, and the servants were loath to enter the great hall without warning the guards of their presence lest an arrow fly past their heads.

Lady Margarite and Seth spent much of their time in their own cottage but they managed to be with Beauty and the Beast often too. Lady Margarite enjoyed sitting with Beauty talking and sewing things for the coming baby and planning for the future. Margarite was overjoyed for her daughter. She had come to adore the Beast and was exceedingly happy with Beauty's choice of a husband, as she was with her own choice. She had stopped haranguing and nagging the Beast and all the castle inhabitants. She now had the look of a well-loved woman, content and joyful. The coming grandchild was a token to Margarite, of a happy future for her daughter and her family.

Gwyneth and Henry were likewise extremely happy with each other and with their lives as man and wife. They continued in their jobs, serving Beauty and the Beast, even though they had both been offered retirement to honoured positions as members of the household. They were grateful for the honour but preferred to work for their living. Still, they did enjoy a status far elevated from the usual servants.

Nate and Claire continued to spend most of their time together. Frequently they were seen holding hands or kissing each other with tender, innocent kisses.

Gradually Claire's emotional scars faded and she started to become the happy lass she was meant to be. She grew prettier as she lost the haunted look she had since coming to the castle. She had come very far with her efforts to polish her speech and comportment, now seeming to be a very refined young lady of some rank. She continued to learn the basic duties of castle management and household tasks from Beauty. Her reading and writing, along with her math skills had improved dramatically.

Nate spent his time, when he was away from Claire, training with the guards. He was very skilful with a sword and a more than adequate archer. He had grown much taller and began to fill out, showing signs of the man he was soon to become.

In fact, the only three people in the castle who were not entirely content were Tom, Beauty and the Beast. It wasn't that there was anything wrong exactly, it was just a few of the minor things.

Tom had been in a foul temper since Lady Althea's departure, only occasionally showing signs of being his old self. The castle staff soon learned to avoid him whenever possible. Beauty took him aside and lectured him sternly on his rude behaviour, an effort that made him act more civil outwardly but utterly failed to improve his mood. It seemed only the return of Lady Althea would accomplish that deed.

The Beast was still frequently demanding and autocratic with everyone even though he had learned how to show his loving nature and how to treat the serfs with wisdom and mercy; even how to get their obedience and loyalty without the use of force or brutality. When his impatience was pointed out to him, usually by Beauty, he would shrug and shake his head ruefully.

For her part, Beauty was awkward and uncomfortable with her pregnancy as her size grew larger. She suffered long bouts of morning sickness, almost constant backaches, swollen and sore ankles, and was very uncomfortable when she slept. She was often moody, sometimes as moody as the Beast. She was very tired of sitting by the fire and sewing. She truly loved the Beast and she valued the infant within her body but she would be greatly pleased when it arrived. She longed to hold the baby in her arms, not within her body.

The Beast also looked forward to the birth of his first child with joy and pride. His only complaint was with Beauty's suffering and strange moods, but that was simply because he was often the target of her temper when a bad mood hit her. He never knew when she would be amorous, angry or burst into tears at the mere sight of him. She also drove him crazy demanding odd combinations of food at strange hours of the day and night. He too would be very happy when the child finally arrived.

There was one good thing about that cold winter in addition to the anticipation of their child; Beauty and the Beast found out the frigid nights were perfect for cuddling up together. They spent long hours talking quietly in front of the fire in the great hall or the smaller more private fire in their bedchamber, and they spent even longer hours entwined with each other in their bed. As her figure grew more and more misshapen Beauty was shy and uncertain about how the Beast viewed the changes in her body, but he reassured her in the best way possible.

He showed her through his actions that he still found her highly desirable. He loved her with exquisite tenderness and care. He repeated this demonstration of his love as often as was humanly possible. The Beast made love to her with extreme passion and delicate touches until she grew too large and even the tenderest lovemaking became too uncomfortable for her.

Even after that he stayed by her side, tenderly holding her and often rubbing her back or stomach. He loved to place his hands on the mound of her stomach and feel the babe within kick.

If the Beast was too busy to spend time by her side at certain periods throughout the worst months of the winter, Beauty would sit in front of the fire in the great hall with her mother and Gwyneth. The three women gossiped and sewed tiny clothes for the coming baby.

One day Lady Margarite sat beside Beauty with a bemused look on her face. She said nothing but just sat there holding a blanket she was supposedly sewing for her coming grandchild and stared off into space, grinning a silly grin. Beauty herself was staring sightlessly at a tiny nightshirt in the throes of one of her own mood swings, but finally her mother's strange frame of mind registered with her.

"Is something wrong?" Beauty asked her mother with concern. "You seem to be in a very odd mood today, Mother. Is aught amiss? Is it Seth?"

"Seth? No. What could be wrong with Seth?" her mother replied absently, smiling gently. "Seth is perfect, he's a wonderful husband."

"So he makes you happy?" Beauty probed.

"Of course, Isabella," Lady Margarite smiled, "he's a wonderful husband. I never dreamed I'd be so happy again."

"Then what's wrong?" Beauty almost yelled. "Mother, you are acting very strange indeed."

"I'm just a little surprised, stunned really. I mean, I didn't even think it was still possible... " Lady Margarite muttered, "and I'm really not sure."

"Mother! Speak out, I implore you," Beauty begged.

"I think I'm... " Lady Margarite began then she stopped completely.

"You're what?" Beauty grabbed her mother by the shoulders.

"With child! I'm with child!" Lady Margaret shouted. "I'm far too old to be carrying a child, of course. It's ridiculous for a woman of my age to be pregnant, but I think I am. I'm sure of it. Almost."

"Mother! That's wonderful news." Beauty hugged her flustered mother. "How can you say you're too old? You're not yet two score years. Just think, we'll have our babies about the same time. Seth must be so proud."

"I haven't told him yet. I wasn't really sure," Lady Margarite smiled softly, "and I'm a little afraid of how he's going to react. We never talked about my having another child."

"He'll react with joy, love and pride, Mother, for that's what he feels for you," Beauty grinned, even as tears of delight formed in her eyes. "We'd better keep up with our sewing. It seems we now have a much larger task facing us than first we anticipated."

Lady Margarite grinned back knowingly. "We have plenty of time, my daughter. In fact, before it's over, it may well seem like an eternity."

"True, but when we feel tired or our bodies ache, we have something we can do about it," Beauty laughed. "We can pester the men and make their lives a living hell."

"They deserve it, 'tis true," Lady Margarite laughed back. "They have the pleasure and we get the rest of it."

"Well, to be fair Mother, we get some of the pleasure too," Beauty laughed.

Just then the Beast entered the room. "Are you two ladies planning something? You have mischief in your faces."

The two women looked at him, then at each other, and laughed aloud. The Beast stood there looking puzzled and helpless, like any other man when confounded by the women in his life.

After looking to her mother for approval, Beauty told the Beast, "Mother was just telling me that she's with child."

The Beast was surprised but hugged his mother-in-law with warmth and joy. "What does Seth say?"

"I haven't told him yet, Sebastian. Do me a favour and don't mention the baby to him until he tells you about it." Margarite's voiced dropped before continuing, "I'm a bit worried about his reaction. Imagine a baby at my age!"

"You will always be young." The Beast kissed her cheek. "Do not worry about Seth's reaction. He'll be very pleased, Margarite, I assure you."

The next day Seth was running all over the castle telling the staff and the inhabitants his happy news. For that day, he was the proudest man alive. He and the Beast hugged each other and sat by the fire talking about their wives and the coming babes.

The touching scene was repeated almost five weeks later, this time with Gwyneth. One day, Beauty and Lady Margarite found Gwyneth sitting by the fire in the great hall. She was staring off into a blank wall with a silly grin on her face. For the first time in Beauty's memory Gwyneth failed to rise as she entered the room. In fact, Gwyneth seemed not to even notice the two women at all. She just continued to sit there and stare at nothing, grinning like a fool.

After a moment, Beauty and her mother just looked at each other and smiled, communicating in that mysterious way women have, the way that doesn't require spoken words.

"Gwyneth, do you have news for us?" Lady Margarite asked gently.

Gwyneth turned to the two women still wearing that silly, dazed grin and whispered, "I'm with child."

They hugged the woman who was more friend than servant. All three women shed tears of joy. All three men strutted as though they were proud roosters.

"We'd better warn Tom," Beauty quipped, "this is getting a bit absurd. It seems to be a pattern."

"I'm not saying a word to Thomas! He's been such a grouchy bear lately. However I am relieved Lady Althea is back at court. Even he would have a problem getting her with child at that distance," Lady Margarite said. "Although she would make a good bride for Thomas."

"I agree, she is one woman who could keep him in his place and make him happy. There is someone else we'd better warn to be careful." Beauty paused. "The other one we had better warn is Nate."

She was only half teasing. "The lad is far more open to love than any of us. He already stands by Claire's side with all the tenderness and support of a grown man, a husband. Indeed, he is almost a man, for all his foolish and childish ways. I do believe he truly loves the girl but nevertheless, he is far too young and she is still suffering too much from her ordeal for them to marry."

"I was the same age as Claire when I married your father, and Tom was born when I was barely fifteen," Lady Margarite pointed out. "So his age, while young, is not going to stop him from loving Claire or prevent him from making any foolish mistakes."

"So Mother, which of us gets to talk to Nate?" Beauty asked. "And make sure he knows what he's doing."

"How about Sebastian?" Lady Margarite suggested. "'Tis better if the subject is discussed man to man."

"But Mother, who gets to approach the Beast and give him this task?" Beauty asked.

"Why Beauty, of course that part of it falls to you." Her mother grinned wickedly.

As it turned out, Beauty wasn't sure who had the worst of it. She found it difficult to explain just why she wanted the Beast to talk to Nate. The Beast completely failed to see a problem.

"The lad's feeling his age, 'tis a passing phase, and he'll soon find something or someone other than Claire to interest him." The Beast dismissed the women's concerns.

"But M'lord, don't you think it's strange that we're all pregnant at the same time? All three of us? 'Tis almost uncanny," Beauty asked him, frustrated. "We just want to make sure that this strange circumstance goes no further."

"No, there's nothing uncanny here. You're all newlyweds with loving husbands. Husbands well able to get you with child and apparently willing to do whatever is necessary to achieve that end. We've all succeeded. What's so strange there?" the Beast replied. "Tis merely a coincidence."

"M'lord Beast, I found out about Nate's romance on the exact same day that I found out about Mother's and Gwyneth's. Now they're both expecting. It seems to be an omen. Please, M'lord, speak to the lad," Beauty pleaded, almost working herself into a nervous frenzy.

Because he had learned that when Beauty was in a mood like this she was not to be swayed, the Beast reluctantly agreed to talk to the lad. However it turned out to be a total disaster. The Beast was better versed in battle strategy than in dealing with such delicate matters as teenage romance. He felt uncomfortable and unsure of what to say. He got nervous and stammered, feeling embarrassed for one of the few times in his life. He decided that he didn't like the feeling. For his part, Nate just laughed aloud and told the Beast not to worry.

"I promised not to do anything to hurt Claire, and I will not," the lad told the Beast. "Tell Beauty everything is fine. I know what I'm doing."

For some reason that statement completely failed to reassure Beauty.

During the deepest part of the winter Beauty began to find herself too heavy and uncomfortable to enjoy having sex with the Beast. It was then that the Beast found another complaint with his life. His problem was that he could not make love with Beauty. He could hold her, comfort her, cuddle with her, love her and desire her, but he just couldn't poke her. The poor warlord was simply horny.

At the worst of the winter the knight worked long and hard in the barn training with his men. Every night he went to bed next to Beauty completely exhausted but it never seemed to help. Beauty's pregnancy dragged on slowly, for both of them. The end seemed to be an elusive goal, in sight, but failing to come any closer.

As the winter finally began to ease and the first signs of spring began to show, Beauty's baby dropped within her. She was very uncomfortable and awkward. One day she was even more uncomfortable than usual. She had slight twinges off and on all day and her back ached constantly. That evening, shortly after dinner, she went into labour. The pains were already coming with some regularity before her water broke.

The Beast assisted her up the stairs and helped her change into a loose shift and a robe. He called for a servant to build up the fires and to fetch Gwyneth and Lady Margarite.

Beauty's mother and Gwyneth arrived quickly and soon shuffled the Beast out of the room. They examined her and told her she wasn't progressing as swiftly as they would have hoped. They suggest that she walk around a bit. The Beast held her arm and gently led her up and down the upstairs corridor of the castle for about an hour, talking all the while about the coming child. Finally her labour pains began to come closer together and with more force. Beauty took to the bed.

The Beast stayed by her side for a while, letting her grasp his hand and curse at him during one of the pains and then relax and speak of her love for him after the pain was over. If he hadn't been so worried, the whole business would have intrigued him greatly. He was shocked at the crudity of the words coming out of her mouth and bemused by the total switch in her personality when she turned tender and loving. He really wanted to stay by her side throughout the whole ordeal and comfort her during her labour but Beauty's mother finally ushered him firmly out of the room.

He found himself relegated to the fireside in the great hall with Tom, Seth and Henry and a few of the guards. Nate and Claire stood together in the corner, almost unnoticed, and watched the men.

The men plied the Beast with stout ale and paced with him; Seth and Henry thinking of their own babies soon to come, and of their own wives soon to face this ordeal. Every time Beauty gave a scream the Beast started for the stairs and the men struggled mightily to restrain him.

Upstairs, Beauty laboured long into the night, almost until dawn with her mother and Gwyneth by her side tending to her. They wiped her brow when she sweated with the strain of her pains. They told her when to push and when to relax and catch her breath. It was almost dawn before the baby's head appeared in the birth canal. Lady Margarite eased the shoulders out of the tight opening. The rest of the baby followed quickly. The small baby needed no prompting to begin squalling vigorously. Lady Margarite handed the baby to Gwyneth who gently cleaned the baby while she tended to her daughter.

"Tis a lad, Beauty," Lady Margarite teased with a smiled. "He's quite a good size. I already know he'll be a very arrogant and demanding brute just like his sire."

"Then I'm most pleased," Beauty said, reaching for her son. "For I love his sire very much."

The two women quickly handed the baby to Beauty who began to nurse him. At the sound of the baby's cries, the men could restrain the Beast no more. He charged up the stairs and into the bedchamber to see his wife and son.

As the Beast held his infant son who they had decided to name James, Beauty knew one thing: The infant had finally completed the task she'd only begun. The baby boy had tamed the mighty Beast. Beauty wept with joy at the sight of her proud husband holding his child with so much love and tenderness.

As spring blossomed fully, Beauty and the Beast spent long hours together with the infant nestled between them. In contrast to his own childhood, the Beast was a tender and loving father. He couldn't bear to be away from the boy. His greatest joy it seemed, was watching Beauty as she nursed the baby. Even changing dirty diapers was a chore the Beast took on with a basic joy.

For the first time he pitied his parents that they knew no such joy. He now realized that they lost much of the joy they could have found with their son, and he lost much with them.

Slowly, Beauty's slim figure began to return. She aided things along by eating a bit less, riding her mare and making sure she took a long walk every day. The spring days were almost idyllic. The only problem the couple had was that the Beast was afraid to make love with Beauty. He felt compelled to give Beauty plenty of time to recover from the strain of childbirth.

Finally the day came when Beauty knew it was time. She wanted her warrior in her arms again and she wanted him most fiercely. She set the scene carefully in their bedchamber with fragrantly scented candles and dark Spanish wine. She wore a shift of the most delicate lace, a gossamer bit of fluff that revealed and titillated more than it concealed. She made sure the baby was well fed and got him to sleep before she sent for her husband.

It worked of course, as the Beast was more than willing to be seduced by Beauty, and Beauty was as saucy and seductive a vixen as he had ever seen. She smiled at him with a cunning look in her eyes and then practically ripped the clothes from his body. She only smiled sweetly when he returned the favour and shredded her gown from her body. He made sure she was ready for him, moist and open, then with a very firm thrust and a few preliminaries, he entered her and ended the long drought. He did try to be careful and gentle with her but Beauty herself made it almost impossible, rising up to meet his thrusts.

At one point, when the Beast was being tender sliding in and out of Beauty's velvet sheath with exquisite slowness and almost torturous gentleness, she wrapped her legs around his waist and drummed her heels sharply on his bare buttocks, urging him on.

"Come on, my love. Ride me," she whispered, even as she kicked his firm bottom sharply. "Take me there, faster and harder. Now."

Not so surprisingly, this ended things dramatically and rather quickly.

"You kicked me! That's what I get for trying to be gentle with you. Thank God you're not wearing spurs," the Beast jested.

"Maybe next time." Beauty kissed him, beginning the passion all over again.

After that night the drought was truly over. Indeed Beauty and the Beast made love every night and many times during the brisk spring days. They made love in chairs, on tables and on the thick fur rug in front of the fireplace. The unspoken watchword for the two of them became "whenever the baby is asleep." As they had before Beauty's mother came to live in the castle, the staff soon learned to knock and await an invitation before entering a room.

When the Beast was occupied with his men, Beauty stayed with her mother and Gwyneth. They were both getting large and uncomfortable with their pregnancies, and were both eager to see their babes arrive.

One night Beauty turned to the Beast before sleep claimed her and asked, "M'lord, do you know what day this is?"

"Nay, Beauty." The Beast was puzzled. "I mean, I do know the date but cannot put any special meaning to it."

"Men are such fools!" Beauty fumed. "'Tis exactly one year since I stood in front of you and bargained for my brother's life."

"Beauty. I'm sorry I forgot the date." The Beast kissed her gently but with a growing passion. "But I remember well the day. It was the luckiest day of my life, even if I didn't know it at the time."

"I remember stripping myself bare and standing there naked, petrified but hoping that you'd find me desirable enough to spare Tom." Beauty stroked his chest, flicking her thumb over his already tight nipples. "Thank God you were merciful that day."

"I was hardly merciful." The Beast moved over her. "But it turned out well, and I promise to spend the rest of my life making sure you never look back on this date with any regret."

It was a long time before sleep claimed them. Then, as they slept soundly, the Beast heard a timid knock at the chamber door. They were awakened with the news that Lady Margarite was in labour.

Beauty kissed her warrior before she slid out of bed and dressed quickly. She bade the servant who had awakened her to fetch Gwyneth. Together the two women made their way to the small cottage where Beauty's mother was indeed, in full labour.

The Beast followed quickly. Henry joined him as he stopped to rouse Nate and Tom. The men tended to Seth, sitting with him and plying him with stout ale. They tried to keep a conversation going and joke with Seth but he was too worried to listen. The Beast watched as his servant paced and worried, and he realized that indeed they had the same feelings, worries and hopes in spite of the differences in their stations in life. Even though Seth was over fifty years of age, this was to be his first child.

After three children, Margarite knew well how and when to push. With Gwyneth and Beauty beside her, she delivered a daughter in only a few short hours. Seth was truly beside himself with pride as he held his tiny daughter. They named the infant girl Alaina.

The night after Alaina was born Beauty went up to nurse James before putting him to sleep, hoping that he would give her a long time with the Beast before demanding more attention from her. However as soon as she opened the door to his nursery, she knew the full meaning of terror. Wolford was there, as evil as a man could be, looming over the crib and reaching for her babe. He held a dagger in his hand. Beauty let out a scream that was cut off as soon as Wolford threatened to harm the babe.

"Yer ladyship," he said with a great deal of sarcasm, "if you want this squalling brat to live you will be silent. You will bring me all your jewels, all your gold coins and you will make sure no alarm is raised. Any sign of yer husband or any of his men and the babe dies."

Beauty fell to the floor, pleading for the babe's life. It seemed like hours, but it was only minutes before he yelled at her. "Cease that wailing, slut. Fetch the jewels and be quick or you will have to bury the brat in pieces!"

Numbly, Beauty nodded her agreement. "Do not harm my child, I beg of you." Tears were streaming down her face as she rose from the floor. "I will do all you ask."

"Hurry about it, then," Wolford sneered, "and I may just let you and your babe live."

Wolford had made one seriously grave blunder. He failed to realize how close the Beast kept to Beauty. To his mind a real man would be down in the great hall, drinking and fondling one of the maids, not waiting nearby while his wife nursed a baby. He never knew the Beast had heard Beauty's short scream. Beauty turned to leave, to fetch the coins and jewels that would buy her precious babe's life, although leaving him in the room with Wolford was the hardest thing she had ever done. She walked out the door filled with dread.

As soon as Beauty left the room, Wolford put the babe down; it was a fatal error. The Beast had indeed heard the aborted scream and instinctively went into action; he had sent a servant to quickly fetch his sword and waited right outside the chamber door, listening as Wolford ordered Beauty to bring him her jewels. When Beauty passed him in the hall he motioned her to be silent, and despite her fear she obeyed, trusting her husband.

He knew he had to chance a rescue, whatever the risk, because he knew Wolford. The man would not leave either Beauty or the babe alive. He would kill them both, the Beast was sure of it. The only question to the Beast's mind was if he would take the time to rape Beauty before killing her.

There was a crack where Beauty had failed to completely close the door, and through it the Beast saw Wolford drop the infant carelessly back into the crib, as though the infant was of no import. Immediately he rushed through the doorway, his sword in hand. He moved so quickly and silently that he caught Wolford by surprise. He put himself firmly between the infant and Wolford. Beauty rushed in behind her husband and grabbed the babe, taking him to safety.

"Give up now, Wolford," the Beast said. "You have already lost all."

Wolford was a coward at heart. Seeing the Beast speed towards him sword in hand with only a dagger in his own hand, he knew he could not win. He also knew what the Beast had done to Gerrin, so he offered little resistance.

Tom and a few of the men came rushing up the stairs in time to see the Beast run Wolford through. As the man dropped to the floor, bleeding badly but not mortally wounded, they grabbed him up.

"Take that piece of trash and drop him from the castle wall," the Beast ordered, "into the pigsty."

The men carried Wolford out to his fate. They never saw the one sight that would have astonished them to the core. They never saw the Beast's knees buckle or the tears running down his face. They never saw Beauty and the Beast clinging to each other long into the night, taking solace in the presence of the babe and comfort from each other.

By morn, the Beast and Beauty had both regained their normal demeanours, joyful that their babe had been spared. As well, there was no trace of the bloody, broken body in the pigsty near the foot of the castle wall.

A few days later Beauty and her mother sat by the fire holding their infants and planning the future they'd like the infants to have. They gently teased Gwyneth about the baby she had coming. The month moved slowly along, especially for Gwyneth and Henry. The two women, well pleased with their infants, were eager for Gwyneth to have hers too.

"Just think Gwyneth, only a short time more and you won't be able to sleep a whole night through," Beauty teased the former maid.

"I thought it was failing to sleep the whole night through that got me into this situation," Gwyneth shot back with a smile.

Finally, just over three weeks after the birth of Lady Alaina, Gwyneth felt her pains begin. The by-now familiar ritual was repeated. The women, Beauty and Lady Margarite, tended to Gwyneth, the woman who was their maid and so much more. The men, the Beast, Seth, Tom and Henry sat by the fire downstairs, paced and drank ale. Both groups thought their tasks were highly important, although the men were hard pressed to explain of exactly what import getting the father-to-be very drunk actually was. Gwyneth gave birth to a son, a boy she named Hank, for her husband. She was the only one of the three women to have ever lost a child to death, so the others really couldn't understand why she wept, in spite of her joy.

About a week later, the three women sat with their babies in the great hall. Gwyneth was nursing Hank, Lady Margarite was changing Alaina, and little James was asleep on the fur rug spread in front of the fire. The men joined them, sitting next to their wives and watching the children that had become the central focus of their lives.

Their quiet days were about to come to an end. They knew it as soon as a messenger came running in, breathing heavily. He caught his breath as soon as possible and gave the Beast his message.

"M'lord, there is a large group of riders coming this way. It appears to be an enormous group, almost an army. I could not be sure who they were, whether they be friend or foe. I left another guard to keep watch for further details but I felt it important to get the message to you as soon as possible." The man drank deeply and gratefully from the tankard of ale the Beast pressed into his hand.

"Finish the ale then alert the men," the Beast ordered, "and have them ready themselves."

In a short while, the second messenger came in from his outpost. "M'lord, I believe it's the King coming here."

The castle was thrown into an instant uproar. Servants were put to work polishing and cleaning everything in sight. The upstairs bedrooms were aired and cleaned, with fresh crisp linen put onto the beds. Henry headed for the kitchen where he set about cooking a feast fit for the King and his men.

Claire and a servant lass were given charge of the babies as Gwyneth, Lady Margarite and Beauty made sure all was in readiness before they quickly dressed in their finest clothes and got ready for the King's arrival.

The Beast went to the men's quarters to warn the guards to put on their best chainmail and clean tunics. He also ordered them to make sure their shields and swords were highly polished. Nate stayed by Claire's side, helping her care for the babies.

Tom merely waited, silently watching and hoping that the King had brought Sir Richard with him. Sir Richard and his men, including one who was no man at all, but a small, pretty, female soldier who held his heart.

Chapter Sixteen

Beauty and the Beast had been together just over a year when the King finally came for his long-awaited visit. It was about one year and three months to the day from the fateful spring afternoon when Beauty had offered herself to the Beast to save her brother's life. It had been a spring of turmoil and tears, followed by a summer of passion and strife. By the fall, the strife had ended and a lifetime of love and passion stretched out ahead of the couple, happiness just waiting to be grasped. By the time of the King's visit, Beauty and the Beast had grasped that happiness and begun to claim it as their own and to spread their joy to others. The infant, James, was barely over four months old.

There were still many conflicts, as there always will be when two such differing people come together. The couple always resolved their small disputes with passion and love; of course, sometimes they also added a little yelling and threw the occasional tankard.

Beauty and the Beast both worked hard to maintain their passion and to nurture their love. Because of their effort, their love continued to grow. The infant, James, was raised with great affection and tenderness by both his parents. The natural way the Beast took to fatherhood was something that Beauty considered a minor miracle, especially when she considered the cruel and heartless manner in which he himself had been raised.

When the King arrived for his visit, he was greeted with honour and love. There was great feasting and celebration. Since the King had announced his intention to visit during the summer, the castle staff had worked very hard all winter to keep everything around the castle in top shape, ready for his arrival.

This time, the King had time to stay for a real visit. He had brought his full retinue of knights and men at arms, including Sir Richard and his men. Seeing Sir Richard beside the King, Tom scanned the soldiers very carefully. He failed to see the one who held his interest. He took a second look at the riders beside the King, this time scanning the women.

Finally he saw Lady Althea riding beside the King. She was dressed in a dark blue velvet riding gown trimmed with gold, and a high pointed headpiece draped with sheer light blue silk. She looked wonderful. To Tom, the day seemed to take on a brighter shade as though the sun were shining with extra brilliance. He quickly donned his best attire and joined the rest of the family waiting in the castle courtyard to greet the King.

The King and his men rode up and dismounted. Servants of the Beast showed the King's soldiers where to stable their horses, and then invited them into the great hall where there were tankards of ale waiting to wash the dirt of the road from their throats. The Beast's family and his closest, most honoured servants stood at the castle doorway and knelt before the King.

"Rise, please," the King gestured to the small group assembled there. "All of you."

The King then greeted the family one by one. He hugged the Beast with great affection in front of everyone. He kissed Beauty's hand and then her cheek.

"So tell me, Milady Beauty, is your child a boy or a girl?" the King smiled, looking around. "I'm most anxious to see the infant."

"'Tis a lad, sire. We've named him James," Beauty smiled back at the King. "He is the pride of our lives."

"Where is the lad?" the King asked with a trace of eagerness in his voice.

"It seemed a bit brisk outside today, Majesty. I thought it best to keep the baby inside," Beauty told him softly.

The King next bowed and kissed Lady Margarite's hand and winked at her.

"How goes it, Milady?" the King asked with humour. "How is your new husband? Are you happy? And are you kept busy watching over your infant grandson? He must be a great joy to you."

"My husband is wonderful, Majesty, he makes me very happy. Truly M'lord, 'tis hard to say which gives me greater pride and joy, my grandson James, or my own new daughter, Alaina," Lady Margarite said proudly, surprising the King.

"You have been busy, indeed!" the King exclaimed. "You have my heartiest congratulations, Milady."

"Seth, you have a lovely wife. I can't wait to meet your daughter." The King greeted the former servant warmly.

"I have been blessed, your Majesty," Seth said with his usual quiet dignity. "I have two beautiful women to love and a wonderful daughter-in-law."

The King next turned to Gwyneth. "And how do you fare, my dear friend? Does your marriage agree with you or shall I remove the knave's head from his shoulders?"

"I'm most happy, M'lord. Beauty and Lady Margarite are not the only ones who have been busy it seems, Majesty," Gwyneth spoke up excitedly. "It seemed to be a trend, a most joyous trend. I also have a new baby, a boy named Hank."

"You suffered so much tragedy at so young an age, my dear Gwyneth. The Lord above should have seen fit to gift you with a loving husband and a child long ago, but He must have known how badly my Sebastian needed you, and how much I needed you for him," the King whispered softly to her. "I'm truly happy for you Gwyneth. Tis no more than you deserve."

"Thank you, Majesty," the maid blushed. "Henry would be out here to greet you also but he's busy in the kitchen cooking. He wanted to make sure everything was perfect for the feast we're having in your honour."

"I'm sure I'll appreciate his efforts," the King laughed. "He's a superb chef as I recall, isn't he?"

"I think so, Majesty," Gwyneth said.

"Nate, how are you?" The King turned around and greeted Beauty's younger brother. "You seem to have been working with the guards and have gained considerable muscle since I was here last."

"Your Majesty, thank you." Nate grinned and boasted, "Tis true I am training daily with the guards. In fact, I beat all but four of them in the last archery contest."

"How's your swordsmanship?" the King asked severely.

"The Beast seems to think it's coming along well," Nate grinned, "but my brother, Tom, is never pleased."

"That's the way of older brothers, it seems," the King grinned.

"Claire, you look wonderful." The King kissed the young girl's slender hand. "I trust the Beast is taking good care of you?"

"Yes, your Majesty," the girl blushed shyly.

The King turned to Beauty's other brother. Although his face was impassive, his eyes narrowed and he seemed to be weighing something as he greeted Tom.

"Thomas, how have you fared?" the King asked with a trace of wariness in his voice.

"I have been well, M'lord," Tom replied shortly, tension showing in his stiff posture.

Everyone watching noticed the slight chill in the air as the two men spoke to each other.

The family also greeted both Sir Richard and Lady Althea very warmly before entering the great hall of the castle. The King, Sir Richard and Lady Althea, all three, forgot the adults as soon as they saw the trio of infants. They admired and fussed over all three. Tiny Hank was very small and cried very loudly. Little Alaina promptly spit up on Sir Richard's best tunic. Of the three, little James was the clear favourite. He seemed to know that he was the centre of attention. He was busy crawling on the soft fur rug.

Before dinner was served, the three mothers discretely took the infants and left the room. Soon all the babies were fed and put down for a nap under the watchful eyes of the servants, and the adults settled down to a feast of roasted lamb and began to visit with each other.

The King looked at the Beast and was struck once again by the changes in the man. The ruthless young knight had indeed grown up. He was now a man of wisdom and maturity. He was now a man who knew how to love, and he valued life. He even valued the lives of his serfs. He also honoured his wife and child.

The King was very pleased. When Beauty was with the King, he saw much more than the perfection of her shape and the exceptional beauty of her features. He saw the beauty of her nature and her love for the Beast and baby James. Her love shone openly in every glance and gesture she made towards the Beast. Her love warmed the room every time she touched and nurtured the baby. They spent a long evening sitting in the great hall, talking and watching baby James as he played on a rug in front of the fire. Later that evening, the King and the Beast talked privately in the nursery.

The King held the baby boy in his arms and looked at the Beast with amusement. "You certainly hurry to please your King, Sebastian. 'Twas only eight months ago, in September, that I told you to marry. I, myself, attended the wedding in October. Almost seven months ago. Unless I'm mistaken, this babe is at least four months old."

The Beast smiled ruefully, "Some tasks are easier to accomplish than others, Sire, when my desires match your orders so perfectly."

"Lady Isabella pleases you then?" the King asked gently. "You are truly happy?"

"I am very happy, Sire. Lady Isabella holds my very soul in her soft hands," the Beast replied. "She's taught me how to love and filled me with passion. Not just passion for sex, although that's certainly a great part of it, but the passion for life and all its miracles."

"'Tis good. You have found both love and passion in your mate." The King paused and gently placed the babe in his cradle. "I took far too long to learn about the difference between love and passion. My first wife and I shared passion but there was no love. There was no respect, no concern for each other or for our children. Only our wealth and prestige were considered important."

"Sire... " the Beast began.

"'Tis true," the King interrupted, "and our children suffered greatly for it. We raised them to be warriors and kings but we forgot to raise them to be simple human beings. Things were no better when my wife died, for the children were already gone to their foster homes and I was at war."

"But then you found your second wife," the Beast prompted, "and had more children."

"I thank God for Lady Alice," the King smiled sadly. "I will miss her always. Before she died she gave me two beautiful children and taught me how to truly love with all my heart and soul."

"As Beauty has taught me how to love," the Beast murmured.

"Lady Isabella has fire, passion, tenderness and a beautiful soul. What more can a father want for his son?" the King murmured, ignoring Beauty's gasp of surprise as she entered the nursery.

"M'lord Beast," she said ominously, looking from the King to the Beast. "Have you been keeping a secret from me?"

She finally noticed the resemblance between the two men. Once she knew to look for it, their family relationship was undeniable. The two men's faces were very similar. There were subtle differences, however. The King had lighter hair and it was streaked with grey. He was fit but his figure was still thicker and stockier than the Beast's.

The King's eyes were the most different however, as they were a soft brown and filled with both quiet contentment and immense sadness. The King's eyes reflected a life lived hard, filled with great tragedy and even greater love.

"'Tis naught, Beauty," the Beast hastened to explain. "I mean, 'tis true he is my father, but I have an older brother who's very good at siring male children. I am not next in line for the crown. I'm somewhere around fifth."

"'Tis true, but your brother should have another heir presented to him in about a month, his fourth, so you'll move down the list again," the King told the Beast, smiling broadly. "Unless 'tis a girl. You and Beauty have a lot of work to do if you want to catch up."

"Loving Beauty is not work, M'lord, tis the easiest thing I've ever done," Sebastian smiled. "'Tis living with her that's so difficult."

"You Beast!" Beauty shrieked, pummelling his chest.

Over her head, the Beast met his father's eyes with a broad grin, "See what I mean, Sire?"

The King made no reply. Smiling, he merely left the room, locking the door on his way out.

"So are we going to try to catch up with my brother?" the Beast grinned as he lowered Beauty to the soft fur rug on the nursery floor.

"He is three babies ahead of us."

"I know not, but it seems we are certainly going to have plenty of our own babies." Beauty kissed her husband, her lover. "I'd wager that our second is already on the way."

"Tis not possible!" the Beast exclaimed, placing a tender hand on her abdomen. "Tis only been a few weeks since the night you seduced me."

"With you, M'lord, a few weeks is plenty of time to do the deed. I'm not certain of course, but for some reason I feel like I got pregnant that night," Beauty told him archly. "Would you be pleased if it were true?"

"I would be stunned and pleased beyond words." The Beast kissed her soundly. "Mayhap this time I'll get a girl with your looks and a nice, quiet disposition."

She laughed openly into his face, "You'll have no such luck, M'lord. I can promise you that."

She reached up and pulled the Beast down on top of her soft body, whispering in his ear, "Love me, M'lord, here and now with the babe sleeping next to us and your father outside the door."

The Beast made no reply but took her into his arms and began to make tender love to her. He kissed and stroked her with tenderness and passion, building her to frenzy that threatened to overwhelm her senses. In a short time they were both sated, gasping with exertion and glowing with pleasure and a little bit of sweat.

That evening as they sat by the fire, the King was fascinated and captivated by Beauty as he watched her with his son and grandson. She was so full of love for them both that he was both enchanted and content with the future he pictured for this family. When the Beast was called away by one of the servants, Beauty and the King sat and talked quietly together.

"Your Majesty," Beauty said softly, "I seem to remember something that troubles me."

"What is that Lady Isabella?" the King gazed at her with genuine affection.

"At our wedding, I made some unflattering references about the Beast's parents and the harsh way he was raised. I want to apologize for my remarks. I did not know he was your son," she said softly.

"No apology is needed, Beauty." The King met her eyes head on. "Your remarks were honest, entirely accurate and very well deserved. The fortunate thing is, I have truly changed and finally learned a different way to treat the people I love. I'm very lucky to have been given a second chance to know my son. He's a grown man now, strong and brave, but also loving and wise. He is a man who I'm proud to call my son but I know that I was not the one who taught him how to be a man. That is something I have to thank you for."

"You honour me, your Majesty," Beauty smiled at him.

"Beauty," the King asked with a seemingly casual tone, "I haven't seen Lady Althea since dinner. Do you know where she is?"

"The last time she was here she spent most of her spare moments in our barn," Beauty replied. Then she remembered just what Lady Althea, the King's daughter, had been doing in the barn. "Training with my bother, Tom."

"Ah yes, she dresses as a man, trains as a guard and travels with Sir Richard. Tis not exactly how I hoped my only daughter would behave." The King shook his head before continuing, "At the wedding, I noticed a considerable amount of affection between her and your brother Tom. Indeed, the air seemed to turn very warm whenever they were together."

"I must admit, Sire, Tom cares very much for your daughter. I truly hope that won't be a problem, Majesty," Beauty said softly.

"I'm not sure how I feel about it. Tis the same for every father, I suppose. No man is ever good enough for his daughter," the King smiled softly. "Whether she be commoner or princess."

"Tom is a very good man, your Majesty," Beauty said, "but I know well what you mean."

The Beast returned to them. "So what mischief are you two brewing without me?"

"We were discussing Beauty's brother, Tom, and his attraction for Lady Althea," the King said. "Tis too bad he can claim no title, not even his knighthood."

"He would be lord of the castle if not for us. I mean, when he inherited from the old lord," the Beast pointed out. "And I was about to petition you to grant him his knighthood. I think he's earned the honour. He has proved to be of rare courage and great service to me and to your Majesty when he saved my life in the battle with Gerrin. His loyalty still astounds me, since for a long time he hated me."

"How did he save your life?" Even Beauty knew not the story, for the two men never mentioned it.

"Whilst I was fighting the renegade guard, Gerrin, one of his men tried to attack me from behind. Tom stepped in at great risk to himself and killed the knave. He was almost felled by the man's sword. He guarded my back for the rest of the battle," the Beast smiled ruefully. "When I first met Beauty he already hated me, and with good reason. He held the loss of his title and lands to be my fault. He believed I was guilty of heinous crimes against women, including the one he had chosen to marry. Of course, he also denounced me for keeping Beauty from seeing her family. And finally, at one point I had ordered him to be whipped and hung. So his show of loyalty to me was even more remarkable than it first appeared."

"Just how did you come to know and love Beauty?" the King asked with great curiosity. "You never told me the whole tale."

"'Tis a tale I'm very much shamed by, Sire," the Beast told him, "even though the results of my actions are better than I ever dreamed. It started this way: There was an accusation of theft against Tom, who at that time worked in my stables. I ordered him to be hung without even bothering to hear any evidence on the matter. Beauty came to me and pleaded for his life. She even offered to give herself to me. In my heartless arrogance, I told her I would hang her brother and still take her virginity. I couldn't seem to realize why this would bother her."

The Beast paused and shook his head, remembering, "She was very brave and strong. She convinced me that there was a difference between taking a woman by force and having someone who was with me willingly. She bartered not only her body but also her willingness and her affection to me in order to convince me to let her brother go free. In exchange, I made her promise to stay with me and never see or speak to any of her family again."

"'Tis a measure of how much you've changed that now you and Beauty are happily wed, and that now Tom would defend you at considerable risk to himself," the King told his son gently. "You should be proud that you were able to make so vast a change."

"'Tis Beauty, I'm very proud of," the Beast told him, "she changed me in many ways and made me happy. I was very harsh with her when she first came to me. I used to tell her she was merely a possession like my horse or my sword. I even struck her for little or no reason. Beauty never once wavered from her course, but she was ever calm, patient and faithful, and very forgiving of my faults."

"What faults?" Beauty quipped. "Your temper, your arrogance, your stubborn streak or your constant refusal to see others as real people?"

"Well yea, those faults," the Beast admitted, smiling. "Although you are as stubborn as I am, Milady."

"'Tis different," Beauty teased him, "I'm not stubborn, I'm merely right more often than you are."

"Cease you two. I've no need to quench any strife twixt the pair of you. I'm still considering your remarks about Tom. Well, I can knight the man," the King mused. "He's certainly earned that. I just have to think on things a bit. I think I'll find Tom."

"Or Althea," the Beast said reaching for Beauty's hand.

"You'll probably find them together," Beauty pointed out as she and the Beast headed for the stairs.

The King was still grinning as he wandered out to the stables. The couple wasn't there. Next, he checked the garden and found them there. They were strolling hand in hand. They stood for a moment by the fountain and exchanged a tender kiss. The King paused to watch them for a moment and saw what he needed to know in their faces. The love between them was real. He returned to the castle without speaking to them. He spent the night deep in thought.

The next morning, he summoned Tom.

When Tom appeared, the King said, "I wanted to speak to you, Tom, for two reasons: First, I know that you've been spending time with my daughter, Lady Althea."

"Lady Althea is your daughter?" Tom paled at the very thought.

226

He had not yet learned that the Beast was the King's son. "I did not know, Majesty."

"Nevertheless, you know that as my daughter, she must have no less than a titled knight. Several good men with great wealth and titles have asked for her hand." The King paused. "Tis true, you do have noble blood. You are by right of title the lord, though your lands were lost to you."

"A worthless title, Majesty," Tom stated calmly. "And no knighthood."

"I have thought long and hard about you and my daughter," the King said.

"And what conclusion have you reached, Majesty?" Tom asked boldly.

"I have concluded that you are a surprising suitor for my daughter," the King replied. "You are not the most powerful nor the wealthiest, nor even the highest born of her suitors, yet it is you who she loves."

"Sire?" Tom asked quietly, but with a trace of humour in his voice. "These other suitors, do they all still have their heads?"

"The knighted ones do." The King eyed Tom with a new measure of respect. "That is the second thing I wanted to talk to you about. The Beast told me that you saved his life in battle. He petitioned me to grant you your knighthood. Kneel."

Tom hid his nervousness as he knelt before the King. It was more than a little intimidating to have so powerful a man holding a sword over his head and touching it to his neck, especially when he's been seen kissing his daughter.

"I dub thee, Sir Thomas." Soon the simple ceremony was complete and Tom was knighted.

"Rise, Sir Thomas," the King said firmly.

"Now, you are a titled knight." The King waited expectantly looking Tom straight in the eyes.

"An empty title with no lands and nothing to offer Lady Althea, your Majesty, else I would beg you for your daughter's hand in marriage," Sir Thomas said softly. "For I do love her very much."

"What if I told you that there's a castle and vast lands included in her dowry?" the King asked. "A castle just over two days ride from here."

"The dowry matters not. Does your Majesty, the King, actually want me to ask for Lady Althea?" Sir Thomas was merely thinking without realizing he'd spoken aloud.

"Ask the question!" the King burst out. "If you are really bold enough to be a knight of the realm, ask the question."

Sir Thomas knelt again on one knee. "Majesty, I humbly ask for the hand of your daughter, Lady Althea, in marriage."

"Lady Althea begged me long ago to let her have some say in choosing her husband. Tis unheard of, I know, but she can refuse any suitor, I have given her that right," the King sighed. "I give you my permission to propose to her. I will approve of the match if she does."

Sir Thomas rose, stunned, and mumbled, "Thank you, your Majesty. You have made me very happy this day."

"Leave me," the King smiled, "I think you have some important matters to attend to." The King smiled as Tom sped out of the room in search of Althea.

Tom found Althea in the garden. He stood silently and watched her for a moment before he approached her. The sight of her took his breath away as it always did. He noticed, however, that she seemed upset and agitated.

"Lady Althea, I have just come from the King," Tom said as he approached her. "And I have a question for you."

"I have several questions for you also, Tom," Lady Althea said nervously beginning to pace. "What are we going to do about my father? He knows about the love between us. He'll never agree to our marriage as long as you're without a title or a knighthood. He may even do something to you to keep us apart."

"Tis going to be aright, you're worried for naught." Tom began to tell her about the conversation he'd had with the King.

"I'm not worried for naught," she interrupted, "he's had several wealthy and titled knights offer for my hand already. He told me I had some say in my choice of a husband but he may yet decide to marry me off to one of them if he fails to approve of you."

"Quiet woman!" Tom roared, then continued softly, "I said, I've just come from the King. If you'll but cease your raving and listen for a minute, I'll tell you what happened."

"Sorry, Tom. I didn't mean to rave." Lady Althea reached for his hand. "I was just nervous."

"I know, my love," Tom smiled at her gently. "I was nervous too when your father first sent for me, but he was very nice. He said I was of nobility indeed, and," Tom flushed with pride, "he knighted me for saving the life of your brother Sebastian. He said that only a knight of noble blood could offer for your hand in marriage. Then he said that if I could gain your consent, he would approve the match."

Tom dropped to one knee. "Lady Althea, my love, will you marry me?"

She leaned over to kiss him before answering. "Yea, my love, I will most happily marry you." Tom rose and returned her kiss with all the passion and love he felt for his woman, his tender warrior.

The newly engaged couple went in search of the King to share their happy news. Pleased and touched, he gave them his formal blessing. Then they disappeared to plan the future and spend the day in each other's arms.

Next, the King sought out Nate and Claire. He had a plan for the future for each of them. He wanted Nate to foster out to Sir Richard as a squire until he could mature and gain his knighthood. He also wanted Claire to visit him at court, to learn more social skills and confidence from the ladies-in-waiting. Then he thought Claire could move into the castle with Sir Thomas and Lady Althea and help them in the organization of their castle.

He knew that as soon as Nate earned his knighthood the young couple would want to marry, and had decided to help them get a good start in life. Both of them were grateful for the King's attention and his offer of help. They were saddened by the idea of leaving Beauty and the Beast, as well as being separated from each other, but they both knew this arrangement would be truly to their advantage in the future. They gratefully accepted the King's offer.

The next day Sir Thomas and Lady Althea had a simple marriage ceremony in the chapel with the King and the rest of their family looking on. The newly married couple promptly disappeared into their private chamber and was not seen except during a few of the meals until they left for their new home.

The next few days were poignant, sad and very busy for both Beauty and the Beast, as so much of their family prepared to move on with their lives. By the day before the scheduled departure, both of them were tense and harried.

On the last day of his visit, the King went to the kitchen and spoke briefly with Henry and Gwyneth before he went in search of Beauty and the Beast.

"I want to spend a day alone with my grandson," the King said gruffly. "I spoke to the lad in the stables and had horses saddled for the two of you. Leave us." He winked, "Go for a ride and have some fun in the woods. Make love in the sunshine, relax together and enjoy each other."

"What if James needs me?" Beauty asked quickly. "Your pardon, Majesty, but you simply can not take care of everything, he's still nursing."

"James will be fine. If I can rule the land, I can certainly care for one small infant," the King laughed, "and Gwyneth is fixing a noontide meal for me to bring to you when the lad is ready to nurse. I'll bring the food and the infant and find you. I'm sure Nate can help me with that. Go spend the day with my son, Beauty, and make an old man very happy."

"If I saw an old man here, I would certainly want him to be happy," Beauty said, "but there's only you, Majesty."

Beauty and the Beast rode out together. As soon as they cleared the castle gate, they took off in an unspoken race. The couple sped across the countryside in a full gallop, heading towards the path that led into the forest. They slowed the horses to a soft canter, although the two steeds still felt the call to run full out. They rode deep into the forest until they came to a narrow path only suited for a slow walk single in file. They followed this path to the river where there was a place they both favoured. They dismounted and tied up the horses.

The spot was a soft grassy bank along the river shore with a tree covering the grass with cool shade. Beauty and the Beast spread out a blanket and sat on it. They talked with joy and sadness of the changes they were facing, especially the hoped for baby, and the departure of Tom, Nate and Claire.

Slowly, as their feelings were released and their fears aired, they began to cuddle in each other's arms. The Beast started kissing Beauty with all his love and caring tenderness. The passion grew as it always did between the two of them, and soon the Beast was gently removing Beauty's clothes.

As she lay nude on the blanket, Beauty looked up at him. With lust in her eyes she watched him shed his clothes and join her on the blanket. He took her into his arms and they made love. They had no need of their tricks, the exotic or erotic positions, the games of tickling, wrestling or playful spankings. No need for exchanging oral sexual favours. No use for the changing of paces, of holding back from the brink and then working towards it over and over again. They just made love with joy, passion and true love.

At midday, the King joined the lovers. Beauty nursed and changed the baby before the three adults ate the meal of cold roasted chicken and fresh fruit with crusty bread and wine. When the meal was finished, the King left Beauty and the Beast to return to the castle, taking the baby with him.

As Beauty and the Beast savoured the remainder of the afternoon, they made love repeatedly. They finally used the tricks, positions, sex play, oral sex and delayed climaxes for the second and third times they made love. By the time they folded the blanket and remounted their horses, that blanket was well used indeed.

The next morning they stood on the castle steps and watched the King and his retinue as they rode away. They had said their tearful goodbyes to Nate, Claire and Sir Thomas, along with Lady Althea, Sir Richard and the King.

"We'll visit them often, Beauty," the Beast said tenderly, "and they will all come to see us from time to time."

"Tis true, my love," Beauty smiled bravely, "and each time, our family will grow larger. We'll have more children, not to mention new nieces and nephews, and we'll love them all whether we get to see them very often or not."

"Tis the way of a family, to love whether they be nearby or not," the Beast said.

"And we are a family full of love, thank God." Beauty kissed her Beast once more before they turned to see the dust of the travellers in the distance. Hand in hand, they went into the castle.

Epilogue

Once upon a time...

There was a castle high on a hill, near a small village. The villagers had planted fields and groves, and had green pastures for grazing their sheep and goats. The surrounding countryside was lush and green. The villagers were very poor but they were also decent and hard working. They were content, free of the strife that affected many small villages because they were ruled by a fierce knight who protected them well.

The lord of the castle was well liked and respected by one and all. He was a fair ruler. He could oft be stern, but he would again and again show a kindly smile. He had a very beautiful wife whom he loved very deeply. The lord and his lady had a nice family: three brave, strong sons and two extraordinarily beautiful, headstrong daughters. Everyone should have lived happily ever after, and surprisingly enough, they all did.

THE HEART OF THE BEAST

Author's Note

When I was young, I fell in love with Beauty and the Beast. When I grew up, I realized that looks were not everything. A man could look like a beast and be wonderful inside. Or vice versa. I did not want to make The Beast hideous, but I wanted him to be cruel and heartless inside. I had fun writing the struggle between these two characters; Beauty's love and patience against his cold temper. Of course, I also had fun writing the love scenes and spanking scenes.

One thing I never wanted to do was make him too tame.

I'm currently working on another romance novel also with some spanking scenes that combines three fairytales and a bit of time travel. It's giving me headaches, but I will finish it. The working title is *Just Another Sleeping Beauty*.

I hope you love *The Heart of The Beast* as much as I loved writing it.

Thanks,

Sue